"I can

She blinked. "Why would I ask you?"

"Because we're old friends, and I'm your neighbor, a baseball enthusiast and former teacher, player and coach." He held both palms out in an "I give up" gesture. "Other than that, no reason I can think of at all."

Amy snorted. "Okay, I think you've made your point."

"Take advantage of the fact I'm right next door."

"Yeah? And what will your girlfriend say about you helping your ex-girlfriend?"

"Are you kidding? It won't bother her at all."

The truth was that Samantha probably wouldn't like it very much but that wasn't going to stop him from helping David. This was about the kid, not Declan and Amy.

They were ancient history.

"Okay. Fine. I'll talk to him."

And then "history" walked out the door, sashaying her butt, leaving Declan to swallow hard and wonder far too much about how history tended to repeat itself.

THE EX NEXT DOOR

HEATHERLY BELL

SPECIAL EDITION

Harlequin®
SPECIAL EDITION™

Recycling programs
for this product may
not exist in your area.

ISBN-13: 978-1-335-18000-1

The Ex Next Door

Copyright © 2025 by Heatherly Bell

 Harlequin Enterprises ULC
22 Adelaide St. West, 41st Floor
Toronto, Ontario M5H 4E3, Canada
www.Harlequin.com

Printed in Lithuania

MIX
Paper | Supporting
responsible forestry
FSC® C021394

Bestselling author **Heatherly Bell** was born in Tuscaloosa, Alabama, but lost her accent by the time she was two. After leaving Alabama, Heatherly lived with her family in Puerto Rico and Maryland before being transplanted kicking and screaming to the California Bay Area. She now loves it here, she swears. Except the traffic.

Books by Heatherly Bell

Montana Mavericks: The Trail to Tenacity

The Maverick's Christmas Countdown

Harlequin Special Edition

Charming, Texas

Winning Mr. Charming
The Charming Checklist
A Charming Christmas Arrangement
A Charming Single Dad
A Charming Doorstep Baby
Once Upon a Charming Bookshop
Her Fake Boyfriend
The Ex Next Door

The Fortunes of Texas: Hitting the Jackpot

Winning Her Fortune

Montana Mavericks: The Real Cowboys of Bronco Heights

Grand-Prize Cowboy

Visit the Author Profile page
at Harlequin.com for more titles.

For Danielle, my favorite single mom.

Chapter One

Amy Holloway pulled up to the rental on Bluebird Lane and viewed the home where she and her children would be living now. Well, it was white with blue trim, so it had that going for it. There was a small porch just outside the front step and the landlord had placed colorful potted flowers along the rails and an old-fashioned bench swing in one corner. Not bad.

Bonus, it was all she could afford. Huge plus.

"Isn't it super cute?" she said, inserting artificial pep in her voice.

Sure, it was nothing like the family home her children had grown up in. That home had finally been sold and Amy had no choice. Bluebird Lane was a quiet tree-lined cul-de-sac in the oldest neighborhood in Charming, Texas. This area, however, was probably the least bucolic part of their Gulf Coast town. A decidedly working-class neighborhood. Every home was almost exactly the same, cookie-cutter homes built from the 1960s.

"Are we really going to live *here*?" This was from her little girl, Naomi.

She hated to think of her twins, Naomi and David, as spoiled because they were good kids. But the home they'd grown up in was twice the size. Unfortunately, the concept of divorce was foreign to them. All they understood was that Daddy would no longer be living with them.

"We're going to have such fun here, just the three of us!" Amy sang out.

"I don't understand why Daddy can't live here, too," David said. "We should *all* live here."

"Maybe Grandma can spend the night and we'll have a slumber party! Won't that be fun?" Amy said.

The twins exchanged an excited look.

"Grandma never spent the night *before*. Yay!" Naomi said.

Finally, a happy note. Amy found changing the subject was the only way to get past this eternal question: Why can't Daddy live here, too?

Because your father decided he was tired of being married.

Imagine that. He worked fifty hours a week and traveled all over the country for his job as an IT cybersecurity expert, but he was tired of his *family*. Amy would never say that to the children, of course. After Rob asked for a separation, to seek direction, she'd read all the books on handling life after a divorce she could get her hands on. She'd consulted Valerie Kinsella, their third-grade teacher, and also spoken to the school guidance counselor.

The tried-and-true still worked: *Your daddy and I still love each other but we can't live together anymore. We'll always be a family. This has* nothing *to do with you. It's between me and Daddy. Grown-up stuff.* Right.

David and Naomi hopped out of the back seat of her economy sedan and ran toward the house. Curiosity, Amy assumed, got the best of them. Or maybe her reframing this whole thing as a type of adventure had helped. At least they wanted to see the place. Her mother had found it, scoping it out ahead of time as a neighborhood in which the kids could still be close to their school.

The key stuck in the door, and Amy had to jiggle it a few times before it turned. She made a note of that to add to the walk-through comments she'd made when she signed the final lease a few days ago. *One year.* After that, she'd see. Maybe she'd have to relocate to a different part of Texas, though if she moved too far, that would be an issue for Rob, who'd moved to Houston thirty minutes away. Also, she didn't want to leave her mother— the only emotional support she had now.

Her small circle of friends, mostly the parents of Naomi's and David's friends, had started to distance themselves. The few times she was around them, she didn't appreciate their pitiful looks. She was working hard to be happy, scraping herself off the floor every morning for the sake of her children.

"It's so big!" Naomi skipped inside the vacant house, holding the book she'd been reading in the car.

Wait until we put all our furniture inside.

It wouldn't look roomy anymore. The single-family home was one large great room connected to a small kitchen. A short hallway led down to the three bedrooms and one bathroom in the back of the house.

"I'm going to pick my new room!" David ran off.

"Me, too!" Naomi followed him down the hall.

Two minutes later, she was hanging her head out of the smallest room. It was just like Naomi to give her brother the bigger room. Had she taught her that, somehow? Had Amy taught her by example to make herself smaller for someone she loved? She adored her brother but that didn't mean letting him have first choice all the time.

This was such a huge change in her children's lives and

Amy wished she could have convinced Rob to attend marriage counseling. At least to try for the sake of their kids. Yet, his mind had been made up.

"Mommy, my door squeaks," Naomi said.

"We'll get Lou to fix that in a jiffy. The hinges just need to be oiled."

"Also, can we paint my room yellow?"

Anything to make you happy here, my princess.

"We'll have to ask our landlord but if she says it's okay, then yes, of course!"

"Yay!" Naomi clapped her hands, looking so joyous that Amy wanted to cry.

She had such good-natured children. But she hadn't been able to give them the one thing they really wanted: parents who loved each other.

The moving truck pulled up outside and Amy ran to meet it. Driven by her mother's boyfriend, Lou, it contained Amy's life for the past ten years. Furniture, pots and pans, her wedding china and silver, clothes and toys. All her memories in boxes.

Her mother pulled up soon after, parking on the street. Moonbeam Miller, child of hippies, was back to the crunchy-granola girl of her youth. Mom turned her back on her parents' nomadic ways and named her only daughter a very safe name. You couldn't get much more conservative of a name than Amy. But Mom had changed after her husband an absolute pillar of everything traditional, had the nerve to die of cancer. It was like she cut loose from some kind of imaginary tether. She now seemed to embrace her flowery past, and in her sixties, she'd gone into business with Lou, buying a garden center in town they called Back to the Fuchsia.

She walked up to Amy, embraced her in a huge hug and

pulled out a wand of what appeared to be dead branches from her beaded purse.

"What's that?" Amy scrunched up her nose.

"It's sage. Normally, you burn it to ward off any negative energy, but we don't want to smoke out the *children*. I consulted with Willow at the gem store, and she said it will be okay to just wave it around."

"Wave it...around?"

"Yes, up in the air like this." She lifted it above her like a torch, looking like a middle-aged Statue of Liberty wearing bangles and braids.

"Mom, I don't know about this."

Her mother had raised Amy in the most traditional of ways, but now often expressed her dismay that Amy couldn't open her eyes and mind. A fortune teller Mom had consulted recently told her that Rob and Amy had been doomed from the beginning. An easy guess when you already knew the outcome. She forecast that Amy was going to meet someone new very soon. And also, that she should watch her high blood pressure. Amy happened to be a few pounds overweight for most of her married life, but her blood pressure had been fine *before* the divorce.

"It can't hurt. And after the year you've had, I think you need all the help you can get."

Amy couldn't argue there.

Naomi and David ran to greet their grandma the moment she walked in the door and then followed her around, watching in fascination.

Outside, Lou opened the back of the moving truck and waved Amy over.

"I'm sorry I can't help much, darlin'. You know, my back." He put a hand low on his back, where he'd been hurt years before in a roofing accident. "Falling two stories was no picnic."

"That's okay, Lou. I've got this." Amy pulled out a box and hefted it into the house.

"Young people. Enjoy your youth, Amy. It goes by fast." Lou followed her up the lawn she shared with her next-door neighbor, carrying Naomi's rainbow unicorn backpack.

"Yes it did." Amy snorted when she set the box down. "Like a blink."

"Aw, c'mon now. You're still a young whippersnapper," Lou cackled. "Where's David? Is he hiding again?"

"David doesn't hide anymore," Amy said. "He learned his lesson."

It was something he'd done as a toddler and preschooler, scaring anyone babysitting him.

"I'll help you, Lou!" David appeared, flexed his bicep and ran outside to the truck. "I can lift a lot of pounds."

"Sure you can, little buddy." Lou patted his head as David flew by him.

A few more boxes came in easily, Amy, Mom, David and Naomi lifting the heavier ones together.

"We can do this," Naomi said, baffled at being able to lift the boxes.

"Don't look so surprised. We can do a lot of things you don't know about as a team," Amy said. "Just wait and see."

The problem came when they were hauling in a particularly heavy box. Mom and Lou stood by directing since the box was so tall they couldn't see ahead of them. Amy pushed from one end and both David and Naomi pulled from the other.

"I shouldn't have packed this one so full," Amy said, winded.

She really needed to work out more.

"You're doing fine," her mother said. "You're got this! Just a few more feet."

Amy pushed and got a few more inches. The kids were of no help whatsoever, not that she blamed them. They wanted to pretend they were helping.

"All right, I can't stand it anymore," said a deep voice Amy couldn't see from her angle with the box blocking. "I've been watching, and I know you can do it yourself, but for the love of God, please let me help. I beg you."

Then he stepped into her line of vision.

Declan Sheridan.

He looked as he always did, a bit like a Greek god if you mixed him up with a Major League Baseball player. Tall, built, tan, blond. Golden. Hotter than a flapjack fresh off the grill.

Surely her mother hadn't called *him*. Amy could take a lot of humiliation, but this was too much to bear. Almost the very last person she wanted to see her in this predicament.

Her high school ex-boyfriend.

"What are *you* doing here?" Amy pushed a stray hair from her sweaty face.

"What do you mean?" He hooked a finger, pointing to the house next door with an Astros flag waving in the breeze. "I live next door."

Chapter Two

Declan Sheridan could handle unpleasantness. He'd lived through plenty in his thirty-plus years. Tragic Dallas Cowboy losses, Houston Astros slaughters, his own rather tepid MLB career, girlfriends slapping and cursing him out, his father breathing down his back, his mother's drastic matchmaking and his brother, Finn, moving out six months ago, just when he'd come to depend on him to help with the rent.

But he was not going to watch Amy push that behemoth of a box another second. Nope.

Not going to do it. That was final.

He'd been watching from his window since the moving van pulled up, surprised to see Amy hauling boxes into the house next door. It wasn't like he didn't know what was happening. He was a bartender at the Salty Dog and was practically a central deposit for all rumors and gossip. Everyone spilled their guts to him over a cold beer. It was all over town that Amy and Rob had divorced. Still, what a loser not to at least be here to help his kids. At least she had *some* help, in the form of Lou and Moonbeam But a pair of sixty-somethings, one of them with a bad back, were not going to get this done.

No need for formalities. They knew each other well even if it had been some time since they ran in the same social circles. Amy had been married and was raising a family. Her friends were other soccer moms.

"Move aside, Amy," Declan ordered. "You're in my way."

"I'm not going anywhere. And I don't need your help."

"Oh, yes you do."

But if she wouldn't move out of his way, this could be difficult.

She was still just as pretty as she'd ever been, a smatter of freckles across her pert nose, her dark hair pulled up in a ponytail. She was his age but looked younger today wearing no makeup and a baseball cap.

"Let him help." This was from Lou. "You know I'd do it if I could."

"Mom, I'm tired," her little boy said, taking a seat on the grass and pulling out a tuft of it.

Her little girl was already sitting on the porch step with a book. Smart kid.

Moonbeam stood beside Lou, arms crossed, eyes blazing, clearly wanting to throttle Declan. But also possessing a keen understanding that they needed his help here. No matter what she thought of her daughter's first boyfriend.

"Ask yourself whether you'd let anyone else help you right now. Anyone that isn't me."

That landed with her. There was only one reason she didn't want his help. He was the ex, and she was projecting her disdain for her current ex on to him. In addition to being a bartender, Declan was an armchair psychologist. Came with the job.

"Fine," Amy said. "If you don't mind, I'd appreciate it."

"I don't mind at all." He forced a smile.

Lifting, he walked the box across the lawn and into the house within a few seconds.

"Wow, you're strong," her little boy said. David, was it? "My dad can do that, too."

"Thank you," Amy said. "I guess you're my new neighbor."

"I am." He then positioned the box out of the way, rubbed his hand and went back outside.

Amy was right behind him. "That was really all we... um..."

He ignored her, carrying in several boxes and chairs.

"Look, moving isn't any fun. But hey, I might need help with the table."

"I wish I could help," Lou said repeatedly each time Declan passed him on the front porch.

He noticed that Moonbeam was keeping to herself, unpacking boxes while Declan and Amy did most of the lifting. She ignored him most of the time, apparently resigned to his help. They worked together as a team even if he did most of the heavier work. It would have been much harder without her.

By the end, he'd helped unload the moving truck, beds included.

"Thanks," Lou said, hopping back into the driver's side of the truck. "I got to get this back into the shop."

"Thank you, Lou," Amy said. "I owe you dinner."

Lou drove off waving to them both.

"What about me?" Declan teased. "Do I get dinner?"

"Yes, if you want." She studied the ground.

"Just a cold beer would do me fine."

"I don't have any beer." She met his eyes and narrowed her own. "And don't you work at a *bar*?"

"Yeah, but the bar's not here right now." He laughed. "I'm kidding. You don't owe me a thing, Amy."

She tipped her head and considered him as if she could

see all the ways he'd failed her years ago and came to a conclusion.

"Yes. I guess you're right."

Declan snorted. "Okay, then. Well, happy moving day!"

He waved and crossed the shared lawn into his house. Bitterness, clearly, was still the order of the day. He'd been *seventeen years old* and a complete idiot when he'd screwed things up with Amy, but she didn't seem to want to cut him any slack. Then again, she was projecting. Yeah, that was it. Either way, he could be a good neighbor to his ex and her kids. Usually, Declan didn't like to over-involve himself in other people's drama and lives. He got enough of that at the bar, and though he was good at listening, he saw no reason to look for drama on his day off.

This was different. A single mom living right next door with her two children. Before long, he suspected, she might not be alone, but until then he would keep an eye out. Unclog any sinks and kill spiders, that sort of thing. Toss around a ball with the boy. This was mostly a safe neighborhood, except for that time a bunch of teenagers broke into a vacant house down the street. All they'd wanted was a place to party but by the end of the deal they'd done some property damage. Stupid kids.

Pizza for dinner tonight, Declan decided. He loved pizza anytime he helped someone move. He'd just finished helping his older brother, Finn, move out earlier this month. Sure, he'd left Declan to pay the entire payment this month by himself, but he couldn't be too upset. Finn was happier than he'd ever been with his new fiancée. At one time, Declan would have laid bets in Vegas that Finn would never again be in a serious relationship after his divorce. So, he guessed it was entirely plausible that Amy would find herself married again before too long. He remembered how important marriage had been to her at seventeen. Far more than it was to him.

And she was still attractive. Still curvy in all the right places. He'd seen her dimples only once today and that had been when talking to her children. It was also the only time her green eyes lit up.

Thanking God for modern food delivery apps, Declan tipped the driver and accepted his pizza. A reward for a job well done. He cracked open a cold beer he found in the cold cut drawer, settled everything on the table in front of the couch and switched on ESPN.

When his doorbell rang thirty minutes later, Declan thought it might be Amy, to apologize for agreeing she didn't owe him anything. A simple thanks would have been nice but maybe ex-boyfriends who hadn't wanted to get married right after high school didn't *qualify*.

Declan swung open the door to find his father there instead. "Hey, Dec!"

"Come on in." He waved him inside, peeking outside to see if Amy and the kids were still out there.

Only the boy, kicking around a soccer ball all alone.

"Slice of pizza?" Declan waved at the box.

"Don't mind if I do."

"I'm watching the recap." Declan jutted his chin to the flat-screen.

Even if he'd been out of majors for years, Declan still enjoyed the sport of baseball. And to be fair, it was about all he had in common with his father. Whenever he dropped by, which was too often now that Finn had moved out, Declan talked stats. If he didn't, his father would start asking about his goals. He insisted that Declan had walked away from his high school coaching position when he should have stuck it out and dealt with the fallout. Obviously Declan disagreed.

A coach for most of his life, Dan Sheridan was a master motivator. The man wouldn't know the word *quit* if it came up and slapped him silly. It was a cool thing for the kids he currently coached in Little League, because if you wanted to believe his father, each one of them was the next Derek Jeter.

"You got new neighbors?" His father said, taking a slice.

"Yeah, Amy and her kids moved in next door. She and Rob are getting a divorce."

"Ah, Amy. Heard about that. Sad situation."

They watched the commentators for a few minutes and then the program cut away to a commercial.

"So," his father said, right on cue. "Have you thought any more about joining me as coach on the Little League team? They could really use the inspiration from a former pro."

Emphasis on former.

"Thought about it. It's not going to fit into my plans at this time."

"And those plans are…?"

Declan scrubbed a hand down his face. "Still formulating."

"Declan," his father sighed. "You are a great player and an even better teacher. Why are you wasting your God-given talent by bartending?"

"I'm not wasting anything. It happens that I'm good at listening to people's troubles and serving them a cocktail."

Not everyone could be a first-class mixologist, and Declan happened to believe the praise he got from his customers.

Best mojito I ever had; thanks for listening; here's a hundred-dollar tip, you're still cheaper than the therapist.

"There's nothing wrong with hard work. I'm a working-class stiff and I like it."

"I appreciate that, but you have a different kind of talent. If you don't share with the world, it's practically a sin."

"A sin?"

Granted, these were new tactics on his Dad's part. He must be getting desperate.

"Tell me. Other than listening to people's troubles and mixing alcoholic drinks, are you contributing to society? Do you have a plan? A goal? Strategy to get there?"

Somebody shoot him now. With Finn now retired from the Olympics and running a boat charter business with his best friend, his father's attentions had turned to Declan.

Even though it was coming up on two years since he'd left the Houston high school, Declan refused to talk about it. Everyone in town knew the reason he'd left and so did his parents. A difference of opinion with the boosters had gone way too far. Declan decided everyone would be better off without him. And though his father was plenty sympathetic when it all went down, by now he expected Declan to have moved on.

He took the job as bartender so he could think next steps. Sure, next steps were dragging but that was his business.

His father needed a new project and Declan looked like fresh and raw material. If he didn't show his father a plan, this wouldn't stop until he did.

"Okay." Declan stood. "Look, I didn't want to say anything to you yet but yes, I have a plan. I intend to contribute to society. Big-time."

"Sounds wonderful!"

Here came the cheering section. It was time for Declan to lay it all out. He whipped out a napkin and grabbed a pen. Far too well, he remembered the younger years: days of charts and graphs and items to check off in the Sheridan house. Both he and Finn were raised on goals and charts.

"I haven't had time to write it all down, but here's the plan." Declan made a graph of the month and slotted in several days. "I'm going to be doing one good deed a day for Amy and her family. And here's the first one—help her move in."

Declan checked it off. "Done. Now, tomorrow, I intend to offer my lawn care services. God forbid that get out of control. I've got it."

"Is this a *joke*?" his father said. "I never understand your sense of humor."

"Not a joke, unless you find something funny about helping a single mom who's just moved into a new house and is probably going to need a lot of support."

For once, he'd left his father speechless. "It's honorable, sure, but just not quite what I had in mind."

"Well, Dad, I know how much you love goals and plans. Now I have one. Make Amy's life go a little bit easier. And I think it's quite meaningful. Beautiful, even." He quirked a brow.

Now Declan was just showing off. Daring his father to tell him this goal wasn't "significant" enough. Because he understood what his father wanted deep down. He wanted Declan to decide he was too talented not to simply enjoy baseball from the sidelines or a recreational team. He wanted Declan to try out for a minor league team and do what he'd been born to do. But for years, Declan had believed that people were meant to do more than one thing. With baseball, he'd been there, done that. His sports career was over, and he had no regrets.

"Well." Realizing he was beaten, at least for now, his father shook his head slowly. "If this is your goal…"

"Thanks, Dad."

Chapter Three

"I assume spaghetti for dinner will be fine?" Amy set the pot filled with water on the stove. "I promised the kids."

"You know Lou. He'll eat anything." Moonbeam unwrapped another kitchen utensil and rolled up the newspaper into a ball. "I'm sorry, honey. I had no idea *he* lived next door."

"It's fine. I have bigger things to worry about than my high school sweetheart."

Still, it had definitely been a shock. Of course, she'd noticed Declan around town, here and there, but not often. They almost lived in two different worlds within their same small town. He worked at the Salty Dog, for one, and she only rarely went into the restaurant. Resoundingly single—color her *not* surprised—he dated an awful lot, according to Amy's best friend, Bianca. But Amy was far more likely to run into Finn, his older brother, who hung out more often at the boardwalk. Especially after the divorce, she used to take the kids to the carnival-style side of the boardwalk on the weekend to cheer them up. Finn and Declan looked so much alike they were practically twins. Naomi and David didn't look that much alike, and they *were* twins.

Both Sheridan brothers possessed those Irish golden-boy

looks that made most women go gaga. Declan still had an athlete's body, all long and muscular legs and wide shoulders.

"I'll never forgive nor forget how he broke your heart," her mother said.

"Um, he was seventeen. I think you're forgetting someone *else* broke my heart far more recently."

Broken her heart and destroyed their family. If there was anyone Amy wasn't likely to forgive anytime, it was her ex-husband, for forcing her to break her *children's* hearts. Their crestfallen faces had looked at her with such confusion.

Daddy and I won't be living together anymore.

"But I remember how you used to adore Declan." Mom unpacked the rice cooker and set it on the counter. "You had such plans. A winter wedding so it wouldn't interfere with his spring training schedule. Such devotion. There's something about first love, I guess. I remember thinking he was so sweet. But then, bam! It was over."

Amy cringed with humiliation at her teenage dreams. She'd been young. What an idiot she'd been thinking she'd marry her first love. Declan hadn't led her on, either, or ever mentioned marriage. She'd just run with it. Both of her parents, especially the father she worshipped, loved Declan, the star athlete.

"Yes, Mom, I know how invested you were in my marrying an MLB player. But that didn't work out for Declan, either."

"Oh, hardly. Your father loved him, but I never cared who you married so long as you were happy." Mom reached to rub Amy's shoulder. "I'm sorry you haven't been lucky in love. *So far.* But don't forget—every flower has to grow through dirt."

Her mother was forever quoting old and tired flower clichés to cheer Amy up. Perhaps now her mother was trying to redirect her current depression with an older version. Maybe she wanted to remind Amy that she'd survived Declan, and in fact went on to date Rob in college. And the rest was history. At least she and Rob had wanted the same things fairly early in life: marriage and children. A home.

Now, her home was in pieces, which reflected her emotions and state of mind. Their beds were not set up but were at least in the proper bedrooms. The couch stuck out like the last item at a garage sale. The kitchen table stood in the corner where Declan had left it. The twelve-person dining set she and Rob had owned would never fit here. It now sat in a storage unit outside town hoping for better days. Their furniture now inside, they had far less space but at least Naomi hadn't said anything. Then again, she was reading a book as per the usual.

When the water began to boil, Amy reached in the shopping bag for the box of pasta she'd bought earlier today. She ignored the tears stinging her eyes and kept a razor focus on the task. Much easier. No, she hadn't been "lucky" in love. But getting in touch with her feelings, at this point, was a useless exercise in self-flagellation. She should have seen the signs of Rob's boredom. She should have lost twenty pounds of baby weight sooner. Shopped for more lingerie. Fallen asleep before ten less often.

But she refused to take all the blame in the divorce. One day, Rob woke up and didn't want to be married anymore. "Marriage," as he'd said, "is more work than I imagined. Maybe it shouldn't be this hard."

When in doubt, change the subject. "Can you still watch the kids Monday while I go on that interview?"

"No problem."

After ten years at home with no work history to speak of, it wasn't going to be easy to find a full-time job. But she'd been lucky to score an interview at an auto car dealership in Houston who wanted someone to work as an entry-level clerk in the accounting department. There would be a commute, but if Amy wanted to be free on the weekends, an office job would be ideal. She could probably find seasonal work at the boardwalk in town, but Amy hoped to do better than serve soft-serve ice cream or work the carnival rides with teenagers.

A few minutes later, Lou waltzed in, David behind him. "Look who I found outside kicking a ball around! He's right at home already."

"Mom, I don't want to play on the soccer team anymore," David said with a whine. "I'm not any good at it."

"Who says, little man?" Lou ruffled David's hair. "I thought you looked pretty fly out there. *Fly* means *good*, by the way. That's what the kids are saying now."

Wonderful. Amy would have to deal with that issue later. David had missed a goal at last week's game and been crabby ever since then. But he hadn't mentioned quitting. She couldn't let him quit just because he'd lost a single goal. Sports for kids David's age were about having fun, teamwork and building leadership skills. It was not about *winning*.

They all ate dinner together, both Lou and David taking two helpings. Afterward, Amy asked Lou to help set up her bed. This was something she had refused to ask "he of the brawny arms" after he'd hauled in her mattress, and that of the kids. Amy could do it herself, but she wasn't extremely familiar with the tools required. Lou had come prepared to put things together.

"Hey, guys, why don't we just cuddle up in my bed tonight? You know, like we used to do when Daddy would go on business trips? That way Lou and Grandma can go home. It's getting late."

"Daddy said I'm too big to do that," David said.

Amy was pretty sure another slice of her heart went with those few words.

"I'll sleep with you, Mama." Naomi took her hand, as always reading the room with the expertise of a fifty-year-old psychologist.

The despair on her face must have been easy to read, because then David said, "I'll just sleep on the floor next to you."

"That's right, little man." Lou fist-bumped him. "You're the man of the house. You can protect your mama and sister."

Noooo, Amy wanted to scream, though she knew Lou meant well. David was not the man of the house. *He's a child and I don't expect him to protect me.* She would protect her son. But David grinned and seemed to like the idea, so Amy let it go for now.

"I don't need protecting," Naomi said, pushing her glasses up her nose.

And just like that, Amy felt a stitch slip over her bruised heart.

That's my girl.

Amy was doing okay. She was raising a strong and independent daughter and God willing would raise a loyal and good man.

The next morning, the lawn mowers woke Amy up. In some ways, this neighborhood was like her old one. Saturday seemed to be the national weekly mowing day. Except in her old neighborhood, most people had a service. Rob did it himself those first years, a proud homeowner, but later decided he was too busy for it. That's when Amy took it up, not willing to pay for something so simple.

Naomi and David were already up, waiting for Rob. It

was his turn to have them this weekend, and to say David was excited would be an understatement. He had his backpack packed, and the soccer ball nearby. Bowls of colored milk were on the table, evidence of their breakfast. Usually, she made pancakes on Saturdays, but she didn't know where she'd packed the mix or the skillet.

Dressed and ready for the day, Amy headed to the coffee machine. She'd made sure to set up essentials last night before bed.

"Morning."

"What time is Daddy coming?" Naomi was still adding things to her stuffed backpack. Mostly books.

"I'll check with him but it's going to be the usual time, I'm sure." She glanced at her Fitbit watch. "In an hour or so."

"We're going to work on my soccer moves today," David said, thankfully forgetting his crabby mood of yesterday. "Next time I'm going to make that goal."

"As long as you have fun doing it."

When Amy glanced out the window, she saw Declan, rolling the mower across his lawn with ease. He wore a baseball cap, old, frayed jeans and a tight-fitting T-shirt so worn she could practically see through it. She was simply enjoying the view of barely concealed six-pack abs when the lawn mower turned and crossed the shared lawn. Yep, he was mowing her lawn.

"Mom, the neighbor is mowing our lawn," David announced helpfully.

"I see that."

"Can he do that?" David scrunched up his nose.

"What do you mean?"

"Shouldn't he ask first?"

Why yes, he probably should. Or not. Truthfully, Amy was a bit out of touch with neighborly rules. In her previous neighborhood, everyone minded their business. The most neighborly thing she'd ever seen Rob do was roll up the recycling and garbage cans for their next-door neighbor once a week when he did their own. When he wasn't in town, Amy would do it because she figured they'd grown accustomed to the nicety. It was no trouble. Declan was mowing his lawn, and just crossed over the boundary.

"He's just being neighborly," Amy explained.

"But this is our lawn," David said. "Daddy should probably do it. Right?"

Rob wasn't here, however. He lived in an apartment where he didn't have to worry about such things. Amy imagined he wanted a bachelor pad where he could pretend at least for a few days a week that he wasn't a family man.

Amy tipped David's chin. "Honey, Daddy isn't going to be mowing our lawn anymore. This is our place, remember?"

David frowned. "He doesn't mind."

"Probably not, but the thing is, *I'm* going to be mowing the lawn from now on."

This got Naomi's attention. "But you don't know how to turn it on. Remember that time you tried, and Lou had to come over and turn it on for you?"

"That's not the point. I learned how."

One of the gifts Rob had given her, if you wanted to call it that, was becoming adjusted to being a single mom in slow and small bursts. Of course, she didn't know she was doing it at the time. But he'd gone on his share of business trips, and she'd managed just fine without him. Now she'd do it permanently.

"I better go and thank him." Amy set her coffee mug down on the kitchen counter and walked outside.

With his back turned to her, Declan didn't see her and would be unable to hear her, so she waited. The seconds ticked by, and Declan shut the mower off and began to wheel it back toward his house.

"Declan!" Amy shouted.

No response.

Amy continued, a little louder, cupping her hands around her mouth to make it a loudspeaker. "Thank you for doing that but you really don't have to. In the future, I'll take care of the lawn."

Still no response. Rude. She ran up to him and touched his shoulder.

"So, Declan! *Hello?*"

He turned to her, removing the earbud. "Oh, hi. I was listening to a podcast."

That at least explained the rudeness. "I wanted to thank you. For yesterday and for, just now, with the lawn. But you—"

"You're welcome!" He grinned. "I really don't mind. I was already going to do my lawn so I thought I'd give you a hand. You must be busy unpacking. It's not that I don't think you can do it, but I'm trying to help."

He'd left her a bit speechless. She did have a lot of unpacking to do. As soon as the kids left with Rob for the weekend, she was going to set up their rooms. She had plans to put up posters, new sheets, comforters and curtains and make them into rooms they'd be happy to sleep in. Amy firmly believed an environment could increase happiness levels. Bright colors and flowers.

Declan's phone buzzed and he put up a finger. "I'll call her right back. That's fine. I have a date with my girlfriend tonight and she's probably wanting to confirm."

"Your girlfriend?"

"Maybe it's too soon to tell, actually. Two dates. We're

going out tonight for number three. I have high hopes, I guess." He shrugged.

Declan? He had high hopes for a third date? Oh, right. Sex, probably, on the proverbial third date. But, she wouldn't know about that. Her pattern was more like four months of dates, with both Declan and Rob. *Two.* She'd had two lovers in her entire life and married one of them.

Maybe two couldn't be called a pattern.

Declan smiled at her. "You're not the only one who wants a couple of kids running around."

Amy's jaw surely dropped. "Really? You want a couple of kids?"

"A least two, maybe three, if I'm lucky."

Amy resisted lecturing him on being sure he wanted to be married, and *stay married*, especially after children. It wasn't any of her business, plus, Declan had waited so maybe he was ready. A lot of people said she and Rob had been too young to have kids in their early twenties. They were right about Rob, but not about Amy. She was happy to be a young mother and only wished she hadn't married a jerk.

"Well, I wish you luck."

You'll need it, she wanted to say. *Okay,* no, *Amy. You're not going to do this. You're not going to join the bitterly betrayed club of divorced single moms. Be nice.* Declan wanted to fall in love and get married. It was a worthy goal. At least he wasn't stuck in an eternal adolescence, or like Rob, feeling that he had to revisit the one robbed of him.

"Thanks!" He and his lawn mower turned to go, but then he stopped. "And if you ever need anything, I mean anything *at all*, please let me know. Walk right over."

"Okay."

She would. Amy wasn't too proud to understand she might be in over her head.

Help would be welcome, even from the ex next door.

Chapter Four

When Rob hadn't arrived, or called, and it was close to noon, Amy broke down and called him.

"Hey, Ames! Whassup?"

God help her, he sounded like an overgrown frat boy lounging poolside. If she recalled, having only seen the place once, the apartment complex had a pool. She was pretty sure Rob had chosen it for that reason alone.

"What's *up*?" Amy hissed. "Where are you? The kids are waiting."

"That's today?" A splash in the background. "I thought it was next weekend."

"No, Rob. You *knew* we were moving in yesterday when you had to pull a late one at the office. But this is your weekend." She lowered her voice and walked out of the living room into her bedroom to shut the door. "I assumed you'd at least take them today. They really want to see you."

"Aw, damn. Unfortunately, I already made plans."

"Cancel them. They miss you. These are your *children*."

"You don't have to tell me that, Amy. Ease up on the hostility, 'm kay?"

"You haven't even *seen* hostile from me. Keep it up, and you will."

The way Amy had always looked at the world, if you hurt

her children, you hurt *her*. There was zero degree of separation. The mama cub came out in full force. It was actually better for someone to hurt her rather than one of her *children*. Hurting her child was like ripping out a piece of her heart, then trampling on it and expecting her to be fine with it. She'd always thought this sort of thing would come into play with a class bully or mean girl and not their own father. But if it were up to her, Rob would not hurt their children any more than he'd already managed just by being himself.

"If you had let me *finish*, I would have explained that I'll cancel my plans and pick up the kids. It will take me about thirty minutes to get there. Have them ready and waiting for me curbside, 'kay?"

"Better yet, why don't I just throw them to you in the car as you swing by? All you have to do is open the door and slow down a bit."

"That's not *funny*. I don't want to waste any more time, that's all. I'm already late. Besides, if I come inside they'll want to give me the grand tour and we'll waste more time."

She wanted to scream that it was his fault he was late today, his fault she was unpacking her entire life, his fault her children had to live in this cottage without their father. His fault for *everything*. But she wasn't going to go down that road. She refused to become a bitter woman. Rob hadn't cheated on her, at least. Best to look on the bright side.

"Daddy's on his way!" Amy said cheerfully, for David's sake.

He'd gone into somewhat of a funk when Rob hadn't shown up earlier, shuffling around the living room and kicking empty boxes. Naomi, for her part, had curled up with a book.

"Why is he late this time?"

Her little boy sounded bitter, and there went another slice of her heart.

"Oh, you know how it is. Traffic, probably."

Rob had decided to rent a place thirty minutes away in Houston, as if he wanted to put more distance between him and his family.

"Yeah," David huffed. "Traffic."

"Should we wait outside?" Naomi sat up, sliding a bookmark into place.

"If you want to. It's a nice enough day, not too hot. We'll wait outside on the porch together."

And that's where Rob found them *forty-five* minutes later.

"Hey, kiddos! Let's go get us some pizza!" Rob said, swinging open the passenger door.

He was dressed in board shorts, dark shades that hid his eyes, a loose T-shirt and sandals, and didn't look like anybody's dad. This was very likely his intent. Amy wore the yoga pants she practically lived in, a dab of smeared peanut butter across *her* T-shirt, hair in a ponytail, looking every bit the harried mother of two.

David and Naomi ran into his open arms.

"Daddy! We missed you."

"Aw, I missed you too, Pumkin'." Rob patted Naomi's head and fist-bumped David.

"I think you should give Mommy a big hug because she worked really hard yesterday," Naomi said with the honesty only a nine-year-old could manage.

"That's okay." Amy held up her palms. "I didn't mind."

"Mommy's fine," Rob said dismissively. "She's stronger than you know."

"Yeah, but good thing our neighbor helped us," David said. "Because *you* weren't here."

"Little dude, I would have been, but I had to work. You

know how it is." The kids buckled up, then Rob shut the rear passenger door and surveyed the house behind her. "So, this is it, huh?"

"It's all I could afford." She crossed her arms.

It might be small for all three of them, but she felt protective about the rental her mother had located in town. It was in an older but quaint neighborhood, with working-class people who struggled for everything they had. Sometimes Amy wished she hadn't gone straight from college to marriage and motherhood. She'd been privileged to stay at home with her children, but it had always been her intent to get her teaching credentials once the kids were in school. She never got around to that, and now she'd never worked outside the home. Her last job had been as a waitress in college.

"Well, I'm up for a raise, and things will be better when *you* get a job." He tapped the hood of his car.

"I have an interview tomorrow."

"Oh, hey, good luck!"

A strange sensation pulsed through her. She seemed to be talking to a stranger, and not the man she'd lain next to in bed for years. The man whose children she'd birthed. The man who'd gone down on one knee when he asked her to marry him and cried when she'd said yes.

What *happened* to that man?

"Of course, once I get a job, we'll need to pay for childcare. I'll let you know how much it is."

Rob frowned. "How much is that going to cost me?"

Amy stiffened. Rob complained about every penny he had to give Amy since he decided he didn't want to be married anymore.

"I don't know. How much is the safety of your children worth?"

Rob sighed, closed his eyes and pinched the bridge of his nose. "I better go."

"Yes, you better." Shame hit her, the feeling she'd crossed a line she promised she would not. Unfortunately, she was bitter. "I'll see you tonight."

"It will be late, around nine."

Amy spent the rest of the day unpacking. In the late afternoon, Mom came over with new princess sheets she'd purchased for Naomi's bed and soccer ball sheets for David's. They set up the beds, decorating the rooms the way they'd been at their home.

After her mother left, Amy appraised the work they'd done. This would never look like the home she'd left and even if it did, her children were too smart to be fooled. From now on, their lives would be different.

Her house was so close to Declan's that she heard his front door slam shut around dinnertime that evening. She looked out the window and there he was, walking to his truck, dressed nicely in slacks and a blue button-up shirt. A sense of melancholy hit her hard and fast, a swift and distant memory of their prom night many years ago.

No matter how hard he played baseball, Declan cleaned up well when he had to. He'd been dressed in a tux the night of their prom, a black one with those shiny shoes. Classy and handsome. She'd worn a hideous yellow dress that at the time seemed cheerful and bright. Lord knew what she'd been thinking.

Declan thought she was beautiful anyway, or at least that's what he'd said.

"I love you, Amy," he'd told her that night and sounded so sincere she believed him.

She allowed herself to briefly wonder what her life would have been like if she'd married Declan Sheridan. They might have gotten back together if she hadn't been so hurt and proud that she refused to listen to anything he had to say.

But there was no world in which she could ever regret being the mother to David and Naomi.

Sometimes, she understood Rob's nostalgia for the old days when they were young and carefree. They'd been parents for so long their youth seemed far away. But if Amy closed her eyes and focused, she could almost feel those days again, and they didn't seem so distant at all.

Right before Declan pulled into his driveway around midnight, he noticed Amy next door. She sat on the porch swing, barefoot, staring out into the dark blue sky.

He shut off the headlights, and Amy stood and moved to the front door.

"Don't go inside on my account," he called out.

She shook her head. "I'm not. It's just…time."

He strolled over, jangling his keys in his fist. "What are you doing out here? Is something wrong?"

"Why would you think that?"

"I don't know… You just moved in." He shrugged and stopped at the bottom step to the porch. "Did everything go okay with settling in? I know you didn't want me to help with anything else, but—"

Amy blinked. "Why would you be concerned with that?"

"Amy." He sighed. "You're going to have to get used to my being neighborly."

Clearly, she wasn't the Amy he remembered from their teenage years. Yeah, that was a long time ago, but his Amy was cheerful and fun. She wore yellow and every bright color under the sun, her long, dark and curly hair always falling loose around her shoulders. You'd catch her smiling far more than frowning, moving more than sitting, and he'd loved her like crazy. He still remembered that.

This new Amy seemed older than her age, and he'd bet she hadn't smiled at anyone other than David and Naomi in a long while.

"I'm sorry. In my old neighborhood, everyone minded their own business."

"Well, now you're in my neck of the woods." He pointed to her and winked. "Your business is my business."

She almost cracked a smile. "That's not true."

"Whatever. Learn to live next door to a concerned ex-boyfriend."

"I don't know if I can. Your being concerned about me is throwing me back a bit too many Thursdays."

"Tell me about it." He sat on the top step. "Seeing you with kids? I don't mind telling you, that's a hard one to get used to."

"My twins are *nine*."

He heard the hint of amusement in her tone. "I know!"

"They saw Rob today."

"Oh yeah?" He turned, hoping she'd sit next to him. Honestly, he wasn't quite ready to go inside.

The date with Samantha tonight had thrown him for a loop. She didn't think she could trust him to be faithful to her. Old girlfriends were apparently talking to each other. Just because he hadn't been ready to settle down for years didn't mean he couldn't be ready now. But Samantha wanted a guarantee. He refused to give her one. It should be enough that he would consider being exclusive and see where it went.

He was talking with someone right now who could tell Samantha that there were no guarantees.

His older brother, Finn, had been married and divorced. Almost all of his classmates in his graduating class, if they'd married, were getting divorced or already divorced. It wasn't just Amy and Rob. Probably half their class. He decided it best not to mention this. His duty was to cheer Amy up, not make her realize she was part of a growing, not-so-elite club.

Amy took the invitation and sat next to him, leaving a healthy two feet or more between them.

"This was to be his weekend, but he had to work yesterday and nearly forgot about today. It's not like this is the first time he's conveniently let it slip his mind or been late to get them. We started doing this a few months ago after he moved out."

"How do they like spending the night away from you?"

"Oh they're fine. *I'm* the one with the problem. I don't know what to do with myself without them." She rubbed her hands up and down her shins. "That probably makes me sound like a neurotic helicopter mom."

"Nah, it makes you sound like a good mom. You love your kids. What's wrong with that?"

"Nothing. Right? Nothing at all."

"Of course, Rob would say I forgot to have fun. That once I became a mom, it became all about them and I forgot who I am as a person."

Ouch. It sounded like the idiot might have a point. After all, his father had some saying about a broken clock being right twice a day. Not that Declan would be caught agreeing with Rob.

"Do you think that's true?"

"No, just ask my kids. I'm full of fun." She sighed. "Not so much lately. It's my job to be the bad guy. Rob has a place with a swimming pool, and he serves pizza and junk food."

"How disgustingly predictable. He wants to be 'fun weekend' dad."

As a rule, Declan knew enough divorced couples to not

make broad statements about any one of them. Some of them even got back together, or attempted to, anyway. Especially when kids were involved. That might even be the case with Rob and Amy. He could see it happening the moment Rob realized Amy was still young and beautiful. Maybe the moment *she* remembered and started dating again.

He remembered now there was something he'd wanted to say to Amy for a long time. It probably wasn't what anyone would expect but it had weighed on his mind for years.

"Meant to tell you, I was very sorry to hear about your dad."

Amy's father died when Declan was away at college. His mother had phoned him, in tears, because a good man was suddenly gone from the world. Declan hadn't come home for the funeral, but he'd heard all about it through his family. The entire town, just about, came out for his wake. Naturally, Amy was devastated to lose the man she'd long considered her hero.

"It feels like a long time ago, but thanks."

"I wanted to call you, but…you know. I figured I was the *last* person you wanted to hear from." Declan held the keys in his fist tighter. "Anyway, a few months ago we had a scare with my dad. It was nothing, but for a while there when I heard he'd been taken by ambulance to the hospital… Let's just say I thought that for a moment, I might know what you were feeling."

"He really loved you."

Declan shook his head slowly. "It was the baseball, Amy. Always the baseball."

Not that Amy's father wasn't a great guy, because he was in every way. But when it came to the people who loved him in this town besides his family, it was all about his baseball career for years.

"How was your date?" Amy asked, completely changing the subject.

He'd almost forgotten he told her about that this morning. But Amy was the last person he wanted to talk to about his love life. It was a sensitive issue for him, the whole trust thing.

"Good."

"Making progress toward your goal of becoming a family man?"

"Slowly. We're not exclusive."

"If you leave it up to her, that won't be for long."

"Think so?"

"All I know is it's hard to find a good man. Even harder to keep him." And with that, Amy stood and moved toward her front door. "I'm going to take my sorry sack inside. Good night, Declan."

All kinds of replies were swirling through him, such as some men weren't worth hanging on to. Like Rob. Such as it wasn't her fault she'd lost herself in her children. It wasn't her fault Rob had bailed instead of trying to rediscover her.

The marriage vows were for better or worse, not "until things get tough."

But instead, all he could say was, "Good night."

Chapter Five

Amy clasped her hands together and remembered the capable, confident woman she'd seen in the mirror this morning. The one who'd kept a household of four running smoothly for nearly a decade. The one whose children were always on time, always clean, always at the top of their class, always respectful and well behaved. The one her children had kissed and hugged before she left as if she was a superwoman going off to conquer the world.

If only this woman across the desk from her, or anyone else for that matter, would see her the way her children did.

"So… You basically have *no* experience?" the human resources representative said, studying Amy's half-page résumé.

Amy repeated what her mother and Bianca had told her to say. "Not outside of the home. But I've balanced our checking account for years, kept track of my hus—ex-husband's business expenses and filed our taxes every year."

"I get it. If only the experience we have as domestic engineers—" she held up air quotes. "—counted in the workforce. It should. I know you can do the work, Amy, and certainly be trained. But we're looking for someone who can just come on board and hit the ground running."

"I understand."

The woman was kind enough to let Amy believe she might possibly still be in consideration by telling her a decision wouldn't be made until next week.

She also walked Amy to the front door. "I've been where you are, returning to the workforce after a long break raising my children. It's taken years to get back to where I was when I left. We say we respect women who choose to stay at home but when it comes right down to it, we don't. If it were up to me alone, Amy…"

"That's okay. I'll find something."

"You want some advice? Take a course at the local community college, then volunteer your services for someone with a business who might need them. Say a friend, or neighbor. At least you will get experience."

"Great idea."

Yet Amy had been working for free for many years. Rob wouldn't like the idea. He expected her to help out now that they had two homes.

It was almost as if the woman could hear Amy's thoughts.

"And your ex? He's just going to have to get used to the fact that you might need a little more time to get back into the workforce. You'll be expected to get back to work but it won't be that easy and he needs to understand that."

"Thanks for your support. It's honestly nice to talk to someone who's been there."

"And come out on the other end fresh as a daisy. You'll get there, honey."

The interview took far less time than Amy had allowed for it. It was true what people said: a no comes a lot faster than a yes. She drove back to Charming and decided to stop by and see Bianca. They'd met at the neighborhood park and become close friends when their children were only a few months apart. Bianca only had one at the time, her son Matthew. Now she had an adorable four-year-old too, named Henry.

Amy felt a bit like a boomerang driving back onto her street in the neighborhood that had come to be known as "IT alley" since so many of the professionals here worked in the field. Apparently she couldn't really leave her home. She passed by it, seeing no one in the front yard. They'd sold it to a couple of childless professionals.

"Hey!" Bianca opened her arms wide to Amy. "Welcome back, you."

"Just got back from the interview. It didn't take long."

"Ugh. I'm sorry."

"It's okay. My first try. I'll get better at selling myself. Though the lady was also a single mom and had some great advice."

She followed Bianca into the kitchen and told her what the woman had suggested.

"Or maybe you could go back to school and get your teaching credentials like you wanted."

"I don't know if Rob would want to give me that kind of time."

"Who cares? He's the idiot. Why make life easier for him?"

Funny, Amy still mistakenly thought of them as a team. The team that got to raise David and Naomi. But in many ways that's what hurt the most. She'd been abandoned by her co-captain in the middle of the playoffs.

The thought suddenly conjured Declan in his baseball uniform, those tight biceps and muscular thighs. Declan had a fastball that went close to ninety miles per hour, according to the town lore. It still surprised her that he thought baseball was the main reason her father had adored Declan.

Sure, it helped, but it was the way Declan treated Amy that her father loved most.

This seemed to be the start of another week of nostalgia for her. She was no longer the girlfriend of the town's best ballplayer and hadn't been for over a decade.

"Matthew wants to try out for Little League," Bianca said, pulling a couple of sodas from the fridge.

Dear Lord, baseball was everywhere now. Next door, in her memories and now at her best friend's house.

"David is still committed to soccer, though he's not getting the hang of it and wants to quit."

"Maybe he and Matthew could join a league together!"

"I don't know, baseball is such a big commitment."

How well she remembered that it took up half of Declan's life, if not more. Away tournaments, fundraisers, practice. And the parents were just as involved as the kids. The Sheridans lived for that kind of thing, which was fine, but Amy didn't think she could do that level of involvement without a partner.

"It's just a city recreational league, not exactly the time constraints of Little League," Bianca said. "I know what you're thinking. You're worried about getting him to practice once you start working. You won't need Rob. I'll do it for you and at least we know we'll see each other a few times a week. The boys, too. With it being summer, I don't want them to lose touch."

She had a point. "I don't know, Bianca. I want him to stick with soccer. He shouldn't just give up. What am I teaching him if I tell him to give up when it's tough?"

"He's just a kid and is just learning what he likes. Trying things is how he figures it out. Anyway, just think about it." Bianca popped open her soda can. "So, a little birdie told me that you moved in next door to your old boyfriend. Did you know Declan lived there?"

"Nope, and neither did poor Mom. You should have seen her expression when he walked over."

"He walked over? What for? Welcome you to the neighborhood?"

"In a way. He helped us move this huge box I overpacked." Amy took a swig of the cherry-flavored ice-cold soda, her favorite.

"Oooooh." Bianca fluttered her hands near her heart and batted her eyelashes. "Declan Sheridan. God of baseball."

Amy wasn't going to mention the little talk they'd had on Sunday night after he'd come back from his date. By the time her children got home at nine in the evening, the kids were bouncing off the walls with a sugar high. David's tongue was blue from the artificially colored powdered candy she'd specifically asked Rob not to give him anymore. It took her hours to get them both calmed down enough for bed, and after the ordeal, she'd simply strolled outside to sit on the bench swing and contemplate her life's choices.

She hadn't expected Declan to roll up at midnight and want to talk. It was a surreal conversation in so many ways, talking about a huge piece of her past. The loss of her father and those painful first years without him. At first, it was like being forced to walk around without a skeleton. With zero foundation, with no bones to hold up the skin, the organs. Her father was the heart of her family and when he was gone neither Amy nor her mother knew quite how to move on.

Amy had turned all her attention toward Rob. Not on graduating from college with honors, as she should have, but with replacing a man who then became the center around which she built her adult life. It was kind of Declan to personally offer his sympathies, but it was a little too late. He'd been the last thing on her mind, and maybe he'd been right to stay away. Maybe he'd been the last person she should have seen then, when her heart was already soft and bruised. The Sheridans had attended the funeral to pay their respects, Mrs. Sheridan holding Amy so tight and close.

"I miss you, honey," she said. "Come by sometime."

Amy never had. She went on to marry Rob after they'd both graduated from UT in Austin. They'd come home, where Rob eventually got a job in IT and started working his way up the corporate ladder. Funny how at one time she'd imagined herself the wife of a professional baseball player, in a supportive role. She'd wound up as the wife of a software salesperson, in a supportive role. Then she'd had children. Another supportive role. The choices were a bit old-fashioned of a millennial such as herself, but her father was a conservative man, and that's the home she'd grown up in.

There was never a time in her life in which Amy built her life around the idea of what she wanted it to look like.

That was going to change.

Tuesday night was slammed at the Salty Dog, and not just because they were short a waitress again. Declan filled orders at the bar and as usual helped wherever else he could. It was summer, and the tourists who came down to see Galveston always made their way to Charming eventually. The board-walk here was the best, with festival rides on one end and restaurants and shops on the other. The Salty Dog Bar & Grill was just one of those establishments, built in an area considered historical because of the last great hurricane.

Declan had been working here for three years now, ever since shortly after the new owners took over and brought it back from the brink of financial ruin. They were great guys, too, three former navy SEALs, and Declan respected the hell out of them. His cousin was a SEAL and Declan knew all too well how much dedication was involved. When Cole decided he wanted to spend less time behind the bar and more time as a silent partner, the hours increased for Declan. It was now his full-time job. Despite the fact he had a degree in physical education, the one year he spent doing the work bored him so much he moved on. Every now and then, he got asked to coach, usually by his own father. But more often, the parent of a child interested in baseball thought Declan could perhaps offer "a few pointers." He always refused politely.

They didn't want to hear what he had to say. What he would tell them wouldn't get them to the top of any team's roster. Because what Declan would say wouldn't win any awards.

Do not make any one thing, whatever it might be, the center of your life.

Yes, that included baseball. Oh yeah, by the way, it also included football, basketball and soccer. All sports. *Want to be the best of the best? Cream of the crop? Top of the heap? Then never mind what I said. Make [insert sport here] the center of your life. Morning, noon and night. Make all decisions based on the sport, including what you eat, where you'll live and go to college, whom you'll marry and when. Then, once you reach the top, look around and notice all you've missed.*

If you're lucky, you'll decide it was worth it.

"Hi, Dec," said Zoey. She ran the boutique downtown and was a frequent guest at the Salty Dog since she became single again. "How's it going?"

"Great, sweetheart. How 'bout you? What can I get ya?"

There was a crowd behind her and she'd been lucky to grab a seat when someone vacated it.

"Just a diet soda, please."

"Comin' right up." He poured from the dispenser and set the iced tumbler in front of her with a napkin. "You meetin' someone new here tonight?"

It seemed to be her modus operandi. Often, she'd get Declan to size up her dates by using his spidey senses to determine if the guy was a player. He'd told her repeatedly he didn't have such powers but she didn't listen. Apparently, he'd been right two out of the last three times and that was good enough for her.

She nodded. "We both swiped right."

That's how Declan met Samantha, so he didn't exactly judge. It was difficult to meet people when almost everyone lived and worked behind a screen.

"Want me to check him out?" Declan winked.

"Yes, please." Zoey sighed. "I'm getting so tired of dating. I wish I could fall in love like Twyla did."

Twyla was her best friend, who ran the bookstore in town.

"Don't worry, it'll happen."

"I hope you're right. I have friends who are getting divorced and I haven't even been *married* yet."

Declan touched her hand, ever so briefly so she'd know it wasn't a come-on, but a supportive pat. "You're beautiful and the right man just hasn't found you yet."

"Aha!"

Both Zoey and Declan startled when Samantha pushed forward from the crowd. He hadn't even seen her arrive.

"Hey, Sam. I didn't see you there."

"Of course not. Otherwise, you wouldn't be flirting and making a date with Zoey!" Her blue eyes were bulging, her cheeks bright red.

"What?" Zoey turned, dark eyes wide. "Oh, no. He just—"

"Save it, sister. I know when two people are flirting with each other."

Declan swallowed the irritation at this latest display of jealousy. He'd been through this with Samantha on their last date, when she'd accused him of checking out every woman in the restaurant, including their waitress. But he refused to avert his eyes and act like he was afraid to see the sun when simply talking to a woman standing right in front of him.

He and Samantha made up the next day with her sending him sweet texts with deep apologies and regret. Now this. She had obviously come here to spy on him.

"What were you guys talking about?" Samantha continued. "I heard you call her beautiful. Did he call you beautiful? Are you making a date? Do you know Declan and I are dating?"

The questions came so rapid-fire that Zoey blinked after each one.

"I was...he was just..."

"Zoey, you don't have to explain a thing." Declan spread his arms across the bar. "Sam, can I get you something? Otherwise, I have customers."

"No, I'm leaving! And don't call me."

"Wait! I'm here to meet someone," Zoey called out, then turned to Declan. "I'm so sorry. I ruined things for you. Let me talk to her."

"Don't even think about it. It's her problem. Not yours."

He went about his night, mixing cocktails, refilling beers and listening to sob stories. Declan had become an expert at listening, which was a gift. No one understood how incredibly difficult it was to listen without offering commentary. One guy was going to ask his wife for a divorce because life was too short and he was miserable, which only made Declan think about Rob the Idiot. Another lost his job, which earned him a free beer and plenty of sympathy from Declan. Eventually Zoey's date showed up, and Declan determined the guy wasn't a player through the process of the size of his tips. Also, he didn't take his eyes off Zoey the entire time, obviously smitten. She happily waved as they left together.

He was cleaning up for the night when the first of the texts from Samantha came. They arrived one after the other, rapid-fire, and he didn't respond to a single one.

I'm so sorry, baby. Please forgive me. I lost my head tonight.

Text me when you get home. I want to apologize in person.

And then the one that really got to him:

It's just that you're so wonderful I can't believe you'd want to be with me.

Far from inspiring his forgiveness, it only made him wonder what he'd done to make her feel that way. Samantha was a gorgeous woman but so incredibly insecure it had become draining. He didn't know where that insecurity had come from, but understood it had nothing to do with him. Maybe someone in her life hadn't believed in her enough, possibly at a young age, and it affected all her adult relationships in the sense that she didn't see herself as deserving, either.

Declan couldn't relate. For all else his parents had ever done, they'd certainly instilled a sense of self-worth in both of their sons. That, plus they had modeled a healthy kind of long-lasting love that while inspiring, was also deeply intimidating. Declan wasn't sure he could ever aspire to reach the goal and it had intimidated him for years. Only once in his life had he had a long-term serious relationship. Come to think of it, in his entire dating life, he could remember only one girl who'd trusted him without any doubts.

He wondered what Amy saw in him all those years ago and why she'd always believed in him.

Chapter Six

"Everyone wants experience with software accounting programs I don't know anything about," Amy said.

Not much demand for those users of home-based accounting systems or basic Excel spreadsheets. That was one requirement for many of these positions, but it was only the tip of the iceberg. They wanted so much more.

"Do you *enjoy* accounting?" her mother asked.

Mom had come over to help unpack the last of the boxes. After a week, there were still boxes filled with books, knick-knacks and all her children's homemade treasures. She would probably now store those due to lack of space.

It wasn't that Amy loved accounting; that was beside the point. It seemed to be the best-paying skill she could use from her years of being home.

"I'm not qualified for much else. There aren't even many receptionist jobs. I could answer phones and greet people but that's all mostly automated now."

"There are a few places left that still prefer the human touch. I'll ask my hairdresser if she could use a backup receptionist."

"Okay."

She had time, but Amy felt discouraged at every turn. Secretary positions at law firms wanted someone who had her paralegal certificate, too. Some preferred someone with a law degree who was working on passing the bar. And every job, from clerical to entry-level sales, required a college degree. At least she had that.

Last night, Amy had further investigated the requirements needed to be a credentialed teacher in Texas, and found it would only take her a few months to complete them. There were some districts in the state so desperate for teachers that with her bachelor's degree in hand, she could start working right away while going through the process. Dallas was one of those cities. Charming was not.

She was not moving to Dallas.

The situation wasn't as desperate as one would think, even if Rob would object to her waiting four to six months to start work as a teacher. She remembered that she wanted to make decisions from this point forward based on her own desires. Yes, she would prefer to teach. It had always been the dream before she married. She would also like to start contributing financially and stop feeling like one of Rob's responsibilities. It was time to break away from him and truly be on her own but it was easier said than done.

Without another thought, Amy filled out the information and sent for the packet to begin the process of becoming credentialed. It didn't matter whether or not Rob liked it, she was doing this. If she could find another job in the meantime, she'd do that, too. Amy felt so good about this, she closed her laptop and stretched. It was satisfying to be on the way to something new and possibly exciting. Her brand-new life.

"I did it," she told Mom.

"Another interview?"

"Nope. But that will come, I hope. I'm applying to become a teacher."

Mom's smile was ear to ear. "Honey! That's wonderful.

It's what you always wanted, and I don't see why you *can't* be a teacher. Don't forget—one day you'll look around and realize that all along you were blooming."

Amy ignored that latest flower metaphor.

"I won't make much money but hopefully enough to help take care of us. It's going to take me a few months to get through the process, and then I'll have to find a job in our district, which might take a little time."

"Perfect. You and the kids will both go to school every day. Summers off. It's ideal."

Amy held up a palm. "Don't tell the kids. To them, six months is a lifetime. I'll probably have to find another job until then anyway. Just something temporary."

The boardwalk was always busy during the summer months, and maybe she could swallow the little pride she had left and dispense kettle corn at the Lazy Mazy counter or saltwater taffy at one of the gift shops. Minimum wage wouldn't cover her half of childcare, but her mother could help some days since she was down to part-time hours at the post office.

Naomi burst through the screen door and it slapped on its hinges.

"Mommy! I found a little girl that wants to be my friend. Her name is Ruby. Can we play?"

Surprisingly, her least-outgoing child had found the neighborhood friend first. "Sure, but play here until I meet her mother."

"Her mom's at work, but her babysitter said okay!" Naomi ran back. "Ruby! My mommy says it's fine!"

Amy exchanged a smile with her mother, as the two girls bounced in and whizzed by her into Naomi's room.

"Where's David?" Amy asked.

He'd been playing a video game when she'd started her online job search.

"He's outside, too. Kicking around that soccer ball but not looking too happy while doing it," Mom said, peering out the window to the front yard.

"What do you think? Should I let him quit?" Amy didn't know what to do here.

On the one hand, he seemed miserable with soccer, and on the other one, Matthew had been bugging him about joining the baseball rec league. David said he'd like to try baseball instead. It seemed the ideal situation.

"I've never subscribed to the theory that a child who's miserable should be forced to finish what he started just for the sake of finishing," her mother said.

"I should probably go talk to him."

Amy stopped mid-step when she noticed David having crossed their shared lawn, holding his soccer ball under one arm, engaged in conversation with Declan. Should she interrupt? It appeared so earnest, with Declan lowering himself in a half crouch to meet David's eyes. The moment made her mind buzz with a sudden remembrance of Declan coaching some of the kids when they'd both volunteered summers with underprivileged kids from inner cities. He'd taught them sports. She'd worked with kids on math skills and science.

She'd often witnessed teenage Declan in that same crouching earnest position giving a kid some inspirational nugget of wisdom. Now it was her own son.

These moments of nostalgia had to stop!

"He's talking to Declan right now," Amy said out loud.

Mom looked up but didn't say a word.

Amy smiled. "Mom? No comment? Should I go stop him from talking to David?"

Mom lowered her head and folded another sheet. "I don't

know. The other day, I pulled out some old photos of you two and I remembered that your father liked him for one important reason. The way he treated you. Whether or not you two wound up together, I guess I can't really hate him anymore. He was a good kid."

"You should have never hated him."

"I just hated the way I saw you hurting after you broke up. But, as you said, it's ancient history."

"He's been helpful so far. I don't see why I can't let him give David some advice about soccer."

Amy went about her business emptying the dishwasher and organizing her shelf space. Twenty minutes or so later, David walked back inside. He set his soccer ball down and came in the kitchen to join Amy and her mom.

"Can I have a snack?"

"Sure." Amy whipped up a peanut butter and jelly sandwich and set it in front of her son. "Did Mr. Sheridan give you some good advice about soccer?"

"Who's Mr. Sheridan?"

"Oh, um, our neighbor. Declan. He's Declan Sheridan."

"He said his name is Declan and that's what I should call him." David took a bite of the sandwich and swallowed it with some milk. "I'm quitting soccer. Declan said it was a good idea."

"W-what? What do you *mean* you're quitting soccer? We talked about this."

"I know, but Dad said I could quit if I wanted to, and now Declan said I should. He said soccer isn't really a sport anyway, 'cept in England. They call it football over there. Isn't that funny?" David chuckled.

Amy didn't think any of this was *funny* at all. A sport only in England? Um, how about the rest of Europe and South America? Outrage burned through her. Teenage Declan used to spout words of encouragement to kids who wanted to play sports. But he'd just told her son, her boy, to give up. Just because something was too tough. Oh hell no, this was not going to happen. She was in charge over here. As for Rob, she'd deal with him later.

"I'll be right back."

This time the screen door slapped on its hinges with enough force to make them whistle, and Amy marched next door to knock on Declan's front door.

Declan opened his door to Amy. She was dressed in tight jeans and a snug T-shirt, her hair down around her shoulders. It was longer than he'd ever seen it before and still had the same waves it always had. Her hair, as always, was as shiny as a copper penny and he wondered if it still smelled like apples.

"Can I talk to you for a minute?" Amy said, with zero preamble.

He waved her inside. "Come on in."

She probably needed help with something like a clogged sink. He was ready to do his duty, and not only because his father would no doubt at some point ask him about his project. The truth was he enjoyed helping kids. Plus, Amy and her children as neighbors happened to be a great improvement to the previous tenants, a middle-aged couple who fought all day and "made up" all night.

Her little boy was a smart kid, easy to talk to. He reminded Declan of Amy, but then so did her little girl.

"What's up?"

"Did you tell David he should quit soccer?"

Ah, well, she was getting right to it. This was just one of the many ways he was helping Amy. Soccer was a useless sport in the United States. *I mean, c'mon.* If you didn't play baseball, you had only two other choices: basketball and football. But everybody knew baseball was the holy grail. The king. The all-American sport. David knew what he wanted, anyway. All Declan did was nudge him a little. David wanted a good excuse to quit because he hated the game. He'd told Declan he wasn't any good with his feet, and what was wrong with putting his hands on a ball, anyway?

"He told me he hates soccer," Declan said.

Amy crossed her arms. "Regardless, we had decided he would stick with it."

"Yeah, he told me that's what *you* decided, but he's the one forced to kick a ball around the field."

"Declan, would your father have let *you* quit baseball?"

Probably not, but that wasn't the point. His father nurtured the desire he saw in Declan in the first place.

"I never wanted to quit baseball," Declan lied. "I loved baseball."

Point being, he *had* loved baseball until it stopped being fun. Until it started to be all about expectations instead of love of the game. Even then it took years to beat it out of him. He hated to see a kid like David forced to play a sport he didn't even like when he was still only a kid. If Declan had sensed any kind of desire to improve, he'd like to think he would have encouraged that. Even if it was, you know... *soccer.*

"You got good at baseball because you stuck with it. Which is all I want for David. How can he know if he's any good at it if he doesn't give it a real try?"

"He *did* try. Don't you want him to have fun with the sport?"

He understood some parents started pursuing the scholarships early on but that didn't sound like the Amy he knew.

"That's all I want for him."

"Well, he's not having fun. And after talking to him, I don't think it's because he isn't giving it his best efforts. It's because soccer just isn't for him, apparently."

"But... He had fun at first, and he wanted to do this."

"Well, that's changed. He talked to me about how he's been doing. Even his coach thinks he should give up."

Amy stared at him blankly. "Excuse me?"

"You heard me. A kid needs to be encouraged by his coach."

Just the idea a coach would have said that to the kid enraged Declan. His father would have words with the man.

"I had no idea his coach said that. Now I'm mad."

"Well, there you go. A good coach makes all the difference. Listen. Why don't you let him play baseball? That's a real sport."

"It's your sport, so no wonder you prefer it."

"It's America's sport, Amy. *America.*"

She cocked her head and smiled. "I see. Baseball, hot dogs and apple pie. I think I know the song. And your preference for the sport has nothing to do with your storied history?"

"It's a great game. The best. I stopped playing because I didn't have what it took for the long haul."

"But you did." She studied him, sincerely assessing him, it seemed. Probably because she knew too much. "You always had what it takes."

He changed the subject. "There's a rec league, so why not do that and see how he likes it? It's not exactly Little League."

"That's the second time someone told me about this, but I don't think I can sign him up. I'll be working as soon as I can find a job, and I can't count on Rob. He travels so much. Bianca said she would help but she's on the other side of town now. It's asking a lot."

"I can do it. All you had to do was ask."

She blinked. "Why would I ask you?"

"Because we're old friends, I'm your neighbor, a baseball enthusiast and former teacher, player and coach." He held both palms out in an "I give up" gesture. "Other than that, no reason I can think of at all."

Amy snorted. "Okay, I think you've made your point."

"Take advantage of the fact I'm right next door."

"Yeah? And what will your girlfriend say about you helping your ex-girlfriend?"

"Are you kidding? It won't bother her at all."

The truth was that Samantha probably wouldn't like it very much but that wasn't going to stop him from helping David. This was about the kid, not Declan and Amy.

They were ancient history.

"Okay. Fine. I'll talk to him."

And then, "history" walked out the door, sashaying her butt, leaving Declan to swallow hard and wonder far too much about how history tended to repeat itself.

Chapter Seven

That evening when Amy tucked the kids into bed after reading to them, she brushed the soft dark hairs along David's hairline. His hair was thicker now, no longer those tiny wisps of fine locks. His smooth skin was still soft as a baby's, though she would never tell him that. She would quietly hang on to those little snippets of his babyhood and tuck them away.

"Why didn't you tell me what your coach said?"

"I didn't want you to get mad and go yell at him."

Oh dear. She was that transparent.

"Well, he shouldn't have said that to you. It's discouraging and just plain wrong."

"Yeah, that's what Dec said."

Interesting. Already calling their neighbor by his nickname.

"If you want to quit soccer, it's okay with me. I want you to have fun. But you have to promise me you're not just going to give up on the next sport when it gets hard. This is it." She tapped the bridge of his nose. "I can't let you give up again. This time, you'll have a good coach. But sometimes persistence is the answer when it's not easy in the beginning. Try and try again."

"For real? You mean I can play baseball with Matthew?

Thanks, Mom!" David reached to give her a hug, and his smile tugged on her heart in a sweet ache.

Her baby. The very least she could do for her son right now, after all she and Rob had put him through, was let him have a fun summer playing the sport he wanted. In the end, it was Declan's sincerity that convinced her to let David try baseball. For an athlete of Declan's caliber to offer help was not something she could take lightly. She would get over her humiliation at accepting assistance from her ex-boyfriend for the sake of her son. The regret she'd carried about Declan was all in the past, unfortunately replaced by Rob's far greater abandonment of his family.

That last year together, she and Declan were about to go their separate ways but neither one of them knew how to handle it. She didn't want to bring up the fact he was going to Arizona with a full scholarship while she would stay in Texas. She loved him and assumed they'd get married after college. He was seventeen and hadn't received the memo her heart sent via the "read my mind" express.

The point was she'd gotten over Declan, which had been possibly the deepest cut to her heart since it was the first. She would get over Rob too.

Just before she turned off the bedroom light and pulled the door halfway closed, Amy thought of one more thing to ask.

"Are you okay? About me and Dad?"

"No, I don't like it. I wish we could all live together again like it used to be."

"I know, honey. But… We've talked about this."

"I know, I know. It isn't my fault, or Naomi's, but Mommy and Daddy can't live together anymore. But I don't see why not!" David threw his hands up.

Because he doesn't want to be married anymore.

How does a mother tell her children their father doesn't

want to be married to their mother? What if they get it into their heads that he might decide he also didn't want to be their father anymore? Amy couldn't explain what she didn't completely understand. For some reason, she and Rob had grown apart. It was all the traveling, all the loneliness, she guessed. When Rob was gone, she and the kids bonded and, without realizing it, they'd failed to include him.

This was obviously going to be a much longer conversation and Amy didn't have any platitudes left in her tonight. She'd given David baseball. Now all she wanted to do was go to bed with a good book and not think about jobs, finances, teaching, baseball and far-too-good-looking exes who lived right next door. Her brain was fried. She'd like to hang up a sign that read, "Gone fishing. Try again tomorrow."

But moms didn't get to take vacations. Actually, she had been hoping David would say, "I'm okay," and a rush of shame hit her. It wasn't her son's job to assuage her guilt. He was simply being honest.

"That's a tough one to explain," she summed up. "Do you know how sometimes you used to ask me and Daddy about a certain joke you heard on TV that you didn't understand and we'd say that's grown-up stuff?"

"Yeah?"

"Well. This is grown-up stuff, honey. I'm sorry."

David sighed and rolled over in bed. "Okay."

Amy pulled the door closed and strolled into the quiet of the kitchen. She wasn't used to all this alone time in the evening, something she used to crave.

Just give me a minute alone, she used to say. Just one or two minutes in which she didn't have demands on her time. For years, it was either the kids or Rob. He'd always been so needy, too, like a third child. If she didn't pay Rob enough attention, he pouted and complained. But if she let go of one of the many chores she did for him to spend time with him instead, he'd also complain. She couldn't win.

Now she had all the time she needed and hated every second. She was truly alone. All her friends were still where she used to be: evenings were family time, and for connecting with the husband. Talking, watching movies, eating the junk food they wouldn't let the kids have. Amy and Rob were the first in their group of friends to get a divorce, and to hear them tell it, no one saw it coming.

Why can't you just be happy, how about that? Fake it till you make it.

Amy poured herself a glass of the Pinot Grigio that Lou and Mom had left behind on move-in day and went outside to the porch. This had quickly become her routine. A glass of wine, sometimes a book if she could concentrate, and her porch swing. From here, she had a nice view of the coastal skyline in the distance and every now and again she'd see the boardwalk's roller coaster make its highest turn and drop. On her right, the lighthouse still beamed its rays even if it no longer led ships to shore.

Next door, the front door opened and Declan walked outside, staring into the black night, apparently deep in thought. She didn't know if this was also his routine and had assumed the other night had been happenstance. The thought occurred she should change her routine and left as quickly as it came. She was done trying to make life easier for men. They could both be out here at the same time. It didn't mean they had to chat.

Declan finally noticed her. "Oh, hey."

"Hi," Amy said and waved at him with her glass.

So much for ignoring each other.

He walked over, which shouldn't have surprised her. Declan had always been a friendly sort, and she imagined he was popular at the Salty Dog with both men and women.

"By the way, I told David he can quit soccer and we're going to try the rec baseball league. I really appreciate your offer to get him there, but for now maybe you could just give him a few pointers."

He stopped at the bottom of the steps to the porch, as if waiting for an invitation. "I'll teach him everything I know."

She'd make room for him on the swing but sitting close to Declan didn't suit her guarded heart. Declan was a tough man to ignore. She might be able to overlook the way he'd bruised her heart for the sake of her son, but that didn't mean her heart was open for business. Besides, Declan was taken.

"That's all I can ask of you."

"Well, you could ask for more but I know you won't."

At this, that old sly grin of his appeared. The one just this side of wicked, which always made him look as if he'd just told a dirty joke. He was an incurable flirt.

"Can I ask you something?" He took a seat again on the bottom step.

The distance was safe and Amy approved. He wasn't encroaching on her space and she could live with this geography.

"Sure, ask away."

"Why did you always trust me so much? When we were going out?"

What a weird question. It seemed to open up some difficult times in their past and Amy would think he wanted to avoid all that right now. But, if they were truly going to be friends, they should probably talk. It was too late to save their old relationship but they could still be good friends.

"Well, it wasn't easy. I'm sure it won't shock you to know women love you."

"You never seemed to mind. It's like you knew I loved you and that was enough somehow."

"I don't think you can have much of a relationship without trust. And I do realize how ironic that is. I'm alone again, and yet I trusted my husband. Just like I trusted you."

"It's not your fault, Amy. Believe that."

"Why are you bringing this up now?" She considered. "Oh, I know. Did your girlfriend already give you a hard time about living next door to me?"

"Nah. But, the thing is, she doesn't trust me. At all. I've given her no reason to doubt me. So, I don't really understand." He rubbed the edge of his jawline with his thumb, and she heard the sound of thick bristle.

"Ah, okay. Let me help you out there. You're a big flirt, Declan. And that can feed a woman's insecurities."

"I can't change who I am." He lifted his shoulders. "Maybe I'm a flirt, but I'm not a cheater."

She'd wanted to believe that. "You had me doubting that, near the end. Not that I blame you entirely. We were young."

"Wait a second—" he interrupted.

She kept talking. "We were going to have to break up and you and I both knew it. And you did it, possibly in the only way you could. At least this way you didn't have to deal with me trying to figure out a way we could have a relationship a thousand miles apart because you know I would have tried."

"Can I talk now?" Declan's jaw was tight in a way she recognized. "Is this what you think just because I didn't want to get married? You're right, I didn't want to get married or talk about getting married or think about getting married. Yeah, I had no idea what we were going to do, but I loved you, and I would have never cheated on you. I want that on the record."

She had a difficult time biting back a laugh. "What record?"

"The history record that exists here, between you and me." He waved one hand in the space between them. "I think it's only fair."

"I wouldn't want to be unfair." She smirked.

"So, this is on the record now—we didn't break up because I wanted to be free to be with other women. Honestly, the relationship we had taught me how to *be* in a relationship. It showed me that I know how to be loyal. I know I can be faithful when I love someone." He shook his head. "I have a tough time getting anyone to believe it. But you did, at least for a while."

"Honestly, Declan, that's not your job. If you're being loyal and honest, then the woman should know it. She'll see it. There's always going to be a little faith involved. A little leap to take. If your girlfriend doesn't trust you, yet, it's probably because she's still getting to know you."

"Maybe you're right."

"Okay." Amy stood. "So glad we had this chat."

"Hey. Are you still looking for a job?"

She turned to see him twirling the neck of the bottle of beer between his fingers. In spite of their discussion, or maybe because of it, the parts of her body not directly connected to her heart kicked alive. He was such a sight, his tousled dark blond hair and formidable athletic build. And she was a woman, even if she was a mother first. Of course she found Declan Sheridan attractive.

"Yeah, still on the hunt but for something part-time now. I'm getting my teaching credentials so hopefully I'll start teaching sometime next fall. It's going to take a few months."

He gave her a slow smile, which seemed genuine. "That's great, Amy."

"It's what I always wanted."

"It's what you always wanted."

They spoke simultaneously and she almost called "Jinx" but instead they both laughed.

"We need a cocktail waitress at the bar. It would just be a few nights a week but it might work for your purposes."

It sounded perfect, actually, because she might not even need childcare. That would make up for the difference in a lower wage, not to mention the tips. Mom and Lou could help out more on the weekends, too, when they didn't work. She'd wanted a nine-to-five job Monday through Friday for the purposes of working days while Naomi and David were back in school, but practically, working weekends and nights made more sense right now. And it was just temporary.

"Really?"

"You have to share your tips with me, though." Declan winked. "That's the setup we have."

"And I assume you share your tips with the waitresses?"

"Correct." He mock saluted her.

Oh, this would be good. Declan would earn astounding tips. Everyone tended to like him. Women thought him handsome, but men weren't threatened by him and considered him a "bro." Probably because of the sports thing.

"I'll go and apply tomorrow."

"I'll put in a good word for you. Honestly, you've pretty much already got the job if I have anything to say about it, which I do."

A warm rush of excitement rolled through Amy. She was going to start her journey toward independence. Soon she'd contribute to the household finances and maybe even make a few new friends in the process. At least she wouldn't be stuck inside the house feeling sorry for herself. It was a new beginning all around. By next summer, maybe she'd be enjoying her first summer off from her teaching position. Her kids would be happy and well adjusted and every moment of pain she'd been through in the past year would be behind her.

"Thanks, Declan. I won't forget this. You can consider your previous record expunged."

"I didn't need it expunged." He stood. "I just needed it *corrected.*"

"Then it's been corrected and amended." She took a deep breath. "And, if there's anything that needs to be *forgiven—*"

"Which, there isn't."

"Well, it would be forgiven if there was anything to forgive since certain people were seventeen."

"Lucky for you and me both, there isn't."

Boy, he wasn't going to let this go. Fine. It was all good. She smiled her thanks, went inside and shut the door, leaning her back against it. After the divorce, after Rob had said those ugly words, *I don't think I love you anymore*, Amy thought she'd never crack a smile again, much less laugh.

Now, she chuckled, remembering the expression on Declan's face as he asked for their mutual history record to be corrected. It was so long ago she'd honestly forgotten most of it even if her mother hadn't. That was okay, she wouldn't soon forget the first man to break Naomi's heart, either. The truth was her own teenage insecurities had fed into the belief Declan wanted someone else besides her, and that was the only reason they'd broken up. Not that he wasn't ready to get married, and she was. All that was in the past.

Amy's old relationship with Declan was gone, replaced with something she would have never imagined.

A sweet and solid brand-new friendship.

Chapter Eight

The Salty Dog Bar & Grill was a throwback to Amy's college days, and she fell right into step after her first day of training. Debbie, who'd been with the Salty Dog back when it was under its previous ownership, was a great help. As it turned out, she was also a single mom and had been able to support herself and her two kids for years. Encouraging, even if Amy didn't see this as a permanent stop. One of the owners, Adam Cruz, had given her an interview, which as Declan had said seemed to be mostly out of formality. She'd filled out a bunch of forms and walked out of the bar with the job.

When Rob made his weekly check-in call to the kids, she'd told him of her plans.

"Really? Waitressing at *your* age?" Rob snorted.

"Until my teaching credentials come through and I can find a position in the district. What did you expect? It's not like I have any experience working outside of the home."

"I thought you'd be able to find something better than *waitressing.*"

It was Rob's attitude about her efforts more than anything that made Amy say her next words.

"I was hired on the spot. Declan Sheridan got me the job."

When they'd split, Rob swore there was no one else. It was immature and childish, but she didn't know whether Rob was already dating someone new. She and Declan weren't dating, and never would be, but Rob didn't have to know that.

"Your ex? Quite a blast from the past."

Rob sounded unconcerned but what did she expect? He'd only be jealous if he still had any feelings left for her. She was silly to play these games with her ex-husband and resolved not to do this again. They were both going to have to move on and be adults about this.

"He's been a good friend to me."

"Well, I agree it can't hurt to have him help coach David. He's got to be good for something, right?" Rob chuckled, as if this was their private little joke. "But I'll be doing most of the coaching, of course."

"Of course." Amy snorted that time. One good snort deserved another. "But naturally, Declan is a gifted athlete so it's a great opportunity for David."

"This is just for fun. We don't need *Declan Sheridan* to train our son for the majors."

"He's not." Amy heard herself defending him. "All he wants is for David to have fun and learn to excel at a sport. That will give him confidence, which will spill over into everything else in his life."

She bit back Declan's other less-than-charitable comments about soccer or any other sport besides baseball.

In the end, Amy found waitressing not that different from mothering with the marked difference of being on her feet far longer. Also, her customers weren't adorable and darling children she'd birthed but demanding adults who didn't like waiting a second too long.

The restaurant was set up so that there was a bar area with some seating and a limited food menu, split from a full-service grill. She worked as a cocktail waitress for the bar side of the restaurant, and on weekends, according to Debbie, they were slammed. Good for tips, not so good for her feet.

"Here we go." Amy settled four drafts on a table.

"Finally!" one of them said. "I was about to *die* of thirst. Next time I'll order something simpler than a *beer*."

How sweet. He sounded like her nine-year-old son.

Amy smiled, thinking, *You overgrown child. Go home to Mommy now.*

If he ordered a sandwich, she might be tempted to cut it into triangles for him.

"Y'all just holler if you need me." She took her tray and was headed back to the station when a couple of women flagged her down. "What can I get for you?"

"Diet soda for me," a beautiful blonde said and then held out her hand. "I'm Samantha. You and I have a lot in common."

"Really?" Amy smiled, taking her hand.

She could use some friends. These two women appeared to be out for a girls' night. She couldn't remember the last time she'd been out with the girls. It was possibly for Bianca's thirtieth birthday party in which Rob behaved as though he should receive a commendation for watching his own children the entire evening so Amy could join her friends for a few precious hours. But those types of girlfriend celebrations didn't happen often anymore. She missed them.

"Declan told me he got you the job. I know you were his first girlfriend, and I'm his latest." She smiled. "Well, and possibly his last."

"If he shapes up," the equally gorgeous woman across from Samantha said. "I'm not sure he deserves you."

This must be the girlfriend Declan had mentioned who didn't trust him like Amy always had. She wanted to help Declan the way he'd helped her.

"You are so lucky," Amy said. "Declan is a great guy. He cares so much and he helps everyone. When I moved in next door, he carried in our heaviest boxes. He—"

"You live *next door*?" Samantha said. "He didn't mention that."

"Yes, my children and I are renting the house. It's…my mother found it…"

"What about your husband?"

"I'm divorced," Amy said, bringing her tray up to her chest like a shield.

Samantha's friend's eyebrow quirked up and her mouth pursed. With that reaction, you would have thought Amy had said, "Declan has a really nice ass." This had all gone sideways on her somewhere along the way. Maybe they thought of her as some wanton divorcee, plying single men to her house to help unclog sinks and maybe get a little action on the side.

Please. *Her?* She could barely spell *divorcee.*

She should have never tried to help Declan and just stayed in her own lane!

"I'll go get your drinks." Amy rushed off.

The rest of the night passed in a blur, and she didn't have any further interaction with Samantha when a couple of seats were vacated near the bar and they joined Declan, who was working a shift tonight, too. He was so busy Amy found herself waiting at the bar station to place her orders.

"What can I get ya?" Declan finally got to her.

"A mojito, a Tequila shot and a draft beer," Amy said.

"Got it."

She waited while Declan made the drinks, wondering how and when she'd mention her faux pas with his girlfriend. She didn't want him to be caught unaware just in case he wanted to preemptively tell Samantha so it wouldn't appear he'd been hiding anything. At the same time, Amy realized she was getting a bit too involved in this matter, but she couldn't help it. Misunderstandings often led to breakups when couples didn't talk.

Amy waited for her drinks while stealing occasional glances at Samantha, who at least didn't seem to be upset. She'd probably just been surprised, but c'mon, Amy was zero threat to someone who looked like *Samantha*. In fact, she seemed to be fending off advances from both left and right.

"Declan," Amy said, and he leaned in. He did that a lot due to the level of noise in the bar. "I'm sorry, but I may have misspoken. I accidentally told Samantha I live next door and she seemed a little surprised you didn't tell her. I don't want to get you in any trouble."

Declan simply shook his head and waved it away. "No problem."

Classic Declan. His attitude had always been rather cavalier, which had been part of the problem. Declan never really seemed to be invested in anyone or anything besides baseball. Amy shook the idea out of her mind and worked hard the rest of the night, getting some great tips from a mommy and me group when a mother recognized her from school pickup.

She caught Samantha and her friend leaving, she blowing a kiss at Declan, he smiling. So, they must have resolved everything. Again, classic Declan. There wasn't much he couldn't smooth over with *those* dimples.

At the end of the evening, Debbie joined Amy. "You did good tonight. Are your dogs barkin'?"

"If that means my feet are killing me, then yes." Amy leaned against the bar and took her weight off one of them.

"Have a seat. Before we leave, Declan always rallies the troops."

"Rallies the troops?" Amy wrinkled her nose.

"Basically we sit and chat, have a soda, and he'll buoy our spirits after a rough night. He's kind of inspirational, actually." Debbie grabbed a stool and encouraged Amy to sit.

She would make excuses to run home for the babysitter, but her mom was her sitter, and already spending the night. Instead, Amy texted her so she wouldn't worry about her being a few minutes late.

"Hey, ladies." Declan carried with him a tray of their sample platter of onion rings, potato skins and jalapeno poppers and set it in front of them. "Compliments of the chef. How was your night?"

"I had a pretentious jackass who had me running back and forth because his steak wasn't cooked to perfection," Debbie said. "It was fine! You want to know how much he tipped me? The worst tip of my night!" She took an onion ring and bit into it.

Debbie worked both sides of the bar and grill, and she didn't stop complaining for ten whole minutes. Compared with her, Amy had a great night.

Declan listened patiently, while he poured Debbie soda into an iced tumbler.

"Some people will never appreciate your true worth," he said. "But I do."

"Sugar, you're the only reason I'm still workin' here. I'm too old for this stink."

"I bet Amy was a huge help." Declan winked.

A wink like that on another woman would probably cause a heart convulsion. Fortunately, Amy was relatively immune to Declan. *Relatively* being the operative word.

"I don't know how I survived without her an entire month!" Debbie leaned in and gave Amy a sideways hug. "Thank you for finding this gem."

He faced Amy, spreading his arms out on the bar. "How about you? You got any complaints?"

She didn't, not really, but wanted to participate. "I guess I'm not fast enough for *some* people."

"You know, you'd think people would realize they can get a cold beer in half the time from their own damn fridge. Going out is supposed to be a social occasion, not a sprint," Debbie said. "What else?"

"Um, well." Amy drummed her fingers on the bar. "My feet hurt."

Debbie elbowed Declan. "Ah, to be young again. She's not likely to get many complaints. Such a pretty girl."

"Aw, thank you."

Amy self-consciously pulled on her work tee. She'd been worried it was a bit too tight around the boobage area but didn't think it would hurt with tips.

"Yeah, this has always been her problem." Declan slid her a slow smile. "Always the prettiest girl in the room. Nothing's changed."

A warm rush of something resembling excitement went through Amy. She shouldn't be so affected by his compliment, but it had been such a long while since she'd felt attractive.

Debbie turned to Declan. "What have you got for me tonight? I could use some inspiration."

"All right. You know what I was thinking? I realized how important we are to the people who come here every night. How important you are." He pointed to both Amy and Debbie. "Tonight, a guy told me that his wife left him two weeks ago and coming here is all he looks forward to. He knows there's going to be a kind word and a cold beer when he gets here. And Debbie's right, it's not about how fast the drink or food gets to them. It's about the social interaction. Connections. We can't forget that part of why we're here. You are very important."

By the time Amy floated outside, she was fairly certain both she and Debbie felt like the Mother Teresa of the service food industry.

"What a gift," Debbie said and waved as she got in her sedan. "I stopped having to go to counseling when Declan started working here."

And to think Amy had briefly wondered why Declan had chosen to go into bartending when he had a college degree and had briefly taught math at a high school in Houston.

You might be able to take the player out of the game, but you couldn't take the game out of the player.

Declan Sheridan was a born coach, whether he realized it or not.

Chapter Nine

The following week, Declan rushed to baseball practice located at the field where the city recreational grade school team practiced. He'd promised David he'd be there, and Amy was also counting on him. While he thought it a good idea they drive together, it worked out that Rob had the kids this week. At the last minute, Naomi didn't want to come with them to the practice, so Amy drove to Houston to pick David up.

Declan planned to meet them but hadn't anticipated Samantha would keep him on the phone so long. She'd grilled him about Amy because he'd made the cardinal mistake of forgetting to mention she'd moved in next door. Sue him, he didn't think it that important.

"What part about *ex* do you not understand?" Declan had said.

"The part where she's young and pretty, living next door and working with you."

"Well, she needed a job. She's a single mom."

"Which means she's available."

Declan sighed. "Look, she's not interested in me, and I'm not interested in her. She was my *high school* girlfriend, for crying out loud. People change. They grow up and move on."

"Regardless, I would like to know where *I* stand with you."

He'd wanted to gouge his eyes out. They'd had five good dates, and the promise that they each were ready for something real. It shouldn't be this difficult to be in a relationship. But Declan had given up so many times before when things got tough that he reminded himself he shouldn't. Not this time. He would try to work it out and see where this went. Samantha was beautiful and nice, but unfortunately desperately insecure. It wasn't his job to constantly reassure her that he was ready for a relationship. He could talk her up, and he did, frequently reminding her she was smart and capable.

"I've got to go," Declan said, seeing the clock and realizing he was running late. "Talk later."

He parked now and quickly rushed to the field where the kids were gathering, catching a glance at Amy out of the corner of his eye. She was seated in an area with the moms, including Bianca, and waved to him. Declan waited on the sidelines, closer to the action, and where David would see him. The coaches had gathered the kids together in groups and when they were dispersed, David caught Declan's eye, grinned and gave him a thumbs-up. The coach looked on the young side, but that was fine. You didn't have to be an expert to coach kids. All you really needed was a positive attitude. If he'd learned nothing else from his father, also known as his coach for half his life, he'd learned that tidbit. Fake it till you make it, sure, but at some point you had to believe in yourself before others would follow suit.

"Declan! What are *you* doing here?"

Declan froze and slowly turned because he'd recognize his father's voice anywhere. "Don't tell me."

"Okay, I won't tell you." His father grinned.

"You're coaching this rec league?"

"Nope. I've come to scout the talent. My Little League team will be starting up soon. Why, are you thinking of coaching? That's great, son!"

Declan was still absorbing the scouting comment, so it took him a minute to correct his father. "I'm not going to coach. I'm just here to support my other, um, project. You know, the one I told you about."

Truthfully, Declan hadn't thought of any of this as one of his goals in a while. Not until he saw his father.

"Ah, yes. How's that going? When I told your mother Amy moved in next to you, she did a little jig. You know how she adored her."

Declan shook his head. "We're just friends."

"That's how it starts." His father clapped Declan's shoulder. "So, which little guy is yours?"

"That's David." Declan pointed. "Amy and Rob's son."

His father crossed his arms and spread his legs, coach style. "Well, let's see what he can do."

"Dad, look. This is a fun league. We just want him to enjoy the sport of baseball, not start grooming a major league player."

"Absolutely. I get it. Going all the way is always up to the kid. But let's face it, it's fun to *win*."

When his father was right, he was right. Yes, winning was fun. That's why Declan was here to watch. He still loved baseball because the desire had never totally dimmed. The game could be fun and winning could be fun. It was just the "at all costs" part he had a little trouble with.

"Your boy is looking good out there," his father said.

David was running near the head of the pack.

"He's enthusiastic, that's for sure."

"When are you coming over for dinner? Your mother wants to know."

"Soon, I guess. I figured you two were happy enough with Finn and Michelle taking up all your time."

Finn had asked his girlfriend to marry him, and the wedding plans were ongoing. Declan had grown tired of hearing about flower arrangements and color hues. He'd check out and was fairly certain Finn did as well but didn't want to admit it. Not in front of his lovely fiancée, in any case. Declan had never seen his brother so in love with a woman and recognized the glassy-eyed "I can't believe I'm this lucky and she chose me" look in his brother's eyes.

Declan had seen it in the mirror once before, a long time ago.

"They're not over all the time. We want to meet Samantha," his father said.

"Sure, at some point you will."

Declan wasn't quite ready to introduce her to the family. He realized that probably said something.

"Still too new, huh?"

"You could say that."

Finally, the coaches organized the kids into positions on the field and it began to get interesting. Levels of talent and experience were almost immediately apparent to Declan. One kid, the one who'd been hanging close to David, was a natural. Declan could see it in his form, in his easy handling of the mitt and ball. They were well-acquainted friends.

David, on the other hand, seemed to be meeting the ball and mitt for the very first time.

"Who is that guy?" Amy overheard one of the moms whisper to her friend. "Is he a dad?"

"Is he single?" someone else asked. "Does anyone know?"

From beside Amy, Bianca elbowed her. "Single or taken, he still has that tight ass and wide shoulders."

"I hadn't noticed," Amy said.

Bianca snorted. "Right. Just keep telling yourself that."

Amy *would* keep telling herself that. Declan was here for her son and while she was eternally grateful for the interest he'd taken in helping him, she wasn't going to allow anything else to permeate her active imagination. Recently, she'd gone back to an old habit of watching old Hallmark movies late at night while the kids were asleep. Quite a few involved reunions and second chances with couples who didn't work out the first time. The idea was certainly enticing because, sure, it would be nice to wind up right back where she started with the one man she thought she'd always love. The one man she never dreamed would let her go. But that was all a fantasy and good material for books and movies. She loved the romance and illusion of it all, but that wasn't real life.

Real life was broken crayons, eternally lost socks and stepping on Legos while barefoot.

The boys were warming up, and Declan and Mr. Sheridan appeared deep in conversation.

"What's Declan's father doing here, anyway?" Amy said.

Though she occasionally saw him around Charming, they hadn't talked in years. She assumed he'd met Declan here for some reason.

"He occasionally comes out to scout talent for Little League," Bianca said.

Amy blinked. "Um, what?"

"You heard me. We have high hopes for Matthew." Bianca sat up straighter. "Mark has been working with him since he was four."

"Aren't they a little young for scouting?"

"Oh, no. You can never get started too young in a sport."

Amy worried now that she'd neglected her son's physical

abilities and certainly Rob had, too immersed in his own career.

"I suppose it's always good for those scholarships."

She and Rob hadn't really saved well for their kids' college funds. When she'd mention it, Rob would say there was plenty of time for that.

"Exactly," Bianca said. "That's what we'd like, a full ride to university. The chances are like two percent so it's extremely competitive."

"I had no idea you and Mark were thinking this way."

"Well, I'd have asked you about it if I'd known your ex was *Declan Sheridan*."

"I wouldn't have been able to help as I hadn't talked to him in years."

"But that's changed."

"Only because he lives next door, and he was nice enough to recommend me for the part-time cocktail waitress job."

Bianca scrunched up her nose. "How's that going?"

"It's exhausting, sure, but the tips are great."

It wasn't exactly a thirty-something-year-old's dream job, but she was proud of how hard they all worked. Valerie, her kid's teacher in third grade, was a waitress too when she'd first returned to Charming. She occasionally still helped out even if she was married to one of the owners now.

"I'm glad you got something. Mark said Rob was complaining how you weren't really trying to get a job because you wanted to stay home with the kids all summer."

"Excuse me?"

"I shouldn't have said anything. I'm sorry."

"It's okay. Rob should know better." Her eyes followed Declan, who was now squatting in front of David.

"Hoo, boy, he's a handsome one. I mean, hell, if I were

single… You better believe I'd go after him, guns blazing."
Bianca chuckled maniacally. "Half the moms here would."

"He's got a girlfriend."

"Hey, if there's no ring on her finger, it's fair game."

Amy huffed. "Regardless, I'm not exactly in the position to date anyone."

"And why not?"

"Because I'm ma—" Amy stopped herself because she was about to say the word *married*. "Oh my God."

"Uh-huh. Did you forget? No, you're not."

It was possible that she still felt married. After all, the past few months hadn't been entirely different from Rob being away on business trips. She'd held down the fort before. But now the fort had moved, and she had a job.

"You're free to date again, to find love again, to rediscover every part of yourself that you've buried."

Amy grabbed Bianca's hand. "I'm not ready."

She truly wasn't ready to be out in the world as a single woman.

"I can't blame you," Bianca said. "I talk a good game, but I don't know what I'd do if I was suddenly single again. It's scary out there. I wouldn't know what to do first. Get a tummy tuck? Boob lift? Or take me as I am? There's a lot of competition out there."

Competition? Bianca made it sound like a sport. Amy loved sports, from the sidelines, cheering others on. She didn't want to be in the game!

"I have children," Amy said.

"Yes, they come first, but what are they going to think if they see their mother wither up and never experience love again? What kind of an example is that? Are they going to feel responsible for you and your future happiness later on?"

Maybe Bianca didn't realize this, but she was making Amy's blood pressure spike.

"I'm just thinking out loud here."

"Well, don't. Please."

Bianca patted her hand. "You're going to be fine. I bet you have someone new before Rob does."

"Is Rob... Is he seeing anyone?"

Bianca's husband and Rob were golf buddies, after all. She might know something.

"I... I don't think so."

But suddenly Bianca became tight-lipped and watching the kids play of the utmost importance. They were really just throwing a ball around the field, practicing catching.

"Bianca." Amy pulled on her arm. "You would tell me, wouldn't you?"

"Yes, of course I would." She straightened. "He's not seeing anyone, but he signed up for Tinder."

Oh my God. *Tinder?* "So I suppose my children will have to be around this woman, whoever she might be."

"Well, same goes for you and whomever you wind up dating."

"I need to talk to Rob about this."

"Don't tell him I said anything!" Bianca hissed.

"No, but if we're going to start dating other people, don't we need to let each other know? Should our new people meet each other? Do we all have to get along? When is the right time to introduce the kids to the new people? Where do we find the new people? What if they don't work out *either*?"

Amy was vaguely aware her voice had increased in volume and pitch to the point she was on the verge of a full-blown anxiety attack.

"Calm down," Bianca said. "Breathe."

"Yes. I'll breathe." Amy covered her face with her hands and rocked back and forth in her fold-up chair.

"It's going to be okay," Bianca said. "You don't need to worry about any of this now. There's time. Hey, look, the boys are having such fun."

Amy looked up just in time to see Matthew toss the ball to David. Not only did he not catch it with his glove, but the ball also hit him in the stomach and knocked him to the ground.

Chapter Ten

"**Y**ou okay, David?" Declan rushed to his side and squatted beside him.

Best not to overreact and give David a chance to show how badly he might be injured, if at all.

He sat up, blinking. "I almost caught it."

"You missed the ball, kiddo." Declan's father stood behind him. "But to be fair, he threw a little low."

"A *little*?" Declan whispered.

"I'm sorry," Matthew said, openly sobbing.

David stood. "I'm okay, Matt. Really. Look, see?"

David proceeded to wiggle his arms and legs in the air to demonstrate. It made Matt laugh out loud and he wiped his eyes with the back of his hand.

"You got a heck of an arm, kid," Declan's father said, patting him on the back. "Fastball. Think about Little League when you finish here."

And work on your aim, Declan thought but kept to himself. These were just kids having fun. Yes, it was fun to win but it was also fun to play. Even getting hurt could be fun. Every boy wanted battle scars.

"Is he okay?" This was from Amy, having now reached them after probably pole-vaulting over all the other moms.

Matthew's mom was comforting him. The coach was now inspecting David and gave Amy a thumbs-up.

"He's great! What a champ! He took that ball and even though it knocked him down, he got right back up again."

Declan slid Amy a smile he'd bet she needed right now. "It happens to all of us."

"Okay, let's huddle, guys!" the coach said and gathered the kids in a circle. "Great effort!"

"It happens to us all," Declan said.

"I don't remember it happening to you," Amy said from beside him.

"You didn't know me when I started Little League. I had my battle scars," Declan said.

"Amy! Sweetheart!" His father came up to them, and folded Amy into his arms. "So good to see you here."

"Mr. Sheridan," Amy said. "It's been a long time."

"It sure has. My wife wants you over for dinner sometime." His father turned to Declan. "Can you bring her, son? Might as well. Two birds, one stone. How about Saturday. Does that work for everyone? Okay, good. I'll tell your mother."

With that he walked away, pulling out his phone, presumably to call Declan's mother.

"Notice how he doesn't wait for an answer. Pay no attention to him," Declan said, crossing his arms and facing the kids. "Apparently my mother heard you live next door and would like to have you over for dinner. I'll make up some excuse for you."

"That's okay. I wouldn't mind seeing them again. It doesn't mean we have to go together."

"Trying to get rid of me?"

"They're great people and I won't lie. This is a great time

for me to be around anyone who actually likes me. Rob's parents blame me for our divorce."

"No kidding?"

Amy nodded. "But I meant we don't have to drive together. Actually, you can probably see them anytime. And Samantha wouldn't like it anyway. So, you stay, and I'll go."

"You want to see my parents that badly?"

"I love your mother's cooking."

"Fine, you go, and I'll watch the kids." Declan wasn't actually joking because he would watch her kids if she wanted him to. It was good practice.

"You want to babysit?"

"How hard can it be? Your kids are angels."

"Thank you, but they have their moments. I might take you up on that because I'm going to have to start dating at some point."

"Yeah?"

"Bianca tells me I may as well get out there. Rob already set up a dating profile."

Yikes. To Declan, that meant maybe Rob had been thinking for a long time about moving on. He was ready. And also an idiot to think he could ever do better than Amy. Declan was still trying, more than ten years later.

"Dating apps aren't the right place for everybody."

"I guess I'll set up a profile and at least try."

Amy sighed, as though she was talking about how she had to go home and take care of her laundry. A chore. Something necessary but unpleasant. He didn't want to discourage her because maybe everybody had to get that sort of thing out of their system after a divorce. Finn certainly had even though he hadn't required the services of an app. His brother was one of the smartest people Declan knew. But those apps were a much safer place for men than women. As a bartender, he'd heard his share of war stories. Well, he'd worry about Amy later.

As the kids were excused, David walked toward them, grinning.

"Did you have fun?" Amy asked, tipping his chin.

"The coach said I'm a badass," David said, puffing up with pride.

"Hey, I want to teach you something about that glove. Can I see it?"

When David handed over his glove, Declan laid it out and punched it a couple of times in some key areas. The best way to break in a glove was with repeated use, but this one felt like it had just come off the conveyor belt. He should take it home and season it with some oil or conditioner.

"The trick is this glove is going to have to form to the shape of your hand. Play catch with it a lot in your spare time. Hit it a few times and knead it when you're sitting down watching TV. It's going to be your best friend, this glove."

Declan handed it back to David.

"Thanks, Dec." He took the glove back and hit it a few times with his fist. "I'm going to practice with my dad this week."

He exchanged a look with Amy.

"Rob has the kids for a whole week a couple of times this summer. This is one of the weeks."

Ah, no wonder she was filling out profiles and accepting dinner dates to his parents' home on a Saturday night. Amy Holloway was lonely. The thought pinched his chest far sharper than he wanted it to. He didn't want to care about his ex-girlfriend being alone. That wasn't part of this. She was pretty and attractive, sure, but he was already dating someone. Plus, she wouldn't want a round two with him even if she liked his family.

Declan drove home, pushing away intrusive thoughts of Amy filling out dating profiles and meeting married men on the make, or worse. He had to protect her from that, but how, and was this even his responsibility? No, it was not, but he still felt protective over her. She was far too easy of a mark for the wrong man. Amy had always believed the best of people, though he considered both he and Rob had proved her wrong more than once.

Declan noticed the sedan parked in front of his house and recognized it as Samantha's immediately. Perfect. He needed this now, a diversion from Amy, and how she'd been wearing a hot pink dress today that accentuated her hourglass figure. There had always been something special about Amy. It was that single almost undecipherable element that once made her the first thought on his mind in the morning and the last in the evening. It happened the first time he ever laid eyes on her. But he couldn't let her infiltrate his thoughts and life again just because she was right next door, in his line of sight, messing with his head.

No, Declan. We're not doing this again. No more FOMO. He was going to stick with a relationship and try. A real effort. Just like in the old days with Amy when somehow, they made it work for a while even when the odds were against them.

Samantha was by his side before he got out of the driver's seat.

"Hey there."

He accepted her hug and a quick kiss, hating the way intrusive thoughts of Amy clawed at him almost instantly. It was only because he'd just seen her, wearing a short dress, and now here was Samantha also wearing a dress. There was nothing wrong with Samantha and he only wished she had a little more confidence in herself. Then again, maybe she sensed his thoughts were running to Amy. He quickly gave himself a mental slap.

"I thought we could hang out a while." She held up a six-pack of beer. "I brought refreshments."

Sure, what better gift to bring a bartender than beer. It came with almost no thought behind it, he'd guess. Declan held back his snarky remark because she meant well. It wasn't her fault that he had Amy on his mind. Her sweet and gentle smile as she'd watched David play. The way she'd hugged his dad, as if little to no time had passed.

And realizing she was lonely.

"You sure had to rush out when we were talking earlier," Samantha said, following him in when he unlocked the front door.

"Sorry about that. I promised David I'd be there and since I encouraged him to play baseball, I figured I should honor that."

"Oh, I thought it was a work thing?" She set the six-pack on the table.

"No, I told Amy I'd meet her there. She had to bring David from his father's place. It was a good practice, I'd say, overall. But David is going to need some coaching. He has to build up his confidence."

He thought about how that ball had hit him, and how that kind of thing could make a kid feel. Weak. Scared. Yet David took it in stride, just like Amy would have. He just got right back up again. That's just the kind of attitude that made champs. David was that type of kid, too, raised by a mother who believed in him.

Within a few minutes, Declan became aware that he was talking about baseball more than he should. Samantha had a glazed look in her eyes.

"Sorry. I'm talking too much baseball."

"Wait. David is *Amy's* son?" Samantha's eyes tightened and narrowed.

"I thought I mentioned that. She moved in next door, a single mom. Two kids, David and Naomi."

"You neglected to mention you're coaching her son!"

"I'm not coaching him, just giving him a little advice here and there. He hated soccer so I suggested he try baseball."

"Which sounds an awful lot like coaching, *Declan*. So, you're basically going to be spending time with your ex-girl-friend, your first love, who lives next door and also works with you? Have I got that right? Am I missing anything?"

"Hang on there. You're overreacting." The minute the words came out of his mouth, he wished he had the super-hero power to stop them.

"I'm *what*?"

"Not overreacting, sorry, I didn't mean that, but I'm not dating Amy. We're friends. What do I have to do to convince you?"

She crossed her arms and jutted her hip. "Remember when we both first swiped right and we had that first incredible date?"

"Yeah."

"We both said we wanted the same things. To settle down, invest time and energy into a relationship and make it work long term. We said we'd explore this spark between us because we both want something permanent."

"I remember. That's exactly what I've been doing here. Exploring this idea."

And so far, he felt that this place that promised so much initially was barren.

"We both have. You know what? In every relationship, there are deal breakers, like cheating and unhealthy arguments."

"I'm with you so far."

"And in addition to that, I believe in every relationship each couple should be allowed to make at least one unreasonable demand of each other. Even if it doesn't make any sense. Only one demand like this is allowed in the course of an entire relationship. It shows a commitment to each other and making it work. This, of course, shouldn't be anything unhealthy or which would intervene with our careers."

"Give me an example."

She shrugged. "Well, let's just say there's a certain guy that relentlessly flirts with me at the ice cream shop in town. Maybe your one unreasonable ask is that I never go in there without you."

"And where's the trust?"

She frowned. "Like I said, it's just a one-off. It has nothing to do with trust. It's our one unreasonable request."

Declan did not like where this was going. "Have you ever done this before?"

"Yes, and it works well. It's a confidence booster. It shows when someone is feeling insecure that the partner will do anything to ease that feeling."

"I'm guessing you already have your demand."

She motioned between them. "If this is going to work between us, you need to stop talking to Amy."

Declan was too stunned to speak for a moment.

"I work with her. Of course I can't stop talking to her!"

"You're right. That does have to do with your career. I guess there's no other solution but to say I'm going to ask that you not help David. The two of you are going to be thrown together too much. I don't like it. This is something I'm asking you to do to reassure me that you want to be with me."

Declan was doubting he did want to be with Samantha with every passing minute.

"This is really how you want to use your unreasonable demand? Your one chance and this is it? I can't help Amy's *kid*?"

"It has nothing to do with him. I'm sure he's a good kid, but you and Amy have history. I'm sorry, but he will probably do fine without you."

"This is *completely* unreasonable."

"Which is the point."

"No."

"No, it's not the *point*?"

"No, I'm not going to do what you've asked. The idea is crazy anyway. If you have to make that kind of demand, something is already wrong."

"Exactly. You're not all in, Declan. Admit it."

She was right, of course, but at this point he couldn't be blamed for wanting out.

"It shouldn't be this hard." He shook his head.

Maybe he should give up on finding a relationship for now. Focus on his goals, like his father kept hammering away at him to do. Though bartending was a good fit for him, he acknowledged it wasn't a career. He couldn't raise a family on his salary. Once, he'd had lofty goals. The major leagues. The World Series. Maybe his father was right and he'd quit too soon. But probably not. Declan's gift was knowing when it was time to go.

When he'd given everything he had in him.

"Samantha, I'm sorry, but this isn't going to work."

Chapter Eleven

"Stop it. You're being ridiculous." Amy wiped the last tear away as she took the turn into Charming. "Okay, big-girl panties. I can do this."

She'd been weeping since driving away from her babies and the apartment they'd be staying in with Rob for the next week. At least the drive to Houston after baseball practice had been wonderful, with David talking about how much fun he'd had. Being knocked to the ground and getting up again, he'd said, meant he had what it took to play baseball.

"That's what Declan said."

He later recounted the story in great detail to Rob and Naomi, beaming the whole time.

Then came the time when she had to leave Rob's bachelor pad and make the drive back home to Charming. Alone.

"Bye, Mommy! See you soon. Don't worry about us," Naomi said. "I'll take care of Daddy."

On the one hand, her chest ballooned with pride. On the other, she wanted to tell Naomi it wasn't her job to take care of her man-child father.

"See ya next week, Ames!" Rob waved. "I'll have them call you *every night*."

The shake of his head and scolding tone in his voice said, "I *know* how you are."

But it would be the first time she'd been separated from her children for so long and this didn't feel like a small thing. Intellectually she understood they'd be okay even if Rob didn't exactly inspire confidence. She didn't doubt that he loved his children. Maybe he'd learn the rest of raising them and the place that guidance and example meant in parenting. Either way, they all deserved a relationship with each other. In the beginning, Amy thought just handling the children on his own might be enough to bring Rob crawling back. But they were good kids, and so he didn't. He truly didn't love her anymore. Didn't even need her.

This was for the best, much as it hurt like an ice pick stabbing her eye. She didn't want a man to stay with her simply for the sake of the kids. She wanted a man to love her through the laundry and the dirty dishes and the clogged sinks. Through the peaks and the valleys of a long-term marriage.

Amy pulled into her driveway just as Samantha was leaving Declan's next door.

More like storming out, actually.

When Samantha reached her sedan, she turned and, red-faced, shouted and pointed to Declan loud enough for the entire neighborhood to hear:

"You don't deserve me!"

Wow. *You go, girl.* How wonderful to have the fortitude to claim those words so loudly. As soon as Amy got a chance to scream where no one would hear her, she'd do the same. For now, Amy found her red-rimmed eyes in the rearview mirror.

"You don't deserve me, Rob!"

She didn't know whether Samantha meant it or was simply once again having a jealous meltdown. But for the first time since her divorce became official, Amy meant those words. Rob did not deserve her or the love she'd showered on him over the years. Whether or not she'd still been in love with him, which could be argued, she was devoted to him and no one could disagree with that fact. She'd built her life around Rob. Maybe it hadn't been smart, or modern, but they had children and she'd assumed she and Rob would grow old together.

So much for assumptions.

Amy waited a moment to get out of her car, for Samantha to drive off and the drama she'd witnessed to subside. Checking her mascara in the mirror, Amy wiped away the last dark smear and tucked a stray hair behind her ear.

Declan stood on the lawn watching Samantha drive away, hands in his pockets, head lowered.

When he caught Amy's glance, he smirked and lifted a shoulder. "My batting average just took another hit. Pretty soon I'm going to stop swinging."

"Are you okay?"

He crossed their shared lawn. "I should be asking you that question."

His head tipped to the side, and it seemed as if the sun itself shone a bright light into her eyes. Leave it to Declan. He'd noticed.

"I feel seen and I thought I was hiding it."

"What is it? Did Rob say or do something to upset you?"

"No. I'm just going to miss my kids."

"It's only a week. Right?"

"Feels like a month."

She pulled down on the skirt of her silly short pink dress. Rob hadn't noticed. She'd even lost a little weight on the "Divorce Diet," which was a real thing, and he'd shown zero interest.

Amy's gaze followed the taillights of Samantha's car, turning at the end of the street. "Did you and Samantha have another fight?"

Declan crossed his arms. "You could say that."

"I'll talk to her for you if she's still jealous."

"Don't bother. We broke up. It's my fault, of course, as usual."

"Oh no, Declan. I doubt it's all your fault, but I'm sorry. If it helps, she sounded unreasonably jealous."

"I don't know, maybe she was right all along. I think she saw something even before I did."

"What's that?"

"I wasn't all in."

She sensed something untenable in that moment, a tiny prickle of awareness. A feeling so long forgotten that she'd almost failed to recognize it. Excitement? Anticipation? None of that made any sense, not with Declan, not here and now, and yet her body wasn't listening. And in the next moment, she didn't think she imagined the lowering of Declan's head and his eyes ever so briefly scanning her bare legs. The tiny prickle grew to a significant tingle that spread down the back of her thighs.

"Sometimes I think I'm looking for the feeling of that first time again. The first time I fell in love, the first time someone else mattered more than anyone else," he said. "I miss that."

So do I.

"Yeah," Amy said, her body buzzing. She couldn't look at him. "I know what you mean."

"Maybe everyone's like that, right?"

"Yeah. I bet."

The moment shifted to being more of a casual one, two friends discussing the challenge of relationships in the age of apps. Not two former lovers remembering they were each other's first. It was easy, of course, to romanticize now. Life was simpler due to being young with few responsibilities. Part of the nostalgia was for their youth. She shook off that sense of intimacy with him she'd felt only moments ago. Her imagination, working overtime. The loneliness didn't help. Before, she'd always had her children.

"I think I'm trying too hard to find someone special," Declan said. "I'm going to stop for a while, and just focus on my personal goals."

"Sounds like a good plan." She moved toward her front door, where in the kitchen freezer a fresh pint of Chunky Monkey awaited her.

"What about you?"

"Me?"

"Are you still going to sign up for those dating app sites?"

She wished she hadn't mentioned that. "I don't know yet."

"You saw how well mine worked out. I don't recommend it." He moved toward his door.

"Declan?" She hesitated, hand on the doorknob, but she had to do this.

He needed the pick-me-up and she could use a little unloading right now. A little honesty and barebones vulnerability when it was her choice.

"Yeah?"

"I never had a chance to tell you this, but you were the best first boyfriend I could have ever had. You made me feel safe, always, and I never doubted that you loved me. Never."

He smiled like the thought cheered him, then nodded. "Thanks for that. Good night. See you tomorrow."

Amy shut the front door and leaned her back against it. She pictured Declan moments ago, standing between a shaft of moonlight and streetlight, illuminating him. Still so attractive to her, with an almost magnetic pull. She'd almost had an out-of-body experience listening to him talk about the first time he'd ever been in love. He was talking about her, she was certain. If it were her saying the same words, she'd mean him.

She covered her face with her hands. No, no. She couldn't, and wouldn't, fall for her first love all over again.

Because that would be stupid.

The next day, Amy's and Declan's shifts at the Salty Dog overlapped. Even though they lived next door to each other, they still hadn't carpooled to work. Declan rolled in about four hours into her shift, twirling his apron between two fingers. He relieved Max Del Toro, one of the owners who occasionally pulled a shift bartending. Amy had already met him and his wife, Ava. A surly and big man, Max was the type to break up bar fights before they even started. People were generally fearful of the former navy SEAL.

Amy learned from Debbie that while bar fights were not the norm, they almost always occurred on a Saturday night during the full moon. And about 98 percent of the time they were disagreements about sport teams. People in Charming took their baseball seriously. Fortunately, the playoffs weren't going to be an issue for another few months so they were in the "safety zone."

"Hey, Declan!" Amy came up to the bar and placed her orders. "Feeling any better today?"

He flipped a glass and caught it in the air with a smile. "Best night of sleep in a while. I did the right thing. No regrets."

Good to know because Amy had seen Samantha in here earlier with another guy. She worked fast. Though she gave Amy a dirty look she didn't deserve, at least her date didn't skimp on her tip. She was beginning to think maybe she'd still work here summers, once she got a job during the year as a teacher. The people were nice, especially the owners. Valerie Kinsella had been David and Naomi's schoolteacher in third grade, and she'd already said she'd refer Amy once she had her credentials. She was working on her first teaching program online in her spare time and had the test scheduled for next month.

Busy, and serving drinks one after the other, at first she didn't recognize the man seated at a table in the bar section with two other men.

"Hey there, I thought that was you."

On second glance, she remembered Paul, who'd worked with Rob at his first tech job. She and Rob ran into him a few times at some of the corporate gatherings. He always seemed to be a bit inebriated at the events, with some beautiful blonde hanging on him. Privately, Rob told her he thought Paul had a drinking problem and a few months later when he was let go, everyone wondered if he'd said something to the wrong person in a moment of drunken stupor. She and Rob made it a practice never to have more than a single glass of wine at corporate parties.

"Guys, this is Rob Holloway's ex-wife, Amy." He waved his arm to the other two men seated with him. "These are some of my buds."

"Well, it's nice to meet y'all."

"You been working here long?"

"Just a couple of weeks."

"If you don't mind my saying, that Rob is an *idiot* to let you go." He gave a smarmy smile. Some women found his type attractive. Very smooth, usually wearing silky Italian suits and driving a BMW. "I always thought he was a jerk."

Amy was not one of the women who found Paul attractive but she smiled anyway.

"Well, thanks. Nice of you to say. What can I get y'all?"

She took their drinks and placed them with Declan, then went to her next table. Throughout the evening, she noticed Paul getting loopier and drunker as she kept serving him beer.

"Don't worry," one of his friends said. "I'm the designated driver."

Still, Amy worried. Obviously, Paul might really have a drinking problem. She'd seen a lot of people get happy after drinks in the two weeks she'd worked here but none that had to be rolled out of here. Yet his buddies were simply encouraging him, as if having a driver was all that mattered.

Amy caught him swaying a bit on the way to the restroom. "Paul? Um, do you think maybe you've had enough to drink tonight?"

"Why do you care?"

"I care because you're my friend and I'm worried you're drinking too much."

"Aw, Amy. You're so sweet. Tell you what, I'll slow down."

He did not. Worse, he got a bit looser with his hands. He kept putting them on Amy even after she asked him nicely to stop. Once, a hand on her back, then lower to her waist. The last time he touched her hip.

It was his friend that finally intervened. "Paul, stop. You've had too much to drink and you're making a gall-darn fool out of yourself."

"Screw you. Amy and I are friends and she likes me touching her." He regarded Amy. "Don't you?"

"Is that why she keeps removing your hands?"

"You don't know what you're talkin' 'bout. You're boo-tiful, Amy. You know that?" Paul pointed and slurred his words. "Maybe we can finally go out now that Rob dumped you."

"Is there a problem?" Suddenly Declan was behind Amy, towering over the group.

"No, we're leaving," said the friend. "Let's go, Paul."

"I'm not leaving. I still have this drink to finish."

"Let's go," Declan said, hooking a thumb to the door. "You've had enough tonight."

Paul scowled. "I'm not going anywhere until Amy says she'll go out with me."

Paul's friend scrubbed a hand down his face. "You've got to be kidding me."

"What? She's beautiful!" Paul yelled. "Rob's an idiot. He took my job, and he had a beautiful wife, too, and now he dumped her."

That's it. If Paul said *dumped* one more time, she was going to throw a glass of water in his face. *Dump* was an ugly word, a word that should only be used when attached to the word "truck."

Paul's friends moved to the door and one of them held it open.

"I'm not asking again," Declan said.

Suddenly every eye in the bar was on them. Amy wanted to shrink and disappear. Somehow, she hadn't handled this right. She should have stopped serving him much earlier, but she thought she'd sound like a mom telling this grown man he had to stop drinking.

Why did grown men still need mothering?

"Who the hell died and left you in charge?" Paul stood.

Everything happened fast after that. It almost looked like Paul was flying, as if he didn't need his legs because his body was propelled forward on its own. But it was Declan behind him, lifting him, carrying him, shoving him forward and out the door.

"Sorry about that," said the designated driver before he shut the door.

"I'm sorry. I should have stopped serving him."

"You didn't know, now you do," Declan said, his hand on her shoulder. "Are *you* okay?"

"Yes, I'm fine. Does Paul do this a lot?" He'd said Rob took his job, something she hadn't heard about before and wondered whether it could be true.

"Seems to be only when he's with his buddies that he gets tanked."

"I'll be ready for him next time."

"Hope he left you a good tip. You deserve it after dealing with him." Declan hooked his thumb back to the bar. "I better get back."

The rest of the night went smoother, and a few of the patrons even asked if Amy was okay. A group of senior citizens called themselves the Almost Dead Poet Society and were among her biggest defenders. Amy knew all of them from the occasional poetry readings they performed at the Once Upon a Book store in town. Mr. Finch worked the register as a volunteer, and Amy was a regular who probably kept them in business. Naomi devoured books.

"I saw Declan propel him out that front door like he had wings," Patty Villanueva, Valerie's aunt, said.

"Declan is the one you want in this kind of situation," Mr. Finch said. "He won't tolerate that kind of behavior."

Of course, they all wanted to know how Amy was doing after "that Rob" left her.

"I'm glad to see you working here," Lois, Mr. Finch's wife, said. "You'll meet someone new in no time at all."

"Honey," Mr. Finch said. "Maybe she shouldn't be in a rush. Take your time, dear."

"You'll need someone who loves children, of course."

Mrs. Villanueva dug through her purse. "I'm sure I know *someone*."

It had come to this now, Amy getting fixed up by these cute senior citizens.

"That's okay, I'm going to sign up for those dating apps when I'm ready."

"The dating apps?" Mrs. Villanueva went hand to heart. "Oh no, you're liable to meet a serial killer!"

"Or one of those people who pretend they're someone they're not," Lois said. "Like a prince."

"Anything else I can get you?" Amy said brightly, after serving their soda and iced tea.

She had to keep moving even if her feet were slowly assassinating her.

As usual, Declan's inspirational talk later that night made her feel as though she'd provided Paul with a valuable service instead of being the one to serve him one too many. Debbie complained about tips, as was her habit, and Declan made her feel better.

"If someone drinks too much? Your own damn fault. I ain't your mama. We provide a service here but it's not day care."

"But I know him," Amy had said. "He lost his job and he said it was because of Rob."

"I seriously doubt that," Debbie said. "Some drunks have a way of feeling sorry for themselves and then it's everybody else's fault."

"Debbie's not wrong," Declan said.

He'd heard it all since working here.

Amy simply nodded. "I'll do better next time. I hate that he must be so unhappy with his life."

"It's not up to you. Even his friends couldn't stop him," Declan said.

"Y'all, I gotta go." Debbie took one last bite of the onion ring on the appetizer platter he'd served them. "My old man is waitin' up for me."

"Have fun." Declan waved.

"I should go, too." Amy stood a few minutes later.

"Hang on." Declan covered her hand with his own. "I'll walk you out."

"All right. I may as well wait for you."

She waited while he cleaned up the area, put the tray in the kitchen and said good-night to some of the staff in the back.

He held open the door so Amy could walk out first. "Maybe I should follow you home. Unless you were going somewhere else first?"

"No, but what are you worried about? Do you really think Paul is out here waiting for me?"

"Just playing it safe." He scanned the almost empty parking lot, which Amy had to admit made her feel better.

There were a few stragglers, as the lot was shared with the boardwalk, which stayed open later than normal in the summertime. But almost everyone would be headed home now. She wondered if David and Naomi were sleeping or if Rob had let them stay up too late. Since she'd had to work, they'd checked in with her earlier and both sounded happy. They'd gone swimming at the complex pool and later minigolf. It was good, she reminded herself, that her kids were okay and not homesick. She didn't want to raise children who were incapable of functioning without her.

At least the silver-bright quarter moon felt like a comfort to her soul.

Because if nothing else, she and her children were sleeping under the same moon tonight.

Chapter Twelve

Declan had been watching from behind the bar much of the night as Paul got more handsy with every drink. Declan's fists clenched as that hand of Paul's just got lower and lower until it sat nearly on Amy's behind. Eventually, Declan started watering down his drinks and to hell with policy. Next he put a parasol in his scotch on the rocks just to mess with him but Amy must have taken it out. Amy, obviously new to this kind of manhandling, didn't know what to do. Plus, apparently this genius was a former coworker of Rob's who was half in love with Amy. That didn't surprise Declan, nor could he blame the man. What surprised him was how quickly everything disintegrated and Declan wound up assuming bouncer duties for the evening.

Tonight's after-work coaching session hadn't helped Amy the way it had Debbie. All Debbie needed was acknowledgment that people were, in general, cheap. But Debbie had been waitressing for decades and she didn't feel guilty about a damn thing.

As he followed the taillights of Amy's sedan into town, he considered that tomorrow he'd be mowing her lawn again. It was also the night his father had invited both of them over for dinner. She was missing the kids, so this would be a perfect distraction. Finn and Michelle would be there and they were always good for a laugh or two. He just had to make sure he got her there tomorrow and that she wouldn't make up some lame excuse.

Plus, he wanted to spend time with her, which he didn't care to analyze too closely.

They were old friends and neighbors so it wouldn't be awkward around his parents, who'd always adored Amy.

He'd become way too sentimental the night before, admitting more than he had cared to. The last thing he needed was for Amy to remember what they'd once meant to each other. He wasn't ready to open up to such vulnerable and tender spots. There was no point.

Amy was standing outside her car admiring the sky when he pulled into his driveway seconds after her.

"Thanks for following me home."

"Turns out, it was on my way," he said with a smirk.

"I hope you don't somehow feel responsible for me."

The words surprised him. He remembered how this had all started with his father, and a challenge and opportunity to help someone in need. But he'd never seen Amy as *helpless*. She was amazing, actually, raising her kids and working while studying for her teacher certifications. Honestly, Amy made Declan feel like he was standing still and she was a whirlwind passing through. This was a big deal for someone like him who'd worked half his life to leave everyone else in the dust.

"Why would you think that?"

"Since we moved in, you always seem to be around."

"Um, I live here?" He put a hand on his chest. "And no offense, but I was here first."

She bit on her lower lip, holding back a smile. "I know that. First, you helped us move in."

"That was out of necessity. Because…the boxes."

"Okay, but the next thing I know, you're mowing the grass every week."

"It's a small shared lawn, no big deal."

"Then, you're helping David with baseball."

"Well, I saw him kicking that soccer ball around and… You know how I feel about soccer."

"And then you got me the job."

"You wanted one, and it worked out."

"So, this is all a coincidence?"

No, it's not.

I wanted to support you and the kids after your divorce, but it's become a lot more than that.

You're one of the best memories I have.

He shrugged, trying to shake it off. "I guess you and I are still connected in a lot of ways."

"I guess we are." She shook a finger at him. "But you're going to have to let me do something for you sometime. No arguments."

"Oh, you're already doing that."

He tipped back on his heels, because man, she left that metaphorical door wide open for him and he was about to walk inside and get himself a beer.

"I am?"

"Did you forget dinner at my parents' house tomorrow night?"

She smacked her forehead. "Was he serious about that?"

"Have you ever heard my dad joke about dinner?"

"Do you really want me there? I thought you could make up some excuse as to why I can't go."

"Why would I do that when it will be easier if I bring someone they can talk to instead of me? Do this for me, Amy. Please."

"That seems like a pretty easy thing to do, but sure. I'll

go to dinner with your parents." She waved, unlocked and opened her front door. "Good night."

He saluted. "Good night."

Declan went inside and grabbed a cold beer out of the fridge. Usually he was a bit too wound up after work to go straight to sleep so he flipped the TV on to ESPN. He wouldn't mind going to *bed* right now, just not alone. His mind kept going to images of Amy in bed with him but he kept pushing them away.

For the first time in weeks, he pulled up the text message from an old friend.

I heard you're between coaching gigs. Could use your help with the varsity baseball team here at Charming High School. Head coach retiring next year. We could always use another science teacher, too. Know it's not what you're used to but we need you. Think about it.

Charming High School, home of the Bulldogs, the first team where he'd played varsity. The place where he'd met Amy. Declan had replied no thanks, that he wasn't ready to go back to coaching ball, maybe never would be.

He found the graph he'd drawn on the back of a napkin and laughed. He'd used the idea to get his dad off his back. Then, he thought he'd outsmarted his father. Maybe now the joke was on him.

He never imagined it would be so easy for Amy to slip back into his life like she'd never left.

"Honey, are you okay? You're not just pretending to be okay, are you?" Mom said. "Lou and I can come over this afternoon, bring you some boba tea."

"You've come over every day this week. Look, I'm fine.

I talked to the kids yesterday like I've talked to them every day. It helps that they're doing fine. It would be awful if I had to force them to go see Rob."

"Well, you've raised two extremely well-adjusted kids and that's *why* they're fine. What kind of tea would you like me to bring you?"

Nice as the tea sounded, Amy didn't have time for her mother today. That sounded awful, but they *had* been spending a lot of time together since the separation. Mom had been there for Amy when everything happened. She'd been there when Rob moved out and Amy fell apart—privately. A good mother didn't let her kids see her depressed. They may have witnessed a tear or two, and they were smarter than Amy sometimes realized. Naturally, her mother worried, and by now Amy understood all too well. Though she was thirty-one and the mother of two, her mom was never going to stop caring and worrying about her only child.

"Actually, I'm kind of busy today. I'm making lots of progress on my certifications with the kids gone, and I'm going to dinner with a friend." Amy bit her lower lip, hoping against hope Mom wouldn't ask.

"Sounds wonderful! What friend?"

Amy diverted. "It's actually dinner with my friend and the family. Not a date or anything."

"You're meeting his *family*?"

"How do you know it's a him?"

"Isn't it?"

"Yes," Amy sighed. "My friend is Declan and it's not as if I'm meeting his family for the first time."

"Declan Sheridan?"

"Yes, he's been really kind and sweet. He's helping David with baseball and he always mows our lawn along with his own. He got me the job, too, as you know."

At that moment, the lawn mower roared to life, and Amy stepped to the window to watch Declan's solid muscular form behind it.

"I suspected he'd come sniffing around again once he realized you were available. That boy has always had the hots for you."

Amy snort-laughed. "Please. It's not like that, okay? It was actually Mr. Sheridan who invited me over when I ran into him at David's practice. So, basically, Declan and I are simply going to the same place at the same time. Nothing more than that."

"Good, because I think it's too soon for you to start dating someone."

"Rob already signed up for one of those dating apps. He'll be dating someone so I don't know what I'm waiting for!"

"Rob did? He did not! Of all the nerve."

"Mom, we're divorced. He's moving on and he's allowed." Amy's phone pinged, and she saw it was Rob's caller ID. "Gotta go. It's Rob calling."

"Hey," Rob said when she clicked over.

"Is everything okay?"

"You're going to be pissed but I got called into work."

"Aren't you on *vacation*?" He'd taken a week off work and still had the kids for a few more days.

"Yeah, Amy. I'm on vacation. But there's a problem at the main office and I'm the guy."

It's not like she hadn't heard this one before. "How long will you be gone?"

"The rest of the week. I'll just add the days to my vacation time next month, and I can have the kids for longer. If that's okay with you."

"When should I come pick them up?"

"I'll bring them to you." He was quiet for a second and

when he resumed talking his voice was hushed. "They miss you, anyway. It's not the same here. They're good kids, and they're trying. But this isn't their home."

For a moment, Rob sounded so discouraged that Amy felt a stab of sympathy. Clearly, this divorce was hard on him, too. He'd been the one to make the decision to end their marriage, but on some level maybe he finally regretted what it had done to their lives. To the kids.

Amy hung up with Rob, then went out front to talk to Declan. She'd have to cancel dinner tonight. Good thing she hadn't gone through too much trouble worrying what to wear.

He looked up to see her waving, stopped the mower and grinned. "Hey."

"I'm sorry, but I can't go to dinner tonight. Rob is bringing the kids by in a few minutes. He had some work emergency."

"Well, too bad for him, but great that you got the kids back early. I know you missed them."

It was awfully insightful of Declan, and not even slightly judgmental that she, as a single woman, wanted to be with her kids instead of other adults.

"Yes, but I'm sorry about dinner. Tell your parents I appreciate the invite and maybe I'll see them some other time."

"Bring the kids. That's not a problem."

"Bring them? Really? You don't think your parents would mind?"

"Are you kidding? My mom loves kids. She can hardly wait to have grandkids. She's been bugging Finn and Michelle since they announced they were getting married."

"Are you sure? I don't want to crash a dinner party intended for adults."

"Clearly, you don't remember my parents. Nothing fancy. It will probably be hot dogs and burgers."

But Amy did remember his parents and they were the

sweetest couple. They always made her feel like part of their family and she'd certainly had many dinners with them. Finn, with his current girlfriend, and her and Declan, together since they were young teenagers. Oh, there she went again with the nostalgic memories. She didn't know whether these feelings of nostalgia were acceptable or whether she should at least make an effort to bury them deep. Declan was trying to be nice and welcoming but she refused to get caught up in remembering too much about how they used to be as a couple. It certainly wasn't going to help to return to the setting where it all happened.

But as it turned out, Amy didn't have to worry about any of that because Declan's parents no longer lived in the same house where they'd raised their boys. They'd downsized. She was grateful that she wouldn't have to see the same nooks and crannies of the home where she and Declan spent hours making out and a lot of other stuff they probably shouldn't have been doing as teenagers.

Declan spoke as he drove all four of them in his extended-cab truck.

"Mom and Dad bought a fixer-upper with a great view of the coast and my father has been working on the house since then. It's like HGTV, but the old Tim Allen version. Power tools, hamming it up, accidents, the whole bit. Believe me, plenty of pension dollars and elbow grease have been going into the house. I think my dad needed a project after retiring from the post office."

The house was set on a small hill on the outskirts of Charming, and Amy grew unreasonably nervous the closer they got. These were old friends, simply people who might have at one time been her in-laws. She would have much rather had them instead of Nancy and John, who'd never thought Amy good enough for their only son. That's the reason she was nervous, perhaps. Every time she'd been to her in-laws, something went wrong. David tripped over something shiny and expensive that Nancy had left out, forgetting children were coming. Or Naomi decided she didn't want to try *Moroccan* food but there was literally nothing else she could eat. Not even peanut butter and jelly.

Still, maybe it was a little bit weird to be going to dinner with her ex-boyfriend. It might be odder if she was still married or if she didn't still feel this intense attraction to Declan. But she was only human, and he really hadn't changed from the person he used to be. He'd simply grown into himself, a bit taller, broader, even more confident. So, considering she'd still loved him when they broke up, and he was pretty much still the same person—except better—it made sense she was still attracted to him.

Though this would have been much easier if she could have had one of those "what was I thinking" moments about having once been so in love with him. Instead, every time she glanced over at him, she thought, *Yeah, that makes sense.*

"Hey, kiddos!" Mr. Sheridan opened the front door to a small beach cottage on a hill. "You're just in time for dinner."

David already knew Mr. Sheridan from the baseball game, but Declan introduced Naomi just before Mrs. Sheridan came up behind her husband.

"The prodigal son returns!" Mrs. Sheridan went on tiptoes to wrap her arms around Declan. "Finn and Michelle are already here, out on the deck enjoying the almost-sunset."

"Dad sanded the deck himself last year," Declan said to Amy.

"I made him hire some help," Mrs. Sheridan said. "He already had arthroscopic knee surgery on one knee. We didn't need problems with the other one!"

"It certainly helped moved the plans right along to get

some assistance. My sons have been too busy to help," Mr. Sheridan said.

"That's right, pile on the old Irish guilt," Declan said.

The three large rooms downstairs were filled with beautiful skylights bringing in natural light. There were large bay windows, wood floors that gleamed and a kitchen large enough for an island that housed modern cabinets in a dark cherry wood.

"The place looks wonderful," Amy said, as she followed the Sheridans to the deck.

There stood Finn with his arm slung low around Michelle's waist. They both turned and Finn bent down to talk to the kids' eye level, something she'd seen Declan do many times. Michelle beamed, too, as she smiled at Naomi.

"Hello! I'm Naomi Holloway." She stuck out her hand to shake.

"I'm David Holloway. It's very nice to meet you." David nodded and also stuck out his hand.

"Well, hello, Naomi and David Holloway. Glad you could make it," Michelle said. "Check out this incoming sunset!"

Beautiful bursts of yellow, red and dark blue framed the coastal skyline.

Amy turned to Michelle, speaking in a hushed tone. "I never had a chance to tell you, but thanks for referring Rob and me to mediation."

They were one of Michelle's first clients last year when she opened her own family-practice law firm. Thanks to her counsel, Amy and Rob saved money and grief by going to mediation, where they both made concessions. Michelle had advised mediation first for couples who had children and that all judges would require it, as they should. At least partly because Michelle found the perfect mediator, a kind middle-aged woman who reminded both of them of their mother, Amy and Rob were able to solve everything amicably.

"And how are you doing?" Michelle briefly touched Amy's shoulder, and there was a world of concern reflected in her eyes.

Probably because Amy had been a walking disaster when she'd arrived at the La Croix Family Law Firm to hire Michelle. Later, Amy would learn Michelle had decided divorces would only be a small part of her practice, but she'd taken one look at Amy and ushered her inside. It wasn't until she'd arrived home and looked in a mirror for the first time in days that Amy noticed her smudged mascara, red-rimmed eyes, her hair partially in a ponytail and partially hanging loose and unkempt. In addition to that, she had been wearing sandals that didn't match. She'd let the separation from Rob come close to ruining her because she hadn't seen it coming.

"Much better, thanks."

"You look happy." Michelle smiled and then her eyes found the children. "And the kids are doing okay?"

Amy followed Michelle's gaze to where David and Naomi were watching Mr. Sheridan flip the burgers wearing an apron that said, "My Grill, My Rules."

"I'm lucky. They're the best kids in the world."

"I agree. You had one of the best divorces I've ever seen, and they're the proof. Just because two people decide they don't want to be married anymore doesn't mean they can't successfully co-parent."

"That's the goal."

To know that she and Rob weren't ruining the kids meant everything to Amy. It came down to the fact that if they were okay, she was okay. Always.

Of course, it hadn't been her decision, but over the last few months she'd started to realize their marriage had turned into a habit. They'd been in trouble for a while and Amy just hadn't seen it. By the time she had, and wanted to save the marriage for her family, it was too late. She'd never make that mistake again.

Amy briefly glanced over at Declan and Finn, their backs to her, both so golden and beautiful in the fading light of the sunrays.

"Oh, wow," Michelle sighed, also looking in the same direction. "Isn't he gorgeous?"

Of course, Michelle was referring to Finn.

"Yes, definitely."

Michelle laughed. "Actually, I meant *Finn*."

"Oh yeah, so did I," Amy lied, biting her lower lip to keep from smiling.

"Right." Michelle smirked. "Sure you did."

Amy was saved by dinner, which turned out to be hamburgers and hot dogs as predicted. The trimmings were a delicious ambrosia-style salad with chunks of pineapple and cherries, homemade French fries and sweet white corn on the cob. The kids ate surprisingly well for being picky eaters, and David asked for a second hot dog.

"Ah, a growing boy!" Mrs. Sheridan said. "Honey, give him two."

There was plenty of talk of Finn and Michelle's upcoming wedding and Naomi tentatively inquired about flower girl status. Amy pressed them on the story of Finn's proposal, which apparently took place at the Salty Dog in the take-out lane. It was the site and one-year anniversary of their first date, and Michelle had arrived to stand in line and pick up their orders when Finn suddenly appeared behind her.

"I was so surprised to see him there I almost got mad. Like, you made me come and get dinner when you were already here? Why didn't *you* get it?"

"She almost ruined it," Declan joked.

But then, surrounded by family and friends seated beforehand, Finn dropped to one knee and asked her to marry him.

"After that, I forgave him."

The two kissed sweetly and Declan threw a French fry. "Get a room."

After dinner, cleanup was a family affair and didn't take long with everyone helping.

Then Mr. Sheridan wanted to show David what an old and well-worn glove would look like after a season of playing, and they disappeared into the garage with Declan and Finn following.

Mrs. Sheridan led them to the patio, where they all settled into Adirondack chairs.

"Mommy, is it okay if I read my book now?" Naomi asked.

She brought one along for every occasion, and Amy pulled it out of her purse for her now. At the moment, she was a huge fan of the old Nancy Drew mysteries.

"She asks for permission to *read*?" Mrs. Sheridan asked. "Where did you get this child? Etsy?"

Amy laughed. "If I let her, she'd read all day, but I want her to play outside, too, and be social."

"I have to find out how it ends," Naomi said, opening to her page.

"I'm the same way." Mrs. Sheridan patted Naomi's lap.

Michelle's phone buzzed and she gave it a quick glance. "Does anyone mind if I take this? It's work. One of my adoptions hit a snag and my parents are freaking out. I'll just be a minute."

"Go, honey." Mrs. Sheridan waved her away. "Take care of business."

"Don't tell Finn," she said with a wink and walked into the house, the phone already to her ear.

Mrs. Sheridan must have seen the puzzled look on Amy's face because she answered the question on her mind: What was that all about?

"It's kind of like you and Naomi. Reading is a good thing but you want her to have a balanced life. That's kind of what Finn wants for Michelle, and so does she. But can I tell you how proud I am to have a future daughter-in-law who can kick butt? It's such a good time for women right now. And as long as we all keep having each other's backs, it will continue."

"Michelle is wonderful at what she does," Amy said. "I have firsthand knowledge."

"And how *is* that all going for you?"

She meant the divorce. Everyone knew about her divorce. She wondered when people would stop asking her, but comparatively, though it had been about a year, it was still new. A year to work through all that.

Amy took a quick look in Naomi's direction, and saw her deeply immersed.

"We're finally in a good place. It was tough for a while, for all of us."

"You must have been blindsided."

"Yes. But… I should have seen it coming."

"Hindsight has one hundred percent accuracy. You probably didn't have the time, as a busy parent, to sit down and evaluate your relationship."

"I should have made time."

Mrs. Sheridan nodded in agreement. "Would you take him back now, if he changed his mind?"

Even Mom hadn't asked Amy that question. Maybe she didn't want to hear the answer because at one time it would have been yes. People made mistakes and as long as he hadn't cheated on her, Amy could have forgiven Rob and insisted on counseling to repair their marriage. But now… Now she saw so many roads ahead of her, so many choices and possibilities for an alternate future, and they all excited her in ways she hadn't anticipated. She could be a teacher and still be a full-time parent.

She could fall in love again and it didn't mean that she'd never loved Rob. He would always be the father of her children and they'd be forever connected. But she understood now that she was no longer *in* love with him. She probably hadn't been for a while. Even so, she would have stayed, because leaving was too scary.

"No. I can say that for sure. For the first time, I'm really excited about my future again."

Almost as if he'd heard, one possible future in the form of a blond, muscular, solidly built male appeared behind the screen of the glass sliders.

"It won't surprise anyone that Dad took David in the back to throw the ball around. Everything okay here?"

Their gazes met, and she allowed herself to fall into those wonderful and warm green eyes that always had a wicked smile in them.

Declan, the man who'd headlined her teenage life, was part of her present.

She could ignore that, or do what her heart wanted, and accept it for the gift it appeared to be.

"Everything is fine."

Chapter Thirteen

Something strange was happening to Declan.

All night long, he kept feeling like he was living the life he should have had all along. It was as if he'd stepped into someone else's metaphorical cleats and found they fit even better than his own. They were the brand and type he'd wanted. But Amy wasn't his and neither were David and Naomi, much as he felt inexplicably connected to them. He rationalized that sense of attachment was due to his relationship with Amy first and foremost. Declan wanted kids, he always had, but certainly never planned on raising somebody *else's* kids.

Amy turned to look in the back seat on the drive home. "Look at that, they fell asleep."

"We tired them out that easily?"

"I'm sure their sleep schedules are all wacky. Summers are usually not a strict bedtime."

"Then again, I guess my dad did throw the ball to David for an hour. Sorry about that. He can be a little...hard to contain sometimes."

"All that enthusiasm. I'm sure it's a good thing."

"It can be." An uncomfortable tension settled in his shoulders, pressing down a memory.

It was one thing to let a kid drop a sport because they weren't enjoying it, like David had. Quite another thing to discourage him from playing because he wasn't good enough. If David was enjoying soccer, Declan would have been the first to encourage him to stick with it. If he loved the sport, he would have only improved with practice.

"I feel like you wanted to say something else," Amy said. "Like there's a *but* following that sentence."

He chuckled. "You're right. *But* I believe a kid should be allowed to play for fun, while they're young."

"One hundred percent agree. Isn't that how you started playing baseball?"

"No, believe it or not, I first wanted to play *ice* hockey."

Amy snort laughed. "Um, what?"

He laughed, too. "Yeah, I know, but I was *seven*. Mom got me the pads, skates, helmet, stick. Everything I needed."

"Except the ice rink?"

"We do *have* them here."

"It's definitely not our state's most popular sport."

He heard the smile in her voice.

"Yeah, especially not in Charming, where baseball is so big. My dad convinced me I should drop it. Basically, that's the only beef I have with him. If you can call it a beef. I wish he'd supported me and I'd had the chance to explore other sports earlier on. But that's in the past."

"I never knew that." She reached and squeezed his shoulder. "You never said anything."

"By the time you met me, I was happily playing baseball. It was my life. I was on fire, which helped. But every once in a while, I wondered if I was living my dad's dream and not my own."

"Oh, Declan."

Nothing had changed. He still had a huge thing for the soft lilt in her voice when she said his name.

"No big deal."

"That's really why you quit, isn't it? Not because you don't have what it takes but because your heart wasn't in it anymore. I knew it had to be something like that. I'd never known you to be a quitter."

But the words stung because he'd quit on her. His life would have taken such different turns if he'd stayed with Amy. He couldn't help but regret his choices now even if never had before. She would have been more than supportive no matter what he chose to do with his life.

"Even though my mom was selling houses to help my father fund both mine and Finn's sports, Finn had always showed the most promise. He was headed to Olympic gold and it just made sense for me to take a back seat. I didn't mind. You want to know something funny? Finn confessed he'd felt guilty all these years that I'd stopped playing baseball. He thought it was his fault and that on some level I must resent him."

"I can't believe Finn even considered that for a minute. It's clear how much you love him. You're *brothers*."

"Exactly. Don't worry, I set him straight."

"Honestly, David and Naomi are close now but my hope is that when they grow up, they'll stay as close as you and Finn are."

"They will."

"All indications are they will, but as they get older and he's interested in teenage-boy stuff while she's interested in girl stuff…"

"News flash, that's the case now. David would still walk through fire for Naomi and she for him. I can tell."

"You're right. And it's a good feeling."

When he finally pulled into Amy's driveway, the kids were still sleeping. They didn't wake up when he shut off the truck or when both he and Amy got out.

She opened the door closest to Naomi's side. "I hate to wake her up but we might have to wake David. He's too heavy. Thankfully, Naomi's still light enough."

He wondered how this would go and whether or not they'd sleep through being moved inside, but then he remembered long family car trips to visit his grandparents. Somehow, he'd magically wake up later in his own bed after falling asleep on the lengthy car ride home.

"I'll unlock the door first," Amy said and went to the front door.

Declan hated being useless, so he carefully undid Naomi's seat belt and lifted her into his arms. Amy's eyes were wide when she saw Declan approaching the door with a little girl in his arms.

"This way." She led him to the bedroom and pulled back the covers.

Declan carefully laid Naomi on the bed. Amy removed her shoes and covered her with a blanket.

"I'll get David," Declan said and headed down the hallway.

"Let me wake him, he's heavier than Naomi." Amy followed him.

"No need." He couldn't possibly be too heavy for Declan.

Not surprisingly David went easily into Declan's arms. Solid sleeper, this one. He didn't budge as Declan carried him into the other bedroom. Amy was already there, the covers turned down. Again, she removed the shoes and pulled up the blanket, then slowly backed out of the room and shut the door.

Declan was right behind her when she did, and also when she turned and they were mere inches from each other. He should take a step back. But he didn't. Even with the bright lights of an interrogation room, he couldn't confess why except that this moment felt natural. If he read any hint of fear, or apprehension, in her gaze he'd leave her alone. Not just tonight, but every day after this. He would bury this ridiculous notion that he wanted to kiss her. He would forget the lilt of her voice when she quietly said his name. He would stop thinking of every single move in his life that had pulled him away from her as a *regret*, and reframe his thinking.

It wouldn't be the first time he'd be forced to sit on an impulse and probably wouldn't be the last.

"Thank you for doing that," she said, leaning against the door. "Even I didn't realize how tired they must be."

"Neither one of them moved a muscle."

"I think they might have…if they felt unsafe in any way. It's instinctive."

"I'm glad they feel safe with me, then." The first move he made was almost without thought, a basic tweak of her chin.

Some people might even think of that gesture as affectionately playful between two good and old friends. Only someone who wanted more would *see* more. At least, this is what he told himself. Funny how the chatter in his mind was always encouraging. Always upbeat, like he had his own eternal cheering section on the sidelines. He supposed he had to thank his upbringing for that. In this highly vulnerable moment, he could use the positive thoughts.

Because Amy wasn't smiling.

The look in her eyes, if he could still read her, was a mixture of surprise, confusion and…desire. Or maybe that was wishful thinking. The coach in the corner was telling Declan to go for it, take that risk, while the cautionary side warned he might just strike out if he didn't take his time. No use swinging at anything that came over the plate.

Lesson learned. Wait for the right one.

Then Amy took a step forward and buried her face in his chest. Her arms went around his neck and she held him tight.

"I also feel safe with you," she said. "And I always have."

Declan held her in the circle of his arms, his hands settled low on her waist. This moment was about a lot more than safety and trust for him. It was about new beginnings, and finding that some roads were circular and led you right back to where you started.

Amy was in Declan's arms and she didn't want to move. This moment should last a thousand years or more just so she could get reacclimated to the sensation of his warm hands on her body again. He'd touched her and it was genuine and filled with raw emotion. She'd missed this. It wasn't just the human touch, or one of a man appreciating her as a woman. This was *Declan* and he obviously still owned some part of her soul. She would have at one time called it the part of her soul that carried with it her youth. Declan owned that part of her because he'd starred in it.

But now he was her present, too, slipping into the role of partner so easily it scared her. He'd carried her children in and set down in their beds the way she and Rob had done so many nights. It should have been jarring to see another man in his place but somehow it wasn't, not after the initial surprise.

Tonight had been spent partially reimagining what could have been. Mr. and Mrs. Sheridan would have been ideal grandparents. Finn played his part as the playful uncle, and Michelle the sophisticated aunt who would advise them on the best universities. Amy went a little "rogue" giving everyone their roles, until she realized those scenarios meant she and Declan would be husband and wife. It was a metaphorical splash of ice water in her face because, yes, maybe she wanted that. Still.

Now, she pulled back and found Declan studying her

mouth. Then he lowered his lips to hers and kissed her, which felt like the single most natural movement. His kiss was tentative, and soft and exploring until she returned it. She fisted his shirt and leaned into the kiss, taking it deeper. But they were against the door to David's bedroom, so she pulled back, took his hand and led him to the couch.

He pulled her into his lap and there was no more talking then, just desperate and feverish kissing. She took it up a notch, daring to reach under his shirt, touching warm, bare skin and then... Amy heard something but...

"Mommy?"

Naomi's voice. Then the sound of the door creaking, that damn squeaky door, but thank God Lou hadn't oiled the hinges. Amy jumped off Declan's lap and smoothed her hair into place.

Before long, as suspected, Naomi joined them, staring at both of them from the hallway.

Naomi rubbed her eyes. "I'm thirsty."

"Of course, honey. Let me get you some water." Amy headed to the kitchen, throwing an apologetic look at the rumpled, tousled-haired, incredibly sexy Declan.

"Good night, you two."

Then he was out the door.

"Why was our neighbor here?" Naomi asked after taking a large gulp of water.

"Well, Declan drove us home, remember? And we were talking. I was thanking him because he carried you and David inside when you fell asleep."

"Oh." Naomi seemed to consider this. She set the glass down and headed back to her bedroom.

Amy followed, handed her a pair of jammies, waited for her to change and tucked her back into bed.

"Good night, sweetheart. Thank you for being such a beautiful, intelligent and sweet daughter."

"You're welcome." Naomi yawned, but stopped Amy on the way to the door. "Mommy?"

"Yes?"

"I love you."

"I love you more." This time Amy didn't close the door all the way but left it cracked a few inches.

She then quickly found her phone and texted Declan:

I'm sorry about the interruption.

She waited, watching as dots filled her screen while he typed his reply.

Takes me back. Instead of parents interrupting us, now it's children. Damn, I think we're old.

He sent an emoji of a man walking with a cane. Amy smiled, shook her head and replied:

Is that a hockey stick or an old man with a cane? Either way, we're not old. We're just grown-up.

Declan:
You definitely feel and look all grown-up.

Amy:
So do you.

Declan:
Sorry if I got you into trouble. Are you grounded?

Amy:
Nope. Guess I'll see you tomorrow?

Declan:
You bet, Tinks.

Years ago, Declan had nicknamed her after the Disney fairy because she was so small in comparison to him. It was said tenderly and always with affection and now it woke up a side of Amy she'd almost forgotten. Yes, once upon a time she was *Tinks*. Not just Amy, or *Ames*, or Mommy.

Before she was Mommy, she was fun and carefree and loved a boy with her whole heart.

Amy:
You haven't called me that in a spell.

Declan:
I'm bringing it back.

Amy:
It's okay with me. Night.

Declan:
Good night. Thank you for the kissing.

Amy didn't know how to respond to that, so she laid the phone down on her nightstand while she got ready for bed. She ought to be thanking *him* for the kissing. Since they'd last kissed, he'd apparently obtained a graduate degree in the sport.

And yes, she wondered, because she was the curious type, what else had improved with age and experience.

Chapter Fourteen

"Thanks for asking David over for a playdate," Amy said. "Both kids miss the old neighborhood."

"We miss y'all so much," Bianca said. "The neighborhood isn't the same without you."

Naomi was visiting with her old next-door neighbor friend, Cathy, and Amy had brought David to play with Matthew.

A funny thing happened. When Amy had driven by their old house today, she hadn't felt the raw lump of tears lodged in her esophagus. Instead, it seemed as though that house, that street, that was another life. And now, she'd taken with her the very best parts into a new world. She was growing in this new place, stretching and learning. Becoming someone new, or maybe just someone old. Someone she recognized.

The boys were throwing the ball back and forth in the yard, never seeming to tire. It was far better than their being holed up inside on a beautiful day playing video games, but Amy was grateful for the shade and the mist fans Bianca had arranged near their chaise lounge chairs. It was just the thing for a hot summer day. The iced tea was nice, too, because she always put the right amount of sugar in.

And then because she couldn't stand it any longer, Amy changed the subject.

"Declan kissed me the other night."

Bianca's jaw dropped and she turned her knees, her entire body pivoted toward Amy.

"Um, *what*? When were you planning on telling me this?"

"When it came up. But it isn't coming up."

"This is something you bring up, girlfriend!" She pushed Amy's shoulder. "For example, eggs are on sale at ALDI's and Declan kissed me."

Amy snorted. "Okay, noted. I'm glad I said something."

"You haven't *said* much!" She leaned forward. "Go on."

"Well, there isn't much else. We kissed and then we've been texting a lot since then. Just stuff about our day but we kind of flirt, too. A little bit, you know, sexy sometimes."

"What are you doing? Where is this going? Have you thought this through?"

"What do you mean? Weren't you the one to tell me to sign up with a dating app?"

"A dating app, not your old boyfriend."

"Why *not*?"

"Oh, dear. I can see we need to have the 'single mom' talk."

"What do *you* know about being a single mom?"

Bianca leaned back, and her neck swiveled chicken-style. "Amy, I read. A lot. I've started a blog."

"That doesn't mean you have experience."

"No, but I know what's going on out there in the trenches. I *know* people. And I know people who know people. You haven't done enough thinking. The thing you need to do is really overthink this whole thing with Declan."

"Overthink?"

"Girl, that's half the fun!"

"Seriously?"

"Yes! You have to play hard to get, too. Don't let him

know you're thinking about him. Don't let him know if the kisses melt you. Maybe set up that profile on the apps anyway. Breed his insecurities. Really rev them up big-time."

"You *can't* be serious."

"Well, honey, until he puts a ring on it, you're a free agent. Am I right?"

Amy coughed. "It's a little soon to think about a ring, don't you think?"

"Is it?" Bianca cocked her head.

"Yes! Look, I have a lot going on. I'm studying for my certifications, working at the bar and raising my children. How do I have time for all this nonsense?"

"That's exactly what you tell him!" She pointed. "That will get you far."

Oh, sigh, it was so much easier to be part of a couple. Amy didn't know if she had it in her to traverse this new brave techy dating world. Had Declan been doing this all these years, and if so, how in the world did he stand it? She was a one-man woman, in one decade going from Declan to Rob with possibly one or two horrible dates in between with men she met at college.

"Is this what you do with Mark?" Amy asked.

"Yes, honey. Every once in a while, I act really disgusted with him, just fed up for no good reason. It's to keep him on his toes. You ought to see how he grovels just to find out what he did wrong. Flowers, candy and *fantastic* makeup sex."

Amy had no idea this went on with her friends. What happened behind closed doors… She wished she'd never asked.

"Does he ever find out what he did wrong?"

"I just make something up, like he left his socks a foot from the hamper."

"Sorry, but that doesn't sound healthy."

"It works for us."

And the casual understated note behind that statement was obvious. Amy was the one divorced, not Bianca. She and Mark usually couldn't keep their hands off each other in public.

"Mom, can we go inside and play video games now?" Matthew asked.

Both boys had sweat pits under their arms and David wiped away a trickle running down his neck.

"Sure, let's all go in. I'll tell your daddy you did your workout today."

Amy followed everyone inside, carrying the glove David had handed her. Bianca strolled to the kitchen and started pulling out snack food for the boys.

"We're so excited about Matt. He's really good, the coach said so. Got a heck of an arm, he said. He wants to work with Matt on pitching. Even Mr. Sheridan said Matt has potential."

"Really? That's amazing! I'm so happy for y'all."

"Thanks. You know how it is. Strapped for cash. House rich, cash poor. Mark said we need Matt to get a scholarship because that would really help the family coffers. And now here we have the chance. We're going to enroll him in Little League in the fall and also pay for a private coach. Mr. Sheridan already talked to us about it."

Amy sincerely hoped that Rob didn't hear about any of this from Mark or he'd want an athletic scholarship for David, too. Amy was all for financial assistance but she thought David had such good grades that if he continued, he'd probably get an academic one anyway.

"It seemed to work for Declan."

"That's exactly what we want for Matt. Do you think you could talk to him for us, get us some advice, now that you have such an in, so to speak?" Bianca arranged the Goldfish crackers on a plate with slices of apple and peanut butter for dipping.

"I'm not sure I have an 'in' any more than I already did, but sure, I'll talk to him for you."

"*You* have an 'in.' You were the ex, now you're the potential new girlfriend. As long as you don't scare him off by being too needy." She put up a hand like a stop sign. "Don't be too needy."

"I'm *not* too needy, so that will be easy."

"Oh, maybe we could all four go out to dinner one night, like a double date!" Bianca said this with the enthusiasm usually reserved for life-changing announcements.

"Um, sure. I'll ask him."

But they were very new. They hadn't really talked about *dating*. They'd just kissed that one time, and then for a little while more the next night when she'd asked him to fix that squeak in Naomi's door. She'd followed him next door afterward with some lame excuse to the kids and spent fifteen minutes in heaven. That was the extent of their dating life.

Her phone buzzed with an incoming message from Declan:

Carpool to work tonight?

She responded with a happy face.

Declan:
What are you wearing right now?

She smiled. Last night they'd texted for an hour, each one getting sillier than the last. Until they got racy.

She responded:

I took the kids to a playdate so what do you think I'm wearing?

Declan:
Pants for sure.

Amy:
Cargo shorts and a T-shirt with sandals.

Declan:
No underwear??????

Amy laughed so hard that Bianca looked up from the snack tray.

Amy:
What are you wearing?

Declan:
A hat.

Amy:
You're so much better at this than I am.

"Is that Declan you're smile-texting?" Bianca asked, looking over Amy's shoulder. Then before Amy could stop her, she grabbed her cell.

"What are you doing? Give that back to me!"

Bianca was reading and thumb texting at warp speed. "You'll thank me later."

"No, I won't!"

Bianca handed the cell back to Amy. "You just don't know how to sext yet. But you'll get there."

The text message was so racy and blue that Amy blushed a thousand shades of pink. She wondered if he'd figure out this wasn't her and was about to text him the truth when he responded.

Declan:
All right, who are you and how do you have Amy's phone? State your business.

"Ha! He knows it's not me."

"Well, that's a problem. You need to work on your skills."

He knows it's not me.

The knowledge spiked a warm thrum of pleasure through her. He *did* know her, in some ways even better than Rob ever had.

Amy:
It was Bianca. She grabbed my phone. How did you know it wasn't me?

Declan:
I know you, Tinks. You've always been shy.

Amy:
I'm going to be less of that now and a little racier.

Declan:
Don't you dare. I like you just the way you are.

"Either way, I put the picture in his head. And I got him all revved up for you," Bianca said. "You are welcome."

"Thank you," Amy said. "You're right. His reaction is exactly what I wanted to know."

It wasn't what Bianca assumed, however. Amy wanted to know whether Declan still remembered her.

And he did.

Late that afternoon, Mom and Lou arrived to babysit.

"Grandma!" Both kids ran to greet them.

"I brought a movie!" Lou held up a DVD.

"Oh," Amy said. "I don't have a player. But I bet you can get that movie on the streaming network."

"I tried to tell you," Mom said.

"What are we supposed to do with all these movies," Lou said. "Nobody wants them."

"Donate them to the library," Amy said.

She strolled into the bathroom to fix her hair and makeup when her cell phone rang. It was Rob.

"Can I have the kids this weekend? I know it's not my weekend but since I had to cut our week short, I thought maybe you'd be okay with it."

Normally this might upset Amy, because Rob always expected her to rearrange everything to suit his schedule. Since separating, he frequently reminded her that he *worked* so they would have to adjust to his schedule. Her plans, then, weren't as important because they were easily rearranged. It was disrespectful of her time as if because she didn't earn a wage it meant she didn't do anything significant. But on the other hand, if she wanted to encourage him to show up on time and have a relationship with the kids, she should work with him when possible. This was one of the many items they'd gone over with the mediator.

"You may not love each other anymore," the mediator had said, "but you both love the same two children. Take

*yourself out of the equation. If it's good for the child, be big
enough to allow it. Children's needs are first, make yours
second whenever possible."*

"That's okay with me."

"Thanks, Ames! You're the best." Rob's voice lowered.
"And I know we said we'd talk about this…um, when the
time came. I wanted you to know that they're going to meet
someone this weekend."

"M-meet someone?"

"Yeah, someone I've been dating for a while now. I think
it's time. Don't worry, it's just a few hours at a park and a
picnic. Something low-key. She thought it might be best to
introduce them that way."

She thought it best. So, this other woman would be making decisions for her children, such as the best time for them
to meet and how. In a way, this was her biggest nightmare.
Someone else, someone she didn't know or trust, having
contact with *her* children. She trusted Rob. She didn't trust
the women he might date because she didn't know them.
This would be a third-party kind of trust. An extension by
way of Rob.

"Amy?" Rob said. "You still there?"

"Yes."

Amy swallowed hard, looking at her reflection in the mirror.

This was a woman who hadn't planned on sharing her
children with a possible future stepmother. This was a
woman who had other plans.

"We knew it would come to this eventually," Rob said
softly. "It's been almost a year since we first separated."

She just didn't think Rob would be first to want the kids
to meet someone special. That should have been her. He was
supposed to be in his happy bachelor era.

"And this is someone you're dating exclusively?"

"Yeah. Not at first, but yeah...now we are."

"Got to be honest, I thought you were going to date and have fun. Free and easy. I thought that's why we broke up. You were tired of married life."

He cleared his throat. "I guess I got it out of my system. At heart, I'm a one-woman man. You know that better than anyone."

"Well, you don't need my approval but thank you for letting me know," Amy said. "I've got to go. I'm getting ready for work."

"Ames, wait." He paused. "You'll meet her, too. I want you to get along. Who knows, maybe this will work out long term."

"Like we did?" Amy couldn't hold back the bite behind the words.

"I don't know why we didn't work. But I think you'll like her because she's a lot like you. A teacher, actually. Ironic, huh? I guess I have a type."

"What's her name? How old is she?"

"Her name is Shannon. She's twenty-five. No kids of her own."

But plenty of time to have them.

"I trust *you*, Rob. You are in charge of our children, not the woman you're dating."

"Got it."

Amy hung up with Rob and got ready in a daze. Rob was right. She always knew it would come to this, but she thought she might have a little more time. So, Rob had someone new in his life. Funny how men just sort of plowed on through relationships, on to the next, without any fear of getting hurt.

And what about you?

Weren't you just making out with your ex-boyfriend?

"Whoa," Lou said, when Amy emerged. "Texas, lock up your sons!"

"You look pretty, Mommy." Naomi smiled up from her book.

"I love those dangly earrings," Moonbeam said.

David just stared at her and didn't say a word, which she interpreted as tacit approval.

She kissed both David and Naomi. "Don't wait up for me. It's a late shift tonight, but I'll see you in the morning and we'll get doughnuts if you want."

Outside, Declan leaned against his truck and waved through the opened screen door at them. "Ready?"

Amy walked over and climbed in the passenger side for the short drive to the boardwalk and pier. It was calm and cool, a light rain earlier having lowered the temps to make the summer night bearable.

She only noticed how quiet she'd been when Declan poked her.

"Hey. You okay?"

"Huh? Yeah, I'm fine." A light breeze blew some of her hair out of its tight hold and she tucked it behind her ear.

"You don't seem fine."

"Just thinking."

"About?"

"The kids are being introduced to someone new this weekend. Rob's new girlfriend."

Declan whistled. "The first time, huh? And are you okay with this?"

"It's not like I'm jealous or anything."

"Are you sure?"

She squeezed Declan's bicep. "Yes, I'm sure."

It didn't seem to bother Declan, but it bothered her that he believed she might still have feelings for Rob and yet be kissing and fooling around with Declan the way she'd been. If she still loved Rob, she'd be heartbroken by the news. The truth was far more complicated. Love was gone, but they'd forever be linked as parents. She was going to have to be friendly with her ex's girlfriend. Just another item in the long list on a single mom's duties.

"Be honest with me. I can take it."

"Declan, I wouldn't be making out with you, flirting and sexting if I still loved someone else."

"Good." He reached for and squeezed her knee. "Because I wouldn't be, either."

Chapter Fifteen

When they split the tips later that night, Declan had the biggest loot for the third shift in a row. The waitstaff were always happy when he had a good night. And to be fair, tonight he'd worked it, smiling, chatting, lending customers a helpful ear. Good people tended to understand that service workers weren't earning a livable wage based on their hourly rate. All they wanted was a friendly server who took their time.

"Declan wins it again." Debbie slapped the bar. "Face it, he's got a gift. We're lucky he shares."

"It must be so *difficult* for a six-foot-two former professional athlete to hustle for tips." Amy winked at him.

"Yeah," Debbie elbowed Amy. "Imagine the poor wretched woman who has to settle for *this* one."

He cut the air with one hand. "Now, now, ladies. It isn't just women. I listen to the men's troubles. Which are usually troubles with the very women who are tipping me."

"Did you give out your number again?" Debbie said.

Declan froze in the middle of pouring fountain soda into an iced glass for Amy. When he turned slightly to glance at her, she'd quickly averted her gaze.

"I haven't taken anyone's number in a while," Declan said, correcting Debbie.

The last thing he wanted was to feed any insecurities in

Amy. She'd just come off a divorce with a man who presumably fell out of love with her. It had to have crushed her, because he knew Amy, and how hard and intense she loved when she did. Honestly, he didn't know what she wanted from him if anything. She'd been on board with some heavy-duty make-out sessions in which they'd relived their glory days. Beyond that, he feared loving Amy again would be like harnessing the wind. And as a pitcher, he'd learned early on the crosswind had a way of changing directions.

"I can see why Samantha might have been jealous," Amy said. "Girls handing you their number?"

"Nope, sorry. She was almost certifiable," Debbie said. "How a girl that beautiful can be so insecure baffles the mind."

"Girls don't always give me their phone number," Declan protested.

"Nine times out of ten they do," Debbie said. "Which isn't bad for business."

They ended the night with a new inspirational quote, all of which were mostly borrowed from his dad. This one Declan found on his own. Debbie always behaved like this was the first time she'd heard some of them, which couldn't be true. She seemed equally blown away by tonight's quote.

On the way home, Amy was quiet, her body turned to face her window, which set Declan's teeth on edge. He did not want her to be jealous and after what he'd recently been through, he almost felt like he had to be proactive.

"You're so quiet," Declan said. "You do believe me when I say I don't accept phone numbers anymore, don't you?"

"Huh? Oh, sure. I believe you. Why would you lie?"

"Exactly. Why would I?" His tight grip on the column of the steering wheel loosened. "What's got you so quiet?"

"Just thinking about the coaching talk today and what that quote means to me."

He snorted. "Coaching talk?"

"You know. When we all sit down after our shift and talk about the night?"

"Yeah but I don't think of it as *coaching*."

"You've got to be kidding me." Amy turned her body to face him and smiled. "You're a born coach. Everything you say just inspires us to keep going, to do better. Honestly, after your talk I leave work feeling less like a cocktail server and more like a facilitator of human connections."

"I started out basically just trying to cheer y'all up after a rough night. But I never thought of it as coaching."

"Because it's not sports. But there's a thing called a life coach, too."

"Yeah, I know. But—"

"You'd be good at that, too. The quote tonight had me thinking about the rest of my life. 'Your self-worth is determined by *you*. You don't have to depend on someone telling you who you are.' Who said that?"

"Actually, Beyoncé." Bet his dad never thought to quote from a musical performer.

"Wow, she really is amazing." Amy shook her head, smiling. "After the divorce, my self-worth spiraled. I felt like everything I had become was tied up in my marriage. First and foremost, I was a wife and a mother. Everything else in life came second. When I started interviewing for a job, I saw that the outside world doesn't value what I've been focused on for the past nine years. I almost forgot who I was and that I had once hoped to be a teacher. I'd forgotten to get around to that."

"I'm glad you remembered, *Tinks*." He spoke softly.

That's the woman he'd never forgotten, and he'd known

even when he'd seen her in town with her family from time to time that she was still in there. He saw it in the playful way she connected to her children. Granted, he saw less joy on the day they'd moved in next door. Then it seemed the weight of failure had colored everything about her. Failure was something Declan knew a little something about. But though failure was never anyone's first choice, in the end it could be the final one. He'd decided to continue failing at baseball because he'd made a decision. Choose failure and move on to something new. The something new had been teaching until he met an obstacle he couldn't work around. Until he realized there could be value in simply walking away. That's something his father never truly understood.

He didn't call it failure so much as an opportunity to learn something.

But Amy was right. Whether or not he wanted to admit to it, coaching was in his blood. He *was* coaching the service workers without even realizing.

You're a born coach, Declan.

She smiled, a world of warmth in her gaze. "Thank you for bringing Tinks back, by the way."

"You're welcome." He pulled into his driveway, shut off the truck and reached for her. "Come inside with me for a while?"

Amy's gaze switched from her house, to his, then back to hers.

"My mom is—"

"Probably asleep along with everyone else."

"She was last time." Amy stroked his cheek. "Why, what did you have in mind, Mr. Hot Bartender? You already *have* my phone number."

"Just talking. Hanging out. I can't go right to sleep after work, I need to unwind."

"Damn, and I was thinking you wanted to move beyond one of our marathon make-out sessions. We are both adults now."

This did surprise him because he was used to shy Amy. She'd been venturing out in more ways than one.

"I don't think you're ready for that. Isn't it three months, if I recall?" He cocked his head, flashing her a wicked smile.

"You remembered, but it's not like I had it marked on a calendar or anything."

"No? It was on mine."

She laughed. "Fine, just a few minutes but then I have to go home before they miss me."

He led her to his home, hand low on her back. They weren't even halfway there before he lifted her hand to his lips and kissed it. It felt so good to touch her. It felt necessary. Natural. He'd never been accused of being affectionate, but Amy brought it out of him. Maybe, in the same way he'd reminded her of who she used to be, she'd done the same for him. But he wasn't kidding himself. They were both a compilation of who they used to be, layered with the experiences and heartbreaks that had shaped and molded them from the minute they broke up and went their separate ways.

But the person he'd been when he loved Amy was someone he missed.

Amy had spent slices of time in Declan's home, occasionally alone for a few minutes, but this was the first time she'd joined him after a late shift. The darkness and quiet of the night brought with it a sense of intimacy she couldn't shake. Despite all that, and the fact she trusted Declan with her life, it didn't mean this was time to lower her guard. This "thing" with Declan, whatever it was, remained new. She didn't know if it could ever turn into anything like what they once had.

Most people would think it bananas to reconnect with their high school boyfriend but safe to say those old boyfriends weren't anything like Declan Sheridan.

If Amy was on the hunt for husband number two, maybe she'd care that Declan didn't seem to have any ambition beyond being a bartender. Luckily, she wasn't looking for husband number two. She also wasn't expecting someone to provide for her and her children. Been there, done that. She was going to be sure, whomever she wound up with, that she'd never be financially dependent on anyone again. However, yes, it would be nice to have a partner, someone to help and share the load the way Rob never had.

But Declan had expressly said he wanted children, and she doubted he'd just take hers and be done with it. Most men would probably want to have their own. Amy didn't know if she could ever go through that again, either. More children, more responsibilities. So much to think about in her new reality, and the possibility had presented itself far sooner than she'd expected.

She was supposed to be filling out app questionnaires, swiping and having dates with complete strangers with similar values and goals. Maybe a single dad with kids of his own. Yours, mine and ours. But she couldn't very well ignore that an extremely handsome, athletic, hot guy who lived next door was interested in spending time with her. Surely she wasn't supposed to reject something that had fallen so easily into her life. It wasn't as if this would be easy. There would never again be simple in her life when it came to love and romance.

Amy took a seat on the brown leather couch in Declan's living room, tucking a leg under her. His home was decidedly masculine with touches of leather and dark muted colors. It desperately required a splash of color somewhere and she determined she'd buy him a colorful plant next time she was at the garden center.

Declan brought her an iced tea and set it on the coffee table. "Do you want to watch something?"

Then he did something shocking. He offered her the TV remote control.

"You're going to let me choose?" She grabbed the remote. "Oh my God, thank you. This is such an extreme honor and I'm truly indebted to you. First, I would like to thank the Academy, and all who supported me—"

Declan swiped it back out of her hand. "If you're not going to take this seriously, smart-ass, I'm taking back my power."

Amy pounced on Declan, reaching for the remote as he moved it higher and out of her reach.

"You had your chance for romantic comedies. Now we move to the sports lineup."

"No, please! Not ESPN. Anything but that!"

She did something a bit underhanded and copped a feel. Just a little stroke of his behind with her hand, but it shocked him enough to lose his focus and loosen his grip. Grabbing it back, she tucked the remote behind her and lay on it.

She crossed her arms. "Say goodbye to your power viewing. It's mine now."

Declan crawled on top of her, keeping his weight off. "I think I somehow knew that the moment you moved in next door."

Oh. How incredibly sweet.

Then he lowered his lips to hers and kissed her, and that… Well, that was even sweeter.

His kisses trailed down the column of her neck, teasing behind her ear, before he met her lips again and again. If she didn't stop this train, they were headed to the station, and yet it wasn't time. There was no prerequisite timeline now for her, just the knowledge she wasn't quite ready for this step. But she would be soon. Very soon.

"Declan," she managed to say when they broke the kiss. "I...you... You never said why you quit teaching. And I always meant to ask."

She bit down on her lower lip because the look on his face was almost laughable as he switched gears. He cooled himself down, realizing without words they weren't boarding that train to paradise, and he was okay with that. The remote long forgotten, he rolled onto the sofa on his back and tucked her into his arms. She lay there, her head on his shoulder, her hand settled over his abs.

"I'm sure you heard I was working in Houston at one of the inner-city public high schools. They hired me on, thought it might look good for their sports department to have my name attached to it. I coached the varsity team."

"But it didn't work out?"

"Their boosters were mostly focused on their football team, which was fine, you know? It's kind of typical at the high school level. I taught biology and calculus. Anyway, it was the old classic 'football star who can't pass his midterm' dichotomy. I was pressured to pass him in my calculus class, but the kid didn't even belong there. He hadn't grasped basic algebra concepts. He was there because another teacher had passed him along. I wouldn't do it. Refused."

"Good for you."

"I didn't mind the thinly disguised hatred among much of the staff when their team started a losing streak after their best player got benched. I had my supporters, quiet though they stayed, and I've been raised to work well under pressure."

"But...?"

"But things got a bit dicey."

"Yeah? What happened?"

Declan let out a long breath. "The kid's father didn't take it well. He became louder than all the rest of the voices when he brought a gun to school."

Amy shot up into a sitting position. "*What?* Why didn't I hear about this? When did this happen?"

Declan tucked an arm behind the crook of his neck. "It was just a blip on the evening news a couple of years ago. Thankfully it was resolved without incident. Well, much incident. Let's put it this way. No one was injured."

He wasn't kidding her. This had changed everything for Declan. He didn't shake easily, but putting guns around children and teachers would be the one thing to do it. She'd heard rumors of teachers who'd either quit or retired early due to gun violence but… Declan. *Her* Declan, whom she'd pictured all these years, when she allowed herself to think about him, living the high life of a professional athlete, attending parties and functions, with plenty of women and plenty of dating. She heard he'd retired early with an injury but she hadn't pictured *this*.

"Oh, Declan." She lowered herself back to him, curling into him, cradling him tight.

He would have blamed himself.

"It's okay." He tightened his arms around her. "The father was arrested and worked out a plea deal of some sort. Anger management. The family moved out of the area, which was probably the best thing for the kid, too. He wasn't going to easily live that ordeal down. Being benched somehow was now the least of his problems. Anyway, after that, I needed a break from teaching."

For the first time, Amy wondered how many teachers were serving cocktails or hawking their wares because they felt safer there than they did in a classroom.

"No one can blame you for stepping away."

"Well, no one but my father. He can't accept that I'm going to let this one event color the rest of my life."

"Are you?"

"I learned a lot about myself through the process and I'm not sure I'm cut out for teaching the upper grades."

"You'd do really well with grade-school kids. David and Naomi adore you."

"It's a thought."

"It would be funny if we both wound up teaching at the same school."

"Got to say, I wouldn't mind seeing you every day in the teachers' lounge."

"I'd always have your back, and I wouldn't be quiet about it, either."

He chuckled and rolled to a sitting position, getting up and offering his hand. "I know."

"It's getting late." She stood, adjusting her tousled hair and straightening her rumpled clothes.

"I'll walk you next door."

They held hands, and when they crossed into her side of the lawn, Declan pulled her close for another deep kiss. It went on for days, forcing her to reconsider going home. She was out of breath when they broke apart. Funny, she would have thought she'd have more questions for Declan, such as "Where is this going? Do we have a future? Are we exclusive?" But Declan had always made her feel so secure and safe. He'd made himself clear without any words. This time, she had the answers for something *he* needed to know before they went any further.

"You were honest with me since the first day we moved in. I know what you want and what you're looking for. But I just ended a marriage not long ago, and I can't promise you anything. I'm just rediscovering who I am. I have kids, and an ex I'll have to co-parent with for the next ten years. Pretty sure I'm going to have my ex's partner involved soon. I don't know what's happening or where I'm going. But I have a plan. You'll just have to be patient if you want to be with me." She sighed, closed her eyes and pressed her forehead to his chest. "But as far as I'm concerned, I want to see where this goes. Where we go this time around."

"Tinks, I'll take whatever you have to give and do it with a smile on my face."

He wouldn't be the only one smiling. It was all she needed to know.

Chapter Sixteen

Amy quietly closed the front door, hoping not to wake Mom and Lou, who'd pulled out the sofa bed in the living room. Lou was on his side, snoring away.

Amy tiptoed halfway to her bedroom when she heard Mom.

"Have a good night?"

She jumped what felt like three feet in the air and held a hand to her throat. "You scared me!"

"Why? I'm just standing here," she said from the dark kitchen.

"In the darkness, like an ax murderer!" Amy hissed, switching on a light.

"You watch too many crime shows. The truck pulling up next door woke me. *About an hour ago.*" The last sentence was said with emphasis.

"Yes, we… It's hard to go right to sleep after working. We were both kind of wound up, so we were just hanging out together…you know, talking about work and stuff."

"It's the *stuff* which I'm worried about."

Mom reached inside the cupboard for the cocoa mix and took the milk out of the refrigerator. Okay, wow, what was with the constant memory dump these days? She remembered this drill, but now she was twice the age she'd been the first time it happened. Her mother wanted to talk and thought a cup of hot cocoa would loosen Amy's lips. It didn't matter whether it was the peak of a summer heat wave or winter, cocoa hit the spot when it came to talks with her mother. Always had.

"Thanks for your concern but I know what I'm doing."

"Do you? You've just been divorced from the father of your children. It's hardly time to reconnect with old boy-friends." Mom grabbed a saucepan and spooned cocoa into the milk.

Amy took a seat at the kitchen table. "Listen. It's time you realize this divorce happened. You act like one day we're all going to wake up and the whole thing will have been a nightmare. Positive thinking is one thing, but I have to rec-ognize and deal with reality. Rob is seeing someone and he's introducing her to the kids this weekend. The truth is, even if Rob wanted me back now, I wouldn't want to."

She glanced up from stirring. "What are you saying? You always have to give him a second chance. He's the father of your children."

"And he's always going to be. We will always be in each other's lives. But I don't love him anymore. I… I want to be with Declan."

It was the truth and saying it out loud now only confirmed what she already knew. A part of her was falling back in love with him. The rushed and heady sensations every time she saw him…the ways she thought of him every day…the way she kissed him… It was all adding up to love.

"Really? So soon?"

"I want to see where it goes. We were young the first time we were together, but maybe now… Mom, there was *always* something there with him. Something real. And nothing has changed."

"Maybe not, but everything else about the rest of your world has changed. Is Declan really going to settle down and be a stepfather to the children? Is he going to be there, day in and day out, supporting you emotionally?"

"I have a lot of faith in him."

"That's not an answer. Is that faith well placed?"

"Why would you *ask* that?"

"I don't want you to get hurt again. The end of a relationship is so emotional and especially for you. You've endured so much loss. First, you lose Declan when you'd pictured a future with him, right or wrong. Then, your father dies unexpectedly. And lastly, Rob decides he doesn't want to be married anymore. That's a lot of loss in the past decade."

"It is, but if there's one thing my dad taught me, it was to believe in people. And he loved Declan even after we split." Amy sighed. "It seems I'm going to have to take a chance with my heart no matter who I date or fall for. Don't worry. If it helps, I'm scared, too."

"No, you're not." Moonbeam set a mug in front of Amy and squeezed her hand. "You're like your father. Always so brave and willing to trust in the goodness of people. I'm the child of hippies but even I can't bring myself to trust people they way you two did."

"That's because your hippie parents trusted everyone a little *too* much," Amy said. "Did you know Declan quit working at the high school because of a gun incident?"

"Yes. A couple of years ago."

"No one told me."

"Declan wasn't even mentioned when it came on the evening news. Only the perpetrator's name. I just happened to hear how Declan was involved later from Lorna when I ran into her at the grocery."

Amy didn't have to ask why Mom never brought it up to her. There would have been no reason to. Declan was fine, and he wasn't even on her radar then.

"It happened because he did the right thing. He refused to give a passing grade to a kid just so he could win the school some football games."

Mom nodded. "You'll have no argument from me that Dan and Lorna raised those boys right."

"Then I wish you'd give him a chance. It would mean a lot to me."

"I will, but please be careful and take it slow."

She planned to. No need to rush when they lived next door to each other, and Amy would have time to introduce the idea to her kids. She'd go easy, let them first realize how much they liked Declan. Naomi would be the easier one of the twins. David should follow easily considering how much Declan had helped him. Once both of them genuinely liked Declan, things should go smoother. She'd explain that she and Declan used to be the best of friends when they were younger and then gradually fell in love. There's no way this could go badly, and as luck would have it, Rob was doing the trial-by-fire version this weekend. She'd take notes and learn to do it better when it was her and Declan's turn. In the meantime, she'd read everything she could get her hands on about blended families. Michelle would have some resources.

After checking on Naomi and David, Amy headed to bed. When she'd moved, she remembered packing her old yearbooks, wondering what a person was supposed to do with them. Recycle? She didn't want them in a landfill somewhere, so she packed and moved them with barely a glance. The books would come in handy now. She reached into the shelf of her closet where she'd stored them and cracked open her senior yearbook. Skimming the pages, she came to the varsity baseball team. There was young Declan, clearly the star, on the pitcher's mound, with the group, his golden looks almost eclipsing his stats. On the "most likely to" page she found the two of them, holding hands, smiling into the camera, looking innocent enough to be approximately twelve years old. She, for her part, had the faith of a child when it came to Declan.

"Most Likely to Get Married" the caption said.

Welp, that hadn't happened. But, safe to say, most high school plans had not materialized either, such as their school's beautiful theater geek, Raquel Martinez, captioned "Most Likely to Win an Academy Award." Raquel had opened a hair salon in town, but she was about as far from Hollywood as she could get. Declan was also captioned as "Most Likely to Win the World Series." Also hadn't happened. And there was no way Harry Delinski was ever going to be president, though he managed an insurance office in San Antonio, last she'd heard.

This had simply been her first dream, and it hadn't been as lofty as the others. Amy was a bit embarrassed that she hadn't reached higher. Or maybe her dreams were simply smaller than other people's. But even then, she'd clearly only seen herself as half of a couple. That was going to change.

Thank goodness for curtain calls and second chances.

The week went by swiftly between baseball practice for David and shifts at the bar. Before long, the weekend arrived. Amy had already explained to the kids they had a choice to spend it with Rob since he'd had to cut their visit short last time. She'd followed Rob's lead, and simply explained they would be meeting "Daddy's friend" this weekend.

"How old is she?" Naomi had asked as if gauging whether or not she should bring her Barbies.

"Um, twenty-five?" Amy said, zipping up Naomi's back-pack.

"That's old."

"Excuse me, young lady? *I'm* thirty-one."

She was almost thirty-two, but never mind.

"Mommy, you're not old! You're a *mommy*." Naomi gave her a hug. "I love you."

"Nice save. I love you, too, my special girl."

David was quiet, which worried Amy. He didn't ask any questions about Daddy's friend and simply packed all his baseball gear because he planned on practicing with Rob all weekend. His dedication lately to the sport had been inspiring. She'd heard him the other night on the phone with Rob.

"Dec says I'm good. I'm just as good as him at nine, which means I'm going to be really, *really* good if I stick with it. Did you know Dec went to college on a scholarship and got recruited to the major leagues?"

Gee, hopefully Rob wasn't getting tired of hearing about Amy's ex-boyfriend the jock. Snort.

Even if Declan hadn't inspired such confidence in her son, Amy would still be grateful for him. Not just for the lawn mowing, but he'd finally oiled those hinges on Naomi's door. He'd also unclogged her kitchen sink once—David had put an apple core in the disposal—and come over when the Wi-Fi went out to troubleshoot. It was like having a husband that went home to his own place every night. She did, however, miss the other perks of marriage but hoped that might change this weekend.

Declan had officially asked her out on a date. He said it was a surprise but would involve water, so she assumed the boardwalk, a place she hadn't enjoyed in years without her children.

As planned, Rob showed up to pick up the kids without his girlfriend.

"Where's your friend?" Naomi asked.

"You'll meet her at the park," Rob said, taking her backpack and stuffing it in the car.

"I hope I like her," Naomi said, giving Amy one last hug.

David said nothing, just hopped in the car and buckled in. "I brought my glove, and it's pretty seasoned now."

Rob chuckled. "Seasoned? Okay, you're trying to sound like a pro."

"I'm really *good*," David said, and Amy thought he sounded a little defensive.

She sincerely hoped David wouldn't compare himself with Matthew, who seemed to have more of a natural-born ability for athletics. But Declan, God bless him, refused to admit it. At least not to Amy and certainly not to David.

Rob shut the passenger door. "So, Declan, huh? Spending a lot of time with him."

"Yes." She was not going to discuss her love life with Rob in any detail.

At this point, even she didn't know where they were going with this. She didn't know if Declan was serious or just having a little fun with an old flame.

"Convenient the kids have already met him," he said with narrowed eyes.

"He's our neighbor."

Amy refused to say more. Too bad if she had an edge because the kids lived with her the majority of the time. She wouldn't talk to Rob about Declan for many reasons, not the least of which she'd already had told him about Declan once. When they'd first met, Declan was that ex she'd talked about.

The one who broke her heart. The one Rob should properly hate. Rob had one of those exes, too, of course. Everyone seemed to in college. It was a relief to unload on someone, but if Rob remembered half the stuff she'd said, when she'd painted Declan as the only reason for the failure of their relationship, he wouldn't have a fair and accurate picture.

Declan hadn't wanted to get married at seventeen and hindsight being twenty-twenty, she'd had no business getting married so young. It would have never worked. Declan would have gone away to college and later been recruited to the majors with or without her. In another scenario, she would have somehow been to blame for his leaving baseball. Instead, it was a choice Declan made that had nothing to do with her.

Amy stood outside and waved as Rob and the kids drove off, then she strolled over to Declan's house.

The door was slightly ajar, and she let herself in since she could hear the TV blaring. Still, no Declan watching ESPN. Instead, the announcer spoke enthusiastically to no one who cared. Amy flipped the remote off and continued walking.

"Declan? Dec?"

She didn't find him in the kitchen, or the back bedrooms. There only one place left to look and she found him outside in his yard, halfway up a fence, trimming the branches of a cherry tree. It was such a domestic picture she had to adjust her eyes by blinking into the bright sunshine. She cupped a hand over her eyes to give her shade. Yep, that was Declan. If she didn't know any better she'd wonder whether he was auditioning for the part of future husband. She used to beg Rob to take care of these gardening chores, especially after the time she'd fallen off a ladder and bruised her temple. Instead, he'd hired a gardener since he couldn't be bothered.

Declan wore a backward baseball cap, a thread-bare Astros T-shirt tight enough to accentuate every muscle rippling and low-rise jeans. Each time he reached higher, the jeans stayed low around his hips and the tee went up, showcasing tanned, taut skin. She'd bet he didn't have more than 10 percent fat on that body.

He turned when he heard the back door slapping shut and his big smile made her heart kick up.

"Hey."

She walked to meet him halfway when he climbed off the ladder, dropping the clippers on the ground.

"Hey yourself. What if I told you *my* tree needed trimming?"

"I would say let me at it." He grinned. "Are the kids gone?"

She went into his arms. "Yes, and I came over to see if I might get a clue about what we're doing so I can dress accordingly."

Declan pressed his chin to the top of her head. "If you dress for an afternoon on the water, you'll be fine."

"We're going to the boardwalk?"

"Near the water, but that's all I'm going to say." He twirled her, and his gaze swept down her body. "Dayum you look good, Tinks."

She was wearing yoga pants and a T-shirt, which she'd thrown on this morning after a quick shower. "Thank you, sir. So do you."

"I still have some errands to run and some prep to do for tonight."

"Sounds like you're going through a lot of trouble. Don't worry about impressing me. I haven't been on a date in… Hmm, actually, I forgot."

For a while, she and Rob had instituted a "date night," but after he'd had to cancel several times because of work travel, it fell off the radar and never came back on again.

"It's not too much trouble. You're worth it."

He kissed her, threading his fingers through hers. It was official. Declan made her feel not only wanted and desired but beautiful and...new.

Chapter Seventeen

Declan didn't know when he'd ever been this excited about a date. Possibly never.

"How much longer?" Amy asked from next to him in the passenger seat. "I still think this is just plain silly."

She wore a red bandanna tied around her eyes because he didn't want her to have clue one where they were headed until they were seconds from embarking. Even if she thought this was silly, she'd been a good sport about it. At this point, she could probably already smell the marina. Thanks to Finn, Declan was able to get a chartered boat on the cheap. Practically free, particularly when they were using him as a guinea pig for their latest model. They'd been wanting to offer a dinner cruise on the bay for a while, which would involve multiple couples. But tonight, they were flying solo. Just him and Amy. Everything was ready for what he hoped would be a great night and a memorable first date.

Considering his actual first date with Amy, years ago, had been at McDonald's, anything would be an improvement. This was already miles ahead of anything he could have pulled off at seventeen.

He maneuvered into the marina parking area closest to Nacho Boat Adventures. "Not yet. I'll come around."

"Good grief," Amy said, reaching for him when he opened

the door. "I can smell the bay and I can hear the waves. What are we doing? Going fishing?"

"Not quite," he said, holding her close and pulling her along.

When they reached the gangplank, he steadied her facing the catamaran. "Okay. Here we go. You can take it off now."

"Oh." She made a little sound in the back of her throat that sounded like a mix of surprise and pleasure. "We're going on your brother's boat?"

"We're having cocktails and dinner." He took her hand and pulled her up the plank. "Surprised?"

"Yes, I hadn't thought of anything this fancy."

"I think you look fancy."

When he'd walked next door to get her, she'd been wearing a short blue dress that reminded him of the pink one he'd liked so much. Amy could definitely rock a dress like nobody's business.

"Welcome aboard. I'll be your captain tonight." Noah Cahill touched the brim of his hat. "We'll be shoving off shortly into some very smooth sailing tonight and cocktails will begin soon after."

"Where are we going?" Amy asked.

Noah bowed. "Just a mile offshore where we'll anchor out and dinner service will begin."

"Oh, y'all added a dinner cruise to Nacho Boat Adventures!" Amy squealed.

"It was Twyla's idea. She read it in a book and hasn't stopped talking about it," Noah said and motioned for them to gather on deck.

Within minutes, they were pulling away from the marina, on the deck rail facing the bay. Declan pulled Amy into his arms, tight around her waist, resting his chin on the top of her head. She was small but fit perfectly in his arms.

"This is so romantic!"

"You sound surprised I can be romantic."

"Sure, it's a lot more than I expected. I just thought we were going to a nice dinner somewhere on the coast. Maybe Galveston, but I didn't think we'd literally be on the water."

"Can't say I didn't warn you."

"Good evening," a voice said from behind them. "I'll be serving y'all the cocktails."

The voice was from Tee, the kid that worked for Noah and Finn. Most often he was in the boat shack where they sold and rented equipment, but Finn mentioned they were trying to give him more responsibilities.

"You should know I'm pretty discerning when it comes to cocktails," Declan said, quirking a brow.

"Oh, dude, yeah. They're the same ones you made and dropped off earlier." He blinked. "I don't think I was supposed to say that."

Amy laughed. "No wonder you had so much to do to prepare before this."

"Oh, you have no idea."

Amy cocked her head. "There isn't going to be a violinist, is there?"

"I couldn't find anyone." Declan shrugged. It wasn't like he hadn't considered it, but Finn had rolled his eyes and told Declan not to shoot so high on the first date or he'd live to regret it.

But he was serious about this and wanted Amy to know it. As a single mom, she wouldn't want to waste time on anyone who would be a one-off. Fortunately, even if he hadn't planned it, he'd told her on the day she moved in what he wanted. What he was looking for. Basically, he wanted what Finn had finally found. What his parents had enjoyed for almost thirty-five years. It existed. But it had to be with the right woman. Amy was that woman, and he grew to be more certain every day.

So, he had no violin, but he had flowers and mojitos— Amy's favorite—and a great meal catered by the new head chef at the Salty Dog. Music that would be piped through the speakers through his Bluetooth.

Once they'd anchored out, Noah and Tee set up a table draped with a white cloth and chairs with a great view facing westward toward the cresting sunset. He held Amy's hand as they sipped on their drinks and ate a delicious seafood dinner of Chilean sea bass with risotto and asparagus.

"Oh, I meant to tell you. You should have heard David bragging about you. He's so single-minded about baseball now, so much more than he ever was with soccer. I guess I have you to thank for that. Along with so many things."

"He's a great kid. They both are." He paused, remembering. "You know what Naomi told me the other day when I was over mowing the lawn? 'Did you know books let you travel without moving your feet?' I laughed about that one."

"Should I be worried about her? Maybe she reads *too* much."

"Nah, she's fine."

She blinked and lowered her head. "I'm sorry. I don't mean to talk about my kids on our date."

"Why not? They're part of our lives."

"I know, but… Everything I've read about dating as a single mom warns against talking too much about the kids." She patted her lips with the napkin. "I'm just learning my way around all this."

"It's different with us."

She met his eyes and smiled. "True, we didn't swipe right for each other."

He was grateful for that. Thankful she'd moved in next

door instead of across town where eventually she would have started dating again via app. He would have never had a second chance with Amy.

"I bet this isn't the way you'd pictured your life going."

She probably viewed her divorce as a failure, and having seen his brother go through it, Declan understood the emotions behind it.

"Not at all. After all, from the beginning, I'd originally pictured my life with you."

It wasn't what he'd expected to hear, but those words deeply gratified him.

"We took a left turn somewhere and lost our way."

"I can't regret my past because I have David and Naomi. There's no world in which I don't want them to be exactly who they are, and that means Rob as their father. But yeah, I do wonder what might have happened if you and I had children. If we had been married instead. Would we still be together? Would we be going through a divorce right now?"

"We were too young."

"I know. I don't think we would have made it. Not then."

"And that would have killed me."

"Oh, Declan." She reached to cup his jaw. "You were always so perfect for me."

The words landed like a gift.

"Well, miss." Declan stood and offered her his hand. "It's time for the dance portion of the evening."

"There's no music." But she glanced around as if she half expected a band to suddenly appear from below deck.

"Ha!" Declan reached for his phone and scrolled to his app. "Wrong again."

The music began to play, a playlist he'd accumulated of every sappy love song known to man. Call him sentimental, but he knew Amy. She loved this stuff. The first song was

Lionel Richie's "Truly," and if he was going to pick a song that perfectly described his feelings, this would be the one. Declan felt every word of the lovesick man singing to his true love. He didn't know how it had happened, how he'd fallen in love so quickly but it seemed there was a cellular memory in his heart surrounding Amy. There'd never been anyone else like her, and he could say that now because he'd experienced this.

They swayed together to the music, holding each other, laughing when Declan decided to spin and dip Amy and she nearly lost her balance. He caught her easily.

Just like Lionel said, there was really no other love like hers. She'd always brought out the best in him. There had never been anyone like Amy for him and he didn't think anything could be more perfect than this night.

"Thank you for a lovely evening," Amy said to Noah and Tee after they'd returned portside.

"Thanks, buddy," Declan said. "I owe you one."

The evening was idyllic. Declan had pulled out all the stops, creating flawless moments. She was stunned at his thoughtfulness to every detail. As they walked to his truck, she was on such a high that she almost feared she'd wake up. How could this be happening to her? Her, no-frills Amy Holloway, ordinary and plain. Wife and mother of two. Declan looked at her as if he saw someone else. A different woman. The woman he apparently saw was some kind of goddess.

"I can't imagine a more perfect evening," she said. "You really outdid yourself."

"It was important. You deserve it, Amy. You do so much for everyone else and rarely think about yourself."

"You're sweet. I do think about myself, though."

"Not enough." He opened the passenger door for her.

"Oh, what's enough?"

While Declan was coming around to the driver's side, she pulled out her cell. They hadn't had any reception on the boat and being apart from her children meant she wanted to be available at all times.

Rob had called her a number of times. She hit Call Back, but it wasn't Rob who answered the phone.

It was Naomi.

"Mommy?"

Amy smiled at Declan as he got in the truck, buckled and squeezed her leg. She mouthed, "It's Naomi."

"Hey there, young lady, what are you doing with your daddy's phone? Everything okay?"

"Mommy, I want you to come quick! David is missing."

Chapter Eighteen

At first, Amy wasn't hugely alarmed.

The words didn't seem to hit her, but instead they sort of flew right past her like a random arrow missing their intended target.

"What do you *mean* he's missing?"

She met Declan's eyes, and his own suddenly narrowed. He immediately started up the truck and backed out of the parking lot.

"We can't find him." Naomi began to whimper. "We were at the park with Daddy's friend. I was on the swings, and I thought David and Daddy were playing catch. Then Daddy came over by himself and asked us where David was. And now we can't find him."

Amy had a lot of questions, such as why her daughter had phoned instead of her ex-husband. Hopefully, he was using his time wisely and looking for their son. The son he'd lost. But no, David *couldn't* be lost. There was some misunderstanding. He must have said something to Rob, and as usual, he didn't listen.

"He probably just wandered off and even though he told Daddy, he doesn't remember it. I'm coming, honey. Don't worry."

"But we've been looking for a long time and Daddy's

friend wants to call the police. But Daddy said no, that David's just hiding. We have to keep looking."

"Where am I headed?" Declan said at the light.

"Houston," Amy said and watched as he made the turn to head toward the interstate. "What's the name of the park, Naomi?"

"Um, I think…um, Miss Shannon? What's the name of this park?"

"Is that your mommy? Can I talk to her?" a woman's voice said, taking the phone. "We're at Donovan Park. I'm so sorry about this. Rob is searching every nook and cranny of this park, but honestly, I don't know why if he's here David won't answer us calling his name."

It had been a long time since she'd seen him do this, but at one time, David used to hide from her.

"Sometimes he hides when he's mad."

"Oh dear."

Rob probably remembered that, too, which explained why he wasn't willing to call the police. He must realize he'd said something to upset David. But he'd never pulled a stunt like this before, hiding in a public place, making them all panic. They'd talked to him so many times about the importance of safety.

What if David *wasn't* hiding? Maybe he was truly missing. Amy's mind rejected the thought at the same time as she couldn't get it out of her mind. What if someone horrible had *taken* her little boy? What if she never saw him again? She didn't want to allow the ugly thought, resisted, but it kept reappearing, terrorizing her. Okay, more than likely David was mad at Rob. Plus, stranger abductions were rare. Everybody said that. It was a *fact*. She repeated this to herself over and over to calm her racing heart.

"We're headed your way," Amy said. "We'll help you look."

It wasn't until Amy hung up that she allowed herself to fall apart. Declan was here and he was her rock. He was her security and safety.

"What if he... I can't think..." She might literally be sick to her stomach as the awful thoughts pressed in.

Declan took her hand and wouldn't let go of it. "Amy, don't go there. We're going to find him and he's going to be fine."

"Yes, yes. We are going to find him. I know. But I'm scared."

"No wonder."

"Did I tell you he used to hide when he was little and mad at me? But, of course, I could always find him. He'd be pouting in his closet because I wouldn't let him have a fourth cookie. And when I found him, he always looked so surprised. Like, 'How did you find me in the closet? I was hiding so good.'" She chuckled at the memory, but tears came out instead.

Finally, they arrived, despite the annoying traffic that had slowed them down. Amy almost didn't wait for the truck to stop before she was flying out the door.

Declan caught up to her. "Where should we start?"

Amy saw Naomi running toward the entrance by the wrought iron gate.

"Mommy! I'm scared." She ran into Amy's arms and held tight to her waist.

Shannon came up behind Naomi. "I'm Shannon. Don't you think we should call the police?"

"Give me a few minutes to find him. If I can't find him in ten minutes, *I'm* calling the police," Amy said. "I don't care what Rob says."

"Now that you're here, I'm going to go find Rob and help him look."

"You go this way, I'll head the other direction," Declan shouted and took off at a run, calling David's name.

Amy grabbed Naomi's hand and they started walking. "Let's try the train structures first."

"Why is David scaring me like this?" Naomi wanted to know.

"Honey, he must be really mad about something. Remember how he used to hide when he was mad?"

"I don't know what I did to make him mad!"

"Nothing. I bet he's mad at your father." She paused every few seconds to call out David's name.

They went winding through the park, checking inside the play structures, calling out his name. Only a few minutes into this routine, Amy heard the most wonderful sound on earth.

"Mom? You came."

It was him. *David.* Her beautiful, beautiful boy. He stood in the fading last rays of sunlight, one hand still holding his baseball glove.

It was Naomi who ran first and threw her arms around him. Though they'd always been the same size, in the past year David had begun the long stretch of growth that would eventually take him into manhood. He stood about two inches taller than her now, and as Naomi clutched him, he lowered his head to her shoulder and patted her back with his free hand.

Naomi pulled back to frame his face. "I was looking for you."

Then all three of them were hugging, Amy coming to her knees to hold her babies tight. Yes, thank you, God, they were all together. No one hurt or injured or lost. She could breathe again. It wasn't time for anger and harsh words and Amy just didn't have it in her anyway.

But this needed to be addressed.

"David, you really scared your sister. You scared me, too."

"I'm sorry." He looked chastised, lowering his gaze, then turning it on Amy. "How did you know?"

"Naomi called me on your dad's phone."

David frowned. "*He* didn't call you?"

An utterly sinking sensation hit Amy. Had David actually orchestrated this to bring her and Rob together somehow? Did he think maybe working together to find their son would bring about a reconciliation? He hadn't done anything like this before, but then again he also hadn't seen his father with another woman until today.

It occurred to Amy that she should let someone know they'd found David, so she texted Declan. He'd let everyone else know where to meet.

She took both Naomi's and David's hands and together they walked to a bench and sat. "What's wrong, honey? Why are you so mad?"

"Mom, Daddy's friend is his girlfriend." He looked at the ground, scowling and kicking with one foot. "I don't understand. You're so much prettier, Mommy. Why does he need a girlfriend when he could be with you?"

Despite everything she'd read and learned about divorce with children, despite the therapy she'd had after the divorce, Amy had nothing. She was hollow. Empty. Everything she had to say was too grown-up for them to understand and she didn't know how to make it simpler.

We grew apart. He doesn't love me anymore. I thought he didn't want to be married but what he didn't want was me. And now, I don't love him anymore. It's too late for us.

"He's right, Mommy," Naomi said. "You are prettier."

"Thanks, sweetie. Listen, you two. You both know that looks aren't everything. Anyway, beauty is in the eye of the beholder."

"I don't know what that means," David said.

"It means that while you and Naomi think I'm pretty, you're sort of looking at me through a special lens. You know, like one of those filters on the phone apps. I'm your mother and you love me so to you, I'm pretty."

"I think Dec thinks you're pretty, too," David said.

"Okay, maybe he does. But see, to Daddy, I'm not as pretty as his *new* girlfriend."

That didn't sound right, either. She was failing here. Sinking fast. Her son didn't like the idea that his father and mother were no longer together. And she wasn't going to be able to make this better for him. Since he'd been born, she'd protected and guided him and Naomi. Cribs with slats the right width apart, car seats tested for accident safety, nursing for optimal health, reading daily, healthy snacks. But when it came to this, possibly the most important part of their lives, she couldn't fix it.

"I don't like this," David said. "I don't need a new mom. Why is she even here? We were supposed to play catch. And all Daddy does is hold her hand and kiss her. It's *disgusting*."

"What? I don't need a new mom, either!" Naomi crossed her arms. "I didn't think about that!"

"No, look, neither one of you are getting a new mom. Or a new dad. Ever. Okay?"

Rob chose that moment to run up to them. He took one long look at the three of them setting on a bench together and his face went nuclear.

"David Robert Holloway!"

"Daddy, don't be mad at him!" Naomi yelled.

"I'm sorry!" David said, swinging his legs and not moving from his spot on the bench.

Rob took several steps until he was nearly in David's face. "You scared *everybody*! You scared your mother! Shannon wanted to call the police!"

"The *police*?" David snorted. "Stupid. I was just mad at you because we didn't play catch enough. I can't get good if you won't let me practice."

"We've talked about this, young man. You cannot hide when you're mad. It's not *safe*." Rob pointed at the air in emphasis, punctuating every word.

Shannon came running up, right behind Declan. If nothing else, Amy hoped the presence of his girlfriend might cool Rob down. He was still in that early stage of the relationship where he would want to make a good impression. But Rob had never been violent with the children. He'd been stern, and too in your face at times, but he'd never hurt them.

"Rob, it's an emotional time," Shannon said. "Maybe you could excuse it just this once."

It was official. Amy really liked Shannon. She liked her a lot and maybe someday, somehow, David would, too. First, he had to give up on the hope that his parents would get back together. Second, he had to understand he would always only have one mother.

Rob deflated like a balloon left out too long in the sun. "Yeah."

"Sorry, Dad. I won't ever do it again." David lowered his head.

Rob finally reached for David and hugged him.

"Okay, let's all go home and talk about this. I'm sorry you're so upset. We're going to fix this, you'll see." He glanced in Amy's direction. "I'll take it from here, Ames.

Thanks for your help finding him. You, too, Declan. Sorry, really, to scare you like that."

"It's okay, I was happy to help. Naomi called me," Amy said.

"And Naomi and I will talk about that later, too." He gave her the side-eye.

"I was scared!" Naomi said.

"Okay, but Mommy doesn't have to come running every time you and I have a problem," Rob said. "We can solve problems on our own by talking about it."

"No, we can't." With that, David got up and slumped away, Naomi following him after giving Amy another quick hug.

She understood what he meant. Words wouldn't fix this for him.

"Well, we better go," Rob said. "By the way, this is Shannon. Shannon, this is my ex-wife, Amy. And Declan, her um, her—"

"Boyfriend," Declan interrupted.

"I'm sorry to meet under these circumstances," Shannon said with a small smile.

"Same here," Amy said. "But it's nice to meet you anyway."

"See you Sunday." Rob turned and held up his arm for a backward wave.

Amy stood there watching them all walk away, intent on seeing Rob catch up to the kids.

"C'mere." From behind her, Declan pulled her into his arms, his head lowering to the crook in her shoulder and neck.

She wanted to collapse. All the emotions sapped from her in the past few minutes ranging from horrific fear, swinging to rising hope and then crashing into despair had taken every ounce of her energy. She turned in Declan's arms, burying her face in his chest.

"Have I ruined him?" She hiccupped back a sob.

"What? No, baby. You haven't ruined anyone. You never could. What you did is fix this. You found your son."

Amy wished it were that simple.

"He's mad because his dad has a new girlfriend. I can't fix this for him, and it hurts."

"Of course it does. You would fix the whole world if you could."

Declan just held her as she cried, his hand sliding up and down her back in slow strokes. They stood there until the sun made its final dip beyond the horizon and the park lights switched on.

The park would be closing soon.

"Tell me you're okay, Tinks," Declan said, tipping her chin to meet his eyes.

"Just take me home."

Chapter Nineteen

The first few minutes of the drive home were spent mostly in comfortable silence, Amy reliving her emotional swings. In one day, she'd experienced more happiness and despair than she had in possibly ten years.

Divorce with children? Not for the faint of heart. Take it from her.

"Do you think David was actually trying to get you and Rob back together tonight?" Declan finally spoke up. "Maybe he thought that if you were united in a common cause, old feelings might resurface."

"I was worried about that for a minute, but David isn't that calculating. It makes more sense he was just mad at Rob. He doesn't spend time with him practicing. And, of course, my son is loyal. When he realized that daddy's 'friend' was actually his girlfriend, reality hit him."

"Yeah, that's what I mean. I guess all kids wish their parents would get back together."

It occurred to her that maybe Declan was sensing uncertainty in this situation.

"Maybe they do, but in my case it's never going to happen. I hope you believe that, too." She reached for his arm. "It's too late."

"Are you sure? I know the divorce is official, but... I

mean, you hear about it all the time. Couples getting back together for round two. Reunions."

"You mean…like us?" She smiled, hoping to change the subject back to them.

They'd had such a wonderful evening and Declan had given her a dream kind of date.

"I meant like parents who have children. They're the primary reason couples stay together."

"Take it from me, it can't be the only reason." She sat up straighter. "Declan, tell me that you don't really think…"

He shrugged. "I don't *want* to believe it."

"Then don't because it's not happening. Here's the thing. I don't love Rob anymore. I'm not sure exactly when I stopped, but I'm a little ashamed to say it was even before the divorce was finalized. He failed me in so many ways. I failed him, too. I would never make the same mistakes again in a marriage. Marriage is *work*. Once you love someone, you've got to nurture that and never take it for granted. I'll always love him as the father of my children but I'm not in love."

"It's enough to almost make me feel sorry for Rob."

"Almost?"

Declan squeezed her hand. "I can't feel too sorry for him. He blew it, so tough luck. Were it me, I'd have never let you go."

Once, even a few short weeks ago, Amy might have bitterly brought up the fact that he *had* let her go. But those two people were a different Amy and Declan. This couple were grown-ups now and their attraction and need for each other were entirely different. To borrow one of Declan's sports analogies, it was like the same team playing on an entirely different field. Maybe even with new equipment.

She giggled at the thought of new "equipment."

"Not that I'm unhappy because hearing you laugh is much better than watching you cry, but what's funny?"

"Silly me, just having an off-color thought."

"Well, you should share." He grinned.

"Maybe later." She cleared her throat and tried to act casual. "Just out of curiosity. What would you have done? When you say you would have never let me go, what would that look like?"

"Well, I wouldn't stalk you." He snorted. "I'd like to think I wouldn't have let it ever get to the point where you fell out of love with me. But if I'd been that stupid, if I'd have allowed that to happen, I would have *groveled.*"

"You? Grovel?"

"You bet. And, of course, I would have gone to the couples counseling, or whatever you call it. Therapy. As you said, marriage is work. I imagine there are a lot of peaks and valleys, too. I've seen my parents go through it over the years."

"I saw mine, too. Funny, we both had great examples of parents who set high standards. But it's also a lot of pressure. I hated failing at my marriage when I'd had such a great example."

"Yep." Declan made a motion around his neck. "Finn and I both say it was like having a tourniquet around our neck. Finn didn't make it the first time, but he learned a lot. And I've been sort of sitting on the sidelines waiting."

Waiting for what? she wondered. The right one, maybe.

When they arrived, they both walked next door to his home without words. Amy held Declan's hand, her excitement comingling with fear. It suddenly occurred to her, rather late, that she had a very different body from the one he'd previously seen naked. After all, she'd been through childbirth now and had the Caesarean scar to prove it. Because she had a daughter, Amy had always been keenly aware not to put an emphasis on her weight or inches. She might be a little plumper than some moms, but she was also happy and healthy. Unfortunately, at the moment she wished she hadn't been quite so apathetic about her size.

"I'd say let's watch TV, but I don't want to get into another battle over the remote." Declan laughed.

It had actually been an easy way to slide into touching each other but a repeat performance would seem boring. She had to think of some new and enticing way to attract Declan. After all, assuming he wanted to have sex tonight meant maybe she'd been flattering herself.

While she was overthinking these matters, apparently he'd left the room.

"Amy?"

She followed him into the kitchen. "Getting a beer?"

"Just a water. Want one?"

Oh, good. Maybe she wasn't the only one nervous. Right now, she could guzzle the entire bottle down because her throat was parched and dry. Maybe the tears had dehydrated her. Either that or she was nervous to have sex for the first time in over a decade with a man who wasn't her husband.

Chances are it was the second one.

Declan was eyeing her carefully after this first guzzle. "I have a confession to make."

Amy swallowed hard. Maybe this is where he would tell her that after tonight he realized he was in over his head. Maybe he was going to give it another try with Samantha. He would try to bow out gracefully, since they would still have to live next door to each other and had started a friendship again.

"Oh. Really?"

"Yeah." He set his empty water bottle down. "This was supposed to go differently."

"H-how was it supposed to go?"

He took a step toward her and then another until he was close enough to tug on a lock of her hair.

"It was going to be a romantic evening—"

"And it was!"

"Yes, but we should have wound up here right after all that romance and instead we took a little detour. I lost your attention."

"You didn't." She sighed. "Maybe you did for a few minutes, but you got it back."

"Did I?"

"Declan, you've always had my attention. I hope I didn't ruin your plans tonight."

He took her hand and brought it up to his lips to kiss it. "First, it wasn't you, and nothing was ruined. A little boy needed his mother. That's all."

"Listen. Romance with me is going to mean a lot of this. Interruptions. Sneaking around so we can be alone. Late nights, waiting until the kids are asleep. And very *early* mornings if morning sex is even a possibility."

He quirked a brow. "Wow. You went there."

"Where did I go?"

"Sex, Amy. You brought up sex. Not just sex, but *morning* sex."

"Was I not supposed to?"

The smile stayed in his eyes, but his lips didn't even quirk. "We don't have to do anything you don't want to do."

"But I *want* to have sex!"

Oh my, she might have blurted that out rather loudly.

"I heard you." This time, Declan's whole face smiled, his eyes crinkling.

She face-palmed. "I'm no good at this."

"Hey," he said, coming closer and taking each of her hands in his. "It's me. No need to be nervous."

"You remember me differently. I'm not a size six. I don't have the body of a teenager anymore."

"Neither do I."

"No, yours is even better." She laughed.

He pulled her close, so they were hip to hip.

"Do you think that's what I care about? I care about you, not your body. But, as a matter of fact, I like the way you look. You still have the world's best butt. It's perfectly shaped. Like a heart."

As if to emphasize his point, his wandering hands slid down her back to her behind and he was hard against her. He trailed kisses down the column of her neck to her shoulder, and gently lowered the straps of her dress. Her body buzzed and trembled under his touch. She stopped her attempts to pull off his shirt and helped him remove her dress, unzipping and lowering it past her hips until it pooled on the floor. The moment of truth. The jagged scar on her belly was not the ugliest she'd ever seen but it certainly wasn't a thing of beauty. Without realizing it, she self-consciously touched it, then lowered her hand, letting him see it, too. He needed to see all of her, and everything he'd missed. All the landmarks.

She stood, nearly naked, vulnerable and unguarded, but still somehow safe.

There was also a quiet kind of strength in this moment. She was proud to be moving on, to enter a new stage, this time with a man she trusted with her life. No matter what happened, Declan would be good to her. And she longed for him more than she ever had any other man.

"You're so beautiful," he said quietly, his fingers sliding over her face.

He took her hand and led her to his bedroom. She pulled

off his shirt, her finger sliding down to the muscles she'd been lusting for, and her knees went absolutely liquid. Under his shirt, she found those muscles were the sinewy strength she'd expected. He was all hard angles and planes, and so utterly...male.

His hand slid from her butt down her thighs, where a quivering heat pulsed and ached. She felt branded by his touch. Everything else in her loud and busy life faded to the background, and she understood this moment was one of no return. After this, she would be his and he would be hers. There was no question.

With the slow, wicked smile she'd never been able to resist, he sat on the edge of the bed and pulled her onto his lap. She straddled him and he kissed her shoulder, the beard stubble rough against her sensitive skin. His fingers threaded in her hair, and he licked the shell of her ear, teasing her earlobe with his teeth. Heat swept through her, fierce and uncontrolled. She'd never wanted anyone like this. Not with this fire.

"I know you're shy, but I need you to tell me what you want."

"I want you." She ran her fingers through his thick hair. "Inside me."

He found a condom and quickly protected them both.

Braced above her, he met her eyes. "I never forgot you, Amy. Never."

His words were sweet, but sweeter still was the way he made love to her. His thrusts tugged at something deep inside her, the friction and pressure mounting, the pleasure building quickly. She wrapped her legs around his back, urging him deeper, closer.

And not for the first time in her life, Amy found herself on the wild and powerful ride that was Declan Sheridan.

* * *

The cold air woke Declan up the next morning, which was unusual even if he ran the AC all night during the summer. Then he realized he was naked, and memories of the night before quickly flooded his synapses. Dayum. Amy had been fantastic. She was passionate and responsive. Insatiable. There seemed to be no off switch once they got in bed. They finally collapsed around midnight, but if he recalled, he'd gone to bed with covers and now had *none*. No wonder he was cold.

As he suspected, all he had to do was turn his head and see Amy wrapped up in the covers like a burrito. So, she hogged covers, the cover-hogger. This could be easily remedied. He rolled close to her, burrowing under the covers with her, becoming her second skin.

"Morning," he said, nuzzling her neck. "Cover-hogger."

"Hmm, I'm sorry," she mumbled. "I steal covers in my sleep. It's a thing I do."

"There are worse things."

"I swear I don't mean it. I don't even realize I'm doing it."

"It's all right, babe."

"Are you cold?" She tried to wrap more cover around him, to bring him into her cocoon.

That was Amy, always generous, last night being a prime example. He could definitely get used to this, waking up next to this gorgeous, amazing woman every day. For the first time in his life, he actually felt lucky. Blessed. He'd done nothing in his entire life to deserve this perfection.

He and Finn used to joke that family folklore was the Sheridan family lost their luck of the Irish in a poker game back in 1876. No luck had fallen into the Sheridan family. Hard work had permeated their lives and they'd earned everything. Declan had always worked for everything he accomplished, having nothing handed to him, unless you wanted to count a God-given natural ability for the sport. Luck had almost nothing to do with his life up until this moment.

But what good fortune of his to have Amy move in right next door, and to have her son become interested in baseball. Okay, so maybe he'd done a little convincing on that end, noticing that David was unhappy with soccer. It eventually turned into a way he might spend even more time with Amy. Because something had stirred in him the moment he'd seen her again and it had been slowly building ever since.

"What do you want to do today?" he said.

"I just want to hang out with you."

"Good. We're on the same page. But do you want to go do something, or just play house?" He nibbled on her ear, indicating that to him this meant not actually getting out of bed except for sustenance.

She rolled on her back and blinked at him through sleepy eyes. "Playing house sounds like fun. I can study later."

"I'll help you."

"I won't be able to concentrate much with you, ahem, 'helping' me." She circled her arms around his neck.

"Why don't I cook dinner for you while you study?"

"You're going to *cook* for me?"

"Why not?"

"I didn't know you could. Are you any good? You make a mean Mojito, but you can cook, too? Where have you been hiding all my life?"

The words were said so sweetly he almost missed the cataclysmic effect they had.

There was a quiet pause when they both smiled at each other. The unspoken message was that, of course, he hadn't been far almost the entire time she was married to someone else.

"I've been right next door."

Chapter Twenty

Later, Declan chopped carrots for the salad while Amy rested on his couch with her laptop. She was taking an online practice test, and he was doing his best not to distract her. He'd already donned his grilling apron because Amy said watching him cook shirtless, wearing only his jeans, was not only seriously distracting but also dangerous.

"Dangerous to whom?" he'd said with a wink.

"You. I don't want you to get burned."

"Okay, good point. I'll put on an apron. I don't want you to jump me while I'm cooking. You're right, that could be dangerous." He'd flashed his chef's knife, the best part of cooking.

All the cool cutlery.

Man, he could get used to this cozy kind of setting. It wasn't the sexiest thing to announce but deep down he was a homebody. He remembered he and Amy had always had a quiet and steady relationship. They'd rarely argued, unusual enough for teenagers that friends used to say they were like an old married couple. And true, they spent nights together watching TV or playing board games. Neither one of them was a party animal and, of course, Declan was forever training for something or the other.

He had to remind himself, though, that it wouldn't always

be Amy and him in their domestic bliss. For at least half the time, David and Naomi would be here, too. Lucky thing he liked kids and especially those two. They were difficult not to like. He and David were especially simpatico, which, of course, made sense. Maybe since David was mad at his father, Declan could now be a sounding board. He certainly understood what it was like to have a less-than-understanding father. What he really could not help David with was an under-involved father. But he could take up the slack there if nothing else.

He chopped and minced, and eventually the smells of garlic and onion permeated the air as he stirred them in olive oil.

"That smells delicious." Amy came up behind him, curling her arms around his waist, then lightly kissed his back.

The move sent a sting of desire slicing through his body. "No distracting the chef."

"I'm taking a break." She came around the other side of the counter to sit on a stool. "And anyway, we should really talk about something kind of serious."

While he didn't like the sound of that, his ears perked up. "What is it?"

"I've been thinking about this a lot and, well… I think and hope you will agree."

This was probably the moment where she reminded him that they needed to take things slow since there were children involved. He recalled her saying something like that right after he'd kissed her for the first time, and he'd understood. But he hoped, and maybe he was pushing his luck here, that after last night something had changed. It certainly had for him. This was what he wanted more than anything, a family with Amy. There was just no one else in the world like her for him. He was already half in love with her but if she wanted to slow down, he'd understand and accept it. Timing was everything. He could be a grown-up about this.

"I know what you're going to say." He held up a hand. "Because of the kids, we should keep this thing between us a secret for now."

She frowned. "Is that what *you* want?"

"What? No, I thought it was what you wanted."

She shook her head and wrapped her arms around her waist. "Actually, I was thinking that we need to tell the kids about us."

Whew. Talking to Amy. Always so easy. Why couldn't it be this easy with anyone else? Cut to the chase. They were always honest with each other, and always spoke up.

He was so flattered, however, it took him a moment to formulate his response. "Yeah. Sure, I agree."

"What do you think we should tell them?"

So, she was going to let him do this. No, she probably only wanted his input. The truth was he figured Amy would know *exactly* what to say to her children. Apparently, calling someone Daddy's "friend" had backfired, so he hoped that she'd learned something there.

He stirred, considering his response. "Can we tell them the truth?"

"I always think honesty is best, but it has to be age-appropriate."

"But not too age-appropriate because 'friend' didn't work."

"No, it didn't." She sighed. "That was a big fail."

Declan set his stirring spoon down and met her eyes. "Can we tell them I'm in love with their mother?"

He watched as Amy's eyes glimmered, shifted and softened.

This time, he'd fallen first. This time, he understood what

he had with Amy and how that was not something to be casually dismissed. Like the risk taker he'd always been, he gave her his heart, just set it at her feet. He did not give his heart lightly or easily, but it was not so much giving it to her as acknowledging that she'd always owned it.

He stepped toward her when she slid off the stool, closing the distance.

"Nothing like coming right out with the truth. You know me, Amy, better than almost anyone in my life. You know I don't lie. I don't cheat. I don't take shortcuts. I work hard and I never give up on the people I love."

Her eyes were shiny and wet. She reached for him, holding on to the straps of his apron. "Oh, Declan."

"Sorry to spring it on you like this. I love you, Amy. That's it. That's all." He pressed his forehead to hers.

"That's everything."

She kissed him, kissed him some more and then she took him to bed, where even if she didn't actually say the words, Declan could feel them. It was Amy and Declan all over again, the 2.0 version. The grown-up one, where two people always meant for each other finally met the right timeline.

This version would last.

Amy Holloway was flying high.

Instead of going back to the kitchen and through all the trouble of getting dressed again, Declan carried the pan of tossed pasta in a creamy tomato sauce into bed with them.

"This is perfect," she said, taking another bite out of the skillet that he placed between them.

"You sure? I feel like it could use a little more…something. Is there anything missing?" he asked, taking a bite, and slowly chewing as if judging his own work.

Nothing at all. She had everything she needed right here.

"It's delicious."

Still, it was not as delicious as the man himself. His incredible body was muscular, with powerful thighs and flat abs. He'd put her at ease immediately, worshipping her body, kissing every inch of flesh until she was a puddle of pure longing. When he said he loved her, he couldn't wipe away all the pain she'd been through in the past year, though he came very close.

She would have never guessed all those years ago that they'd someday wind up back together again. Certainly not like this. For a short while, she'd fantasized Declan followed her out to her college, declaring he'd changed his mind. He'd then go down on bended knee in front of the sorority she'd just pledged and beg her to marry him. All the girls would faint dead away at her handsome fiancé and realize she was clearly the coolest girl at the sorority house if not the entire college. Those were the dreams of a self-centered young adult who wanted everything in her life to happen immediately. Marriage. Children. *Hurry up, life, give me everything I want. Now.* She had zero patience.

Now, she wondered why she'd been in such a rush. Now, her children were growing up, her mother was aging, and so was Amy. Now, she found herself wishing time would occasionally stand still. Like this moment, here, in bed with the single-most-desirable man in all of Charming, Texas. Okay, so maybe she was a bit biased.

She leaned against Declan. "I've got to go home, but I don't want to."

"And I don't want you to."

"Do I really have to be a grown-up?" she groaned.

"Afraid so, babe. We both do. Or at least fake it till we make it."

She loved her children, but she'd forgotten what *this* was

like. This complete unraveling of her soul and swimming in a passion like she'd never had before. A whole carnal side of her she'd been ignoring for too long while throwing herself into raising her kids and running a household.

"Okay, I'll be a grown-up if you will."

Taking the lead, Declan grabbed the empty pan and rose from the bed, carrying it into the kitchen. He was already halfway dressed in his boxer briefs. When he returned, she remained in bed, pouting. He offered his hand to her and guided her toward the bathroom. They took a shower together, which was sensual even if it couldn't end in seduction. She towel-dried her hair and they dressed together, going through the motions as if it were the start of their day and not a Sunday night.

Declan walked her next door. "So, the kids have every other weekend with Rob, right?"

"Yes," she said, a smile tugging at her lips. "I'm counting the days, too."

"I'm giving you something to remember me."

He kissed her then, long and hard and filled with such passion that her knees were liquid when they broke apart and came up for air.

"I'll see you tomorrow," she said with a gasp, still holding on to his hand as she walked away. She stretched as far as she could before being forced to let go.

Amy went inside to wait for the kids. She straightened up the living room but since she hadn't been here most of the weekend, everything looked the way she'd left it on Saturday before her date with Declan.

A few minutes later, Rob was at the door, right on time.

"Bye, Daddy!" said Naomi, giving her father a kiss and hug.

"Bye, Princess."

David waltzed inside the house without a word to Rob, much less a hug goodbye.

"Hey, Mom," he said to Amy, then headed straight to his room.

Rob scowled, following David's retreating back with his eyes. "He's been this way all weekend."

"I'm sorry. I guess we didn't do a very good job in preparing him for this moment."

"I tried talking to him." Rob shuffled his feet and looked at the ground.

"Don't worry, I'll see what I can do."

"I appreciate that. He listens to you." He beckoned Amy to step outside.

"I'll be right back, sweetie," Amy called out to Naomi. "Just going to talk to Daddy for a minute."

She was sitting on the living room couch, unzipping her backpack. "Okay."

Outside, Amy closed the front door and faced Rob. "What is it?"

"So, you and Declan?" He nudged his chin in the direction of the house next door.

"That's right. We're...back together."

"With the guy who broke your heart? You're giving him another *chance*?"

"Um, I find this quite ironic coming from you, but yes."

"It's just... What if it doesn't work out, again? The kids have already been through you and me breaking up and that's bad enough."

"Well, what if you and Shannon break up?" She crossed her arms, hating the double standard Rob attached to everything.

"Okay, I deserve that, but the thing is, Shannon and I are a blank page. We haven't already *failed* each other once."

"Wow. Declan was *seventeen* when we broke up because he didn't want to get *married*."

He scoffed. "All I know is he's all I heard about when we first met, and how the man shattered your heart."

"Did you ever consider you were only hearing one side of the story?"

"Forgive me for wanting to save you from some grief and pain, Amy." He shook his head.

Amy quirked a brow. He must be joking.

"Fine! I screwed up, too." He held out his palms. "Okay, I screwed up *worse*. But you have to admit, it wasn't right between us for a long time. We weren't... We weren't *happy*."

"Yes," she said. "I know that now. You were right."

"Wait. *What?*" Rob jerked his head. "I was?"

"I wish I'd seen it earlier. You weren't happy and neither was I. Somewhere along the way we lost each other in the hustle and bustle of raising kids and putting them first. We're both to blame. I don't know about you, but I learned my lesson. I'm never going to take love for granted again. I'm going to—"

Rob blinked. "Love? You're already *in love* with him again?"

Until Rob repeated what she'd said back to her, she wasn't even aware she meant the words. But they were true. How easily she'd slipped back into a love that fit like a worn-out glove. No, not a worn-out glove. A *seasoned* glove. It fit. It was the perfect size and worked because it had molded itself to her soul early on. They'd failed for one reason only. They were too young.

"I... I don't know. But let's just say the possibility is there."

Rob grimaced like she'd socked him in the stomach.

"Oh brother! Well, whatever you do, don't say *that* to the

kids. It's all they can handle with both of us seeing other people."

With that, he climbed into his sedan and was off without another word.

Amy headed back inside, finding Naomi still on the couch but now she'd pulled out a book and was drawing inside it with her markers. She wondered if she should wait a little while before she told the kids about Declan. Rob had a point.

Amy sat next to her little girl, draping a hand around her tiny shoulders. "Did you have a good time yesterday after the park ordeal?"

"Shannon said I never have to call her Mom, that she's not my mom and only wants to be my friend. I call her Shannon and she's not Daddy's friend, but she's mine now, I guess. We played dolls for a little while." She shrugged and used her blue pencil to color in the clouds she'd drawn over a little cottage.

"But David… He's still upset?"

"Yeah." Naomi sighed like the little worrier she'd already become. "I tried to tell him Shannon isn't going to be our mom. He still doesn't like her."

Amy was about to go into David's room to talk to him when he came wandering out himself, tablet in his hand. "Could I have a sandwich?"

"Sure!" She shot up. It seemed to be their way of bonding and talking. "How about you, Naomi?"

"Cookies," she said. "And milk."

David followed Amy into the kitchen and sat at their little table in the corner while she fixed him his favorite, a PB&J. He played a game on his tablet, the one with the annoying song on repeat.

"I'm so sorry about what happened yesterday," Amy said,

taking the peanut butter and spreading it evenly on the wheat bread.

He said nothing.

"Naomi said that Shannon explained she doesn't want to be your new mother. Just a friend to you both. It's nice to have another adult friend."

David grunted.

"This is a lot of change to get used to. Daddy and I living apart, then we move to this new house. Now Daddy has a girlfriend. It's a lot."

"Yeah. It's super stupid. At least you don't have a boyfriend." David snorted.

Amy froze in the middle of spreading the grape jelly. "W-why would that be stupid?"

"D-uh," David said, his thumbs flying over the tablet. "Because if you have a boyfriend and Daddy has a girlfriend, then we're *never* getting back together."

No. Not this. A sharp ache stabbed through her chest. Routines were good. They kept order in an emotionally chaotic world. Throat tightening, Amy cut the sandwich into four triangles, the way she did when her life was far less complicated. David and Naomi were little, and she could protect them. There was so much. Stranger danger, carbon emissions, dirty water, pollution. High-fructose corn syrup, food dyes and pesticides, overly processed foods, too much screen time and hormones in their milk. She'd done her best to keep them healthy and happy but that hadn't been enough.

In the end, she'd ruined her children by being one half of the couple who had ruined their family.

"Here you go." She set the sandwich down.

"Thanks." David barely looked at her, not even noticing the triangles as he used one hand to take a bite.

"What did we say about eating and electronics?"

"They don't go together." David paused his game and took two huge bites of his sandwich.

Amy sat in the chair across from him, wondering how best to put the truth to him. She had to be at once firm but also compassionate. Her little boy wanted something she was never going to be able to give him, and to say that stung was an understatement.

"David, look at me."

"Yeah?" He did, his beautiful eyes so filled with hope it nearly killed her.

"Daddy and I are not going to get back together." Her voice cracked and she cleared her throat.

"You never know!"

"I do know, honey." Meeting his gaze, she refused to look away from those hazel eyes so like her own.

"Why won't you give him a chance?" David whispered and he sounded so grown-up she had to blink for a moment.

"Honey, it's not that simple." She reached for his hand, but he pulled it away.

"Yes, it is!"

"Remember we said some things are too complicated for kids to understand? This is one of them."

"Why? You always *say* I'm super smart."

Amy struggled for an analogy that might make sense to a nine-year-old boy's emotional maturity.

"Well, remember when soccer just didn't work out for you, even though I made you stick with it? Even though I didn't want you to quit? You tried, I know you did, but it just wasn't a good fit. It wasn't fun. Then you found baseball and you could see what you were missing. You're good at baseball and you have fun, too. Right?"

No, this wasn't right, either. *Terrible* analogy. She was sinking fast and could only think that Declan would know what to say. He was so good at positive self-talk, so good at being someone's personal cheerleader.

All of these intense feelings David had expressed were real and complicated and there was no place for more platitudes here. Only real talk, age-appropriate.

"Never mind. That might be a bad example." She gave up and tried again. "What I mean is—"

"It's because of Daddy! All this is his fault, and I *hate* him!"

David stood up from his chair so fast that it made a scraping sound across the tile floor.

"David, honey, wait," she said but he left the kitchen, taking his tablet with him.

In a fantasy world where Amy reigned as queen and everyone else were her subjects, of course it would be wonderful to be the favored parent. The great unblamed. The favored.

Let the kids take their anger of the divorce out on the father they once adored. Realistically, it was his fault anyway.

In the real world in which she lived and functioned, this hatred was going to cause more division and anger that wouldn't serve anyone. If left to grow, it would infect her children like a parasite. David hated the world right now, because he was almost a year behind Amy and Rob in terms of acceptance. He'd only now come to the full-blown realization that his perfect and previously protected bubble had popped and forever shifted.

And all he wanted to do was get his world back in order again.

She was David's mother, and so she felt his suffering like a blade knifing through her heart, looking for the best place to cut the deepest. Amy blinked back tears.

"*Mommy!* What about my cookies and milk?" Naomi called out from the living room.

Right. Amy rose, poured milk and plated some cookies. This was something she could do. Feed her children. Read them a bedtime story. Sit and cuddle. Love them.

The rest of this might never get any easier.

Chapter Twenty-One

"I was surprised to get your call. But can I just say I'm ecstatic?"

"Let's not get ahead of ourselves," Declan said, leaning back in his chair. "I said I'd *consider* this."

After months, he was in the office of the principal of Charming High School, Tyrone "Ty" Jefferson, who also happened to be a former classmate. He was four years ahead of Declan in school, but they'd played varsity baseball together. Unlike Declan, Ty also played football and was in fact an all-star. After a short career in college football with the Crimson Tide, Ty had quickly advanced through school administration and eventually returned to Charming. Ever since he realized Declan had quit teaching in Houston, he'd been trying to recruit him back into the fold.

"You'll find it's different here." Ty ran a hand through his dark close-cropped hair. "Not that I haven't lost a few teachers over the years due to both retirement and burnout. But we're a smaller high school, lots of parental support and an exceptional safety record."

"We had great security at my school in Houston, too," Declan reminded him.

It was the only reason his student's father hadn't been able to get far. He'd been tackled by the peace officer on-site who'd risked his life to save the kids. From time to time, Declan still pictured the day's events and how easily it could have all gone sideways. The man was looking for Declan, and if he'd known that, he would have presented himself front and center. But how many innocents might have been caught in the crossfire? They'd never know, and he thanked God for that every day.

"It's a different world now, isn't it?" Ty said, tugging on his tie. "We should probably all get hazard pay."

"Yep." Declan nodded. "But I'd like to hear more about the position."

For a week after the school-related incident, Declan had trouble leaving the house. Then, when he did, he kept a loaded handgun in his glove compartment. It wasn't unheard of in Texas to carry, but he wasn't into hunting or shooting the way some of his old friends were. The handgun was protection for himself and others. He considered it a major achievement the day he'd locked it up for good and put it high on a shelf of his closet. He'd never gone back to teaching at the high school, however, feeling maybe everyone would be safer without him around. In the aftermath, the student and his family had moved out of the area for a fresh start. Let's just say some staff remained unhappy with Declan and the loss of their star player.

Which meant he'd been working at the Salty Dog Bar & Grill now for close to three years. Huh. He'd never planned for it to be that long. It was to be a temporary stop while he considered his options. Either he went back to teaching somewhere else, went back to school for a graduate degree or went out for a minor league team and hit the road. That last one didn't have much appeal for a man who wanted a family sooner rather than later.

And all this time, his father had hammered away in his ear

like a woodpecker, trying to drill into him that he still had work to do. Important work. Yeah, Declan got it. Or maybe he'd finally simply accepted the fact that he wanted more out of life. That he was done with one bad experience coloring his entire view. He loved kids, and given his experience with David and Naomi in particular, they didn't have to be his own flesh and blood. He loved teaching and coaching, given his propensity to do both even off the field.

Maybe Amy was right. *You're a born coach, Declan.*

Just like his father.

But hey, if he could program a running recording of affirmations into a young person, whether it be his own child or another's, maybe he could do some greater good in the world. Maybe that kid with the positive encouragement running in his head 24/7 wouldn't choose violence when he ran into a problem.

Ty continued to discuss in depth the position as an AP calculus teacher he was recruiting and took Declan through a tour of the building. The gym was new, and the fields freshly chalked. Outside, those fields smelled like fresh-cut grass, spring and the middle of the season. He met teachers, some who'd taught him in their first years, now suddenly not all that much older than Declan.

His coach, of course, had retired years ago and the school hadn't found a good replacement.

"That's where you come in," Ty said. "I'll be honest. With your name and experience behind us, I feel like the Charming Mustangs could go all the way next season."

"What do you think the team morale is like right now?"

"Honestly, I'd have to say it's at an all-time low."

"Sounds like I'd have my work cut out for me."

"We do have a few good players. I mean *really* good. One

of them reminds me of you, but let's just say, he's not Irish," Ty joked. "More like me."

Declan chuckled. The year he belonged to the team, he was practically the only white player, surrounded by Latinos and African Americans who'd been playing the sport as long as he'd been.

"For his sake, I hope his head is not nearly as big and swollen as mine was in high school. I think the only thing that kept me levelheaded was my girlfriend."

"Ah, yes. Amy. Who could forget the two of you, walking through the halls like you had matching halos." Ty elbowed him.

"Yeah, Amy was the only one of us that deserved that halo."

"If I recall, you two were voted Most Likely to Be Married." Ty quirked a brow. "You missed that boat, didn't you?"

Declan smiled and shook his head but didn't say a word. *Not yet, Ty. Not yet.*

"I guess I don't have to tell you about my experience with grade expectations. The truth is, I won't give in to pressure. If a kid doesn't deserve a passing grade, he's not getting one from me. If that means he's benched, so be it. If I accept the position, I'm going to demand your full support and that of the administrative staff."

Ty nodded and fist-bumped with Declan. "Not a problem. We do it differently here in Charming. And though I wouldn't say this in front of my boosters, high school football isn't everything."

Declan chuckled. "Just don't say that too loudly."

They left the meeting with Ty expressing his intent to send an offer of employment and Declan promising to give it full consideration. Maybe he was finally on the way to bridging that gap that for so long had held him from moving forward.

As his father continually instructed him and Finn early on: the only person who can truly hold you back is the same one you'll see in the mirror.

Tonight was the rec team practice for David, so he drove straight there after his meeting. Amy would be there early with the kids so that he could go over a few drills with David and maybe throw the ball a bit beforehand. Naomi would no doubt bring her book and Declan smiled at the thought of the girl who reminded him so much of Amy.

He hadn't told Amy about the interview with Tyrone or the fact he was actually considering going back to teaching and coaching. They had so much going on right now with the kids getting used to their father being in a relationship with someone new. He wouldn't blame Amy for wanting to hold off on telling them about what they'd started up again. The most important thing to Declan was that *she* knew he was all in. But the last thing Declan wanted was to hurt these kids any more than they'd already been by the loss of the home they'd had for the first formative years of their lives. They were still adjusting and coping with their new reality.

Last night, Amy had texted him about David. He wasn't much happier with his father than he'd been the day at the park. If anything, she'd said, his attitude had worsened.

He saw Amy turn when she heard his truck drive in the lot and park, and the smile she gave him lit up a flame in his heart. She had so quickly become...everything. He knew he'd walk through fire for her without a second thought *and* for her children because they were a part of her. He tugged off the tie he'd worn to his interview and rolled up his sleeves.

It was David who reached him first, running up to him. "Dec! We're doing a scrimmage today with another team."

"Oh yeah? That ought to be fun." He tousled David's hair.

Amy and Naomi brought up the rear.

"Hi, Declan!" Naomi said, waving.

"Hey there."

Declan followed Amy's lead when it came to PDA. If it were up to him, he'd put his arm around her, but he had no idea what she'd told the kids and after the display at the park he'd wait for a sign. He didn't have to be a Neanderthal who would claim his woman.

"Do you think they're ready for that? A scrimmage?" Amy said, holding Naomi's hand.

"Usually that term is used with football because of the scrimmage line. But yeah, a scrimmage is just a pretend game, like a practice for the real thing. It's good experience, right?"

"Yeah." David bobbed his head. "I tried to tell her."

Declan reached in the cab of his truck and pulled out his old glove. "This is the one I was telling you about."

"Whoa," David said, almost reverently. "Is that the one you used when you pitched in college?"

"That's right." He slipped it on and strolled toward the field. "Walk with me."

He practiced catch with David for at least thirty minutes under the clear blue sky and then the rest of the team began to arrive. Matthew, David's pal, rushed right up to them and joined in. A self-assured man followed him wearing a business suit complete with red power tie.

He stood behind Declan and offered his hand. "I'm Mark Burrows, Matthew's father."

"Good to meet you. I'm Declan Sheridan." Declan shook his hand.

"C'mon, Dec! Throw it back," David yelled.

Declan threw the ball back to him and he caught it easily.

"Oh, I know who you are." Mark chuckled and tipped back on his heels. "We're very excited to see you helping out around here. The coach is a little young, don't you think? He really doesn't seem to know what he's doing."

Declan, who'd been taught to respect the chain of command, so to speak, couldn't bring himself to go there. Besides, it was a *recreational* league.

"He'll learn."

"Yeah. Apparently your father sees real promise in Matthew."

Sometimes, Declan wished his father didn't try to recruit everyone he met into competitive sports.

"He's good." Declan caught the ball and threw it to Matthew.

Unfortunately, Matthew was looking at something else and the ball sailed right past him.

"Sorry!" he yelled and went running after it.

"See that? His only problem is he isn't taking this seriously enough," Mark said.

Declan was stopped from engaging in a mini lecture on fun versus competition in sports at an early age. There was plenty of time for that later. A lifetime.

The coach and the rest of the team had arrived, and it was time for the scrimmage to begin.

Amy tried to keep her eyes on the game, but it was tough with Bianca chirping in her ear nonstop, Mark yelling "encouragements" to their son and Declan looking so smoking hot wearing slacks and a button-down. He'd rolled up the sleeves, displaying those powerful forearms. Maybe she was a wanton woman for noticing this, but the man was yummy.

"Mark took off early from work so he could be here," Bianca said. "He's being so supportive."

"That's good. I'm sure his support means a lot." She glanced at her phone again to note the time.

She'd told Rob about the practice, and he was supposed to be here. Not that David would be happy to see him but being a parent meant you couldn't just give up trying because your kid was mad. After her talk with David, she'd texted Rob with an honest update. He'd been less than thrilled, accusing her of borderline alienation and reminding her they promised they'd never take sides against each other. Withholding the less-than-kind words she wanted to hurl at him, Amy composed a text advising him she was doing no such thing. She encouraged him to come to the game and show his support, omitting the fact Declan would be there in case that might discourage him.

She texted Rob a reminder of the time and location again. Within minutes he texted back:

Can't make it. Huge problem at the office. Tell David I'll catch him at the next one.

"Why is Declan dressed in slacks and a button-up?" Bianca said.

"I don't know, maybe he had to go into work for a bit."

"He looks good. Notice all the moms checking him out. What a great ass. Is he really just going to *bartend* for the rest of his life?"

"I don't know, Bianca. I haven't asked."

"Why isn't Rob here? You did tell him, didn't you?" The tone sounded borderline accusatory, and Amy flinched.

"Of course. Why would you ask that?"

"Well, no offense, Amy, but I see how you'd want to slide Declan in there to take Rob's place. He is pretty hot, and amazing, but he's not David's *father*."

A slice of irritation hit Amy hard. "I know and I'm *not* trying to replace him. In fact, funny thing, but David mistakenly believed that Rob was trying to get him a new mother when he met his new girlfriend this weekend. We both made sure he understood that wasn't true."

"Oh brother." Bianca rolled her eyes. "Rob is blowing it right and left."

Amy refrained from defending Rob but just barely. They were trying, damn it, and it was *tough*. No one liked a divorce, least of all the children. But Rob wanted to move on and so did Amy. There was nothing wrong with that and she deeply resented people judging them. She'd judged the situation enough herself. It was a mistake, but it happened, and they were both to blame.

Before she spoke, Amy checked and saw Naomi still sitting a few seats over with a friend who'd showed up to practice with her brother, who was on the other team.

Amy kept her eyes on the game, not wanting to miss when David went up to bat. Batting was his weakness and he tended to swing at anything that came over the plate. Declan told her it was a common enough mistake and told her not to worry. He didn't really have to tell Amy twice as she worried about real-life stuff, not a game.

"I'm not making the same mistake. Which is why I'm not telling the kids about me and Declan," Amy said quietly.

"Ooooh, and how's that going?" Bianca said, turning her folding chair to face Amy and away from the game. "Did you two get jiggy with it?"

"Hey, ladies. Mind if I join you?" Declan's deep voice interrupted from behind them, and they both turned.

He stood in the sunlight, practically bathed in the golden rays. *The golden boy.* At least, he'd been her golden boy, now a man.

"Hey, Declan!" Bianca practically giggled. "So *good* to see you here!"

"Good to see you, too." With no extra seat, he crouched beside Amy.

Usually, Declan stayed close to the action, observing as if he couldn't tear himself away from the game.

She was flattered he'd come to find her.

"Hey," he said, taking her hand in his. "Missed you."

She squeezed his hand. "Me, too."

She was still living on the memory of their lazy Sunday together and for the first time since the divorce looking forward to when the kids went to see their father. Safe to say she would no longer be crying herself to sleep or falling asleep in her daughter's bed. It had been a tough time, grieving the loss of a marriage and partnership, but now she was on the other side of it. And while she'd never expected this with Declan, she would luxuriate in the sharp sweetness of the moment.

"So, Declan," Bianca said. "Mark and I were talking. Can we hire you for private coaching lessons? We want Matthew to go all the way with this. He shows such promise."

"Is he having fun out there?" Declan asked, looking at the field.

It was not lost on Amy that he'd carefully avoided answering the question. She didn't see when he'd have time to coach but he'd already made such a difference with David simply in his casual spare time.

"Oh yes!" Bianca went on, her back still to the game. "We're signing him up for Little League, for sure. Mark is talking about pitching clinics and camp. What do you think is the best-rated one in the area? Should we go to Houston?"

"You could do any of those things, but why not just let him have fun for right now?"

"Yeah, fun's great but competition is stiff. Nine is really a good age to start training, isn't it?"

"It can be, with the right kid. Unfortunately, I'm not going to be available for private coaching. Looks like I'm going back to teaching and coaching at the high school level."

"Really?" Amy whispered. "You're going back?"

He nodded. "If the employment offer comes through as expected, I should start in the fall."

"In… Houston?" she hesitated, worried about him dealing with big-city high school booster politics.

"Actually, right here in Charming. Funny, right? Our old alma mater." He grinned. "They've been wanting to talk to me for a few years, but I wasn't ready until now."

"Declan, that's perfect."

Both of them would be teaching right in Charming, he at the same school where they'd first met.

"Thanks, Tinks."

"Yeah, that's awesome," Bianca said, getting the answer to the burning question of whether or not Declan would bartend for the rest of his life. "That's where Matthew will be going to high school. Hopefully by then he'll be one of your all-star players."

Loud male voices rose from the field.

"Are you kidding me, Coach? He's not out! Is there something wrong with your eyesight?"

"I hate when parents get out of control like this," one of the mothers sitting behind them said. "And it's always the dads."

"Girl, wait until they get to Little League," another one said. "You ain't seen nothing yet."

Bianca had turned her entire body to watch the scene play out. It was *her* husband reading the riot act to the poor harried coach.

"Oh, Mark," Bianca said, covering her face with her hands. "Nooooo."

Declan stood. "I'll be right back."

She watched as he strode purposefully toward them right into the middle of the melee. He shoved his big body between the coach and Mark, who was still angrily pointing from Matthew to the plate.

"He's been under a lot of pressure at work," Bianca said. "This is so humiliating."

"Don't worry. Declan will get it under control." Amy pushed her chair closer to Bianca and draped her arm around her shoulder. "I'm sure it will be fine."

But Amy suddenly wasn't so sure of that as she watched Mark storm off.

Chapter Twenty-Two

After practice, or scrimmage, or whatever you wanted to call it, Amy thought her kids deserved a treat.

"How's pizza for dinner?"

"Yay!" David said.

"Thanks, Mommy!" Naomi said.

Since both Amy and Bianca were upset to see a grown man behave the way Mark had, Amy could only imagine how the *kids* were feeling. Bianca took Matthew home, apologizing to anyone who would listen for her husband's behavior. Amy promised to call her later and drop by for a playdate soon.

Then Amy and Declan took a detour to The Pie in the Sky, home of the best pizza in Charming, Texas.

"Did I ever tell you that your mom and I used to come here all the time?" Declan said.

"Really?" David asked.

"Yeah, she was my best friend."

"You never told me that," David said.

"Mommy, you were best friends with a boy?" Naomi's eyes went wide.

They'd chosen to sit across from each other, and she gazed at him now with tender familiarity and what she could only call love. Yes, in many ways he'd been her best friend. She'd heard it said that the best relationships started with a friendship, and that's how she and Dec had started out.

Declan was amazing and understanding. He did not want to push anything and have a reaction similar to the one David had with Rob's girlfriend. She appreciated him more than she could say.

"We both had other friends, of course, and all my other friends were girls. All his other friends were fellow baseball players. But yes, Declan was my best friend. We were close."

"Like me and Matthew?" David said.

"Yes, kind of like that."

"But we were older," Declan said. "Teenagers."

"I'll still be friends with Matt when we're teenagers," David said.

"I think so, too," Declan said.

"Mommy, why was Matthew's dad yelling at the coach?" Naomi said.

"Um, well, it sounds like he needed to take a time-out. He got a little too excited about the game," Amy editorialized.

Best not to explain to Amy that Mark was probably having a career crisis and might be struggling with his own self-worth. With Matt presenting an aptitude, he felt he had to jump on that. She couldn't blame him or Bianca for wanting to support their son's interests and abilities, but she hoped they wouldn't make Matt's talents about them. It seemed Mark already had.

"He just wanted us to win so bad," David explained to his sister. "And he got upset because Matt struck out."

"You did good." Naomi patted his shoulder. "You hit the ball."

"Yeah, but I got out pretty quick." David shook his head. "I flew right to the second base."

"It happens," Declan said. "You have your strengths elsewhere. So did I, by the way. I once led my team in the season's strikeouts."

"So, you were the worst player?" David stared, jaw gaping.

"No, he wasn't." Amy shook her head. "He was the best pitcher by far."

"Hey, you miss 100 percent of the swings you never take." Declan laughed. "Anyway, don't tell your coach I said that."

After they finished their pizza, David and Naomi wanted to play some of the arcade games, so Amy gave them some change. She'd now at least have a few minutes alone with Declan.

"Tell me more about the job." She reached across the table and squeezed his hand.

Surely this small amount of PDA would be allowed. The kids were busy, after all, and maybe she could let some of her feelings seep through. She loved this man, loved everything about him, and couldn't believe she'd forgotten him for so many years. Part of that forgetting, of course, had been self-preservation.

"Remember Tyrone? He's the principal at our old high school and has been trying to recruit me since I left Houston."

"What made you change your mind?"

He shrugged. "I think it's time."

"We're going to miss you at the Salty Dog. What will Debbie do without her nightly coaching talk?"

Declan laughed. "You're the one who made me realize it's in my blood. I can't escape who I am, and just being around David has brought the rest to me. Damn it, I love baseball. Always have, always will."

"I know you do. And I bet you're a great teacher, too. I've already seen how good you are with David."

"You won't be working at the bar much longer, either. I'm sure you'll get an offer as soon as you're ready."

"Let's hope."

They just grinned across the table at each other, and she felt caught in a love spell. This was how they'd been all those years ago but without all the experiences and changes between them. They were like two different people, who simply looked like older versions of the previous Amy and Declan.

"I have an idea. We should pretend we don't know anything about each other, like this is the first time we've ever met. Start over, blank slate." She swiped at an imaginary whiteboard.

He cocked his head. "Right here, right now?"

"Sure. Like one of those speed date thingies they used to do back in the day." She offered her outstretched hand. "Hi, I'm Amy Holloway, nice to meet you."

"I'm Declan Sheridan. I work as a bartender, but don't hold that against me. I give great advice on any given night. I played major league baseball until I got injured, then I taught and coached high school baseball. Thinking about going back to it. How about you?"

"You see those little people over there? They're mine. Twins, nine years old. Naomi and David."

"I love kids and I'm not just saying this but yours look exceptionally smart." He leaned back in his seat. "So, Amy. Are you thinking you'll have any more kids? Or is two the limit for you?"

The question made her heart jerk as if coming out of a trance. These were exactly the type of questions asked on a first date. Or a dating app's questionnaire.

After David and Naomi, she swore she wouldn't have more children. How could she when she'd been gifted with both a boy and a girl at the same time? But everything had changed. She was looking across the table at a man who, in her humble opinion, should procreate because those perfect genes deserved to be spread around. And that wasn't even mentioning his emotional intelligence. He'd be a great father.

"I want more kids. Yes."

"Good to know." He cleared his throat. "And I'm to assume that you're not soured on marriage, since it didn't work out the first time?"

"I would get married again to the right person. I like being married."

He touched his chest. "I've never been married."

"I won't hold that against you."

"Any old boyfriends out there I should be worried about?"

"Actually, yes. There is someone."

"Ah. Thanks for the warning. Is he still in your life?"

"He reappeared again after a long absence, but he was always someone very special to me. If you want to know the truth, I've always loved him, and let's just say if he decides he wants another chance… Well, you're going to have some stiff competition."

"Good to know."

If only Amy could freeze time, she'd take this moment and relive it over and over again. This moment when Declan heard her admit she loved him, and his face…changed. Every hard angle in his face relaxed and softened. In those few seconds, she saw shades of the young man he'd been juxtaposed to the one he'd become. She also saw a hint of the older man he'd be when his perfect face acquired some deep crevices and wrinkles. His golden looks would never leave him.

She could almost see the years stretching head of her, the children they would have, a home, jobs, vacations, the illnesses, their aging parents. She would love him through every piece of it.

Her golden boy.

Later, after he'd taken Amy and the kids home and managed somehow to sneak a kiss, Declan went home, switched on the TV and caught up on the sports recap. One thing he hadn't done in a long time is call his father to discuss the league standings. Dan Sheridan lived for that stuff even more than Declan.

It occurred to him that on some level he'd been punishing his father. Without realizing it, he'd created this distance between them because he'd sensed how much they were alike. When exploring this through the lens of harsh parental judgment, Declan honestly didn't want to be like his father. He'd tried like hell for years to be his own man but today had reminded him of something significant. His father was never one to call out or criticize a coach, whether it be pro sports or Little League, *even* in instances where his own knowledge superseded the coach's by leaps and bounds.

The sad state of affairs he'd witnessed today reminded him that winning was *all* that mattered to some people. But not his dad. He'd told him early on he was only in competition with himself. For years, Declan hadn't listened, or more than likely, he'd heard the louder voices. The voices telling him he'd never be anyone if he couldn't make it to the major leagues. But his father, again, had been at him like that damn woodpecker.

"You never give up on something you love. If you can no longer play the game, there's always another way to give back."

Declan had let one bad, okay, horrible experience sideline him and that wasn't how he'd been raised.

He picked up the phone and dialed. "Hey, Mom. Is Dad around?"

"Watching the sports wrap-up," she said. "How are you, sweetie?"

"Looks like I'm going back to teaching soon."

She might be trying to disguise it well, but even Declan heard the thick emotion in his mother's voice. "Oh. That's... wonderful. Just wonderful."

"I'm finally ready."

"I'll get your father." He heard the sounds of her wandering through the house. "Dan? Dan! Turn that down. Here, it's your son."

"Which one?" His father took the phone and the sounds of ESPN finally muted. "Hello, son!"

"Hey, Dad. Number two here."

"Hello, number two! Did you get a chance to see that line drive today? It was a thing of beauty."

For a few more minutes they discussed the season so far. Lots of hopes for their beloved Astros, looking good but still a long way to go to the playoffs.

"Looks like I'm going back to teaching and coaching," Declan finally said.

"Is that right? How about that."

Declan heard the smile in his father's voice.

"Yeah, don't act so surprised. There's no way I could stay away forever. I love baseball, and I always have. I just... I guess I needed that break from all the things I have to do that *aren't* baseball. You know?"

"I know. And for what it's worth, I might have done the same in your position."

Declan doubted it but it was kind of his father to say. Dan Sheridan just never gave up on people, and he'd been a shining example to his sons. Not just for positive thinking and setting goals, but for loving a woman and dedicating his life to their family. It was the one way in which Declan hoped to emulate him most.

"In case you didn't know, I was yanking your chain about the project next door. You know, the chart I drew up on the back of a napkin?"

"Like I didn't realize that," his father snorted. "I still had to admire your tenacity."

"No doubt you'd find something to admire if I rolled up in a corner like a potato bug and refused to move."

"Sure. I'd compliment your form." Dan chuckled.

"Also, um, Amy? She and I... We're seeing each other again. If there's something I've learned the hard way, it's that you don't turn your back on a second chance. And she's giving me one."

"I always liked Amy."

"Of all the things you taught me, Dad, loving your wife was probably the most important. Finn and I both had the best example of how to be a good husband and father. I admit I didn't always want to be just like you, but I've accepted that I am. And I'm lucky."

"Hang on a second," his father said, not exactly what Declan had expected him to say.

A moment later, his mother was back on the phone again. "Honey, what did you say to your father? He's crying."

Declan laughed, wiping one of his eyes with the back of his hand.

"Nothing but good things, Ma. Nothing but good things. I'm sure he'll explain. Tell him I'll talk to him later. Anyway, just give him this message—me, too."

With that, Declan hung up and went to find his planner. It was tucked away in the drawer of his nightstand, and he hadn't looked at it for a while. But now it was time to plan the next few months and how he would make the move from bartender back to teacher and coach.

Chapter Twenty-Three

The summer temperatures had turned outside into a sauna, so two days later, Amy and Bianca made the boys stay inside on their playdate. They were playing video games on the console in Matthew's room. Naomi had decided to spend the afternoon with Mom and Lou at the garden center.

"Is Mark doing any better after the scrimmage?" Amy tentatively asked.

She'd almost been afraid to bring it up because the ordeal had so upset Bianca.

"Much better," Bianca said, pouring iced tea from a pitcher. "That night, he called and apologized to the coach. Believe me, he won't make that mistake again. He's letting tensions at work get the better of his temper."

"Well, at least he showed up. I have to give him credit there. Rob hasn't made it to a practice yet. I can't help but think that David is feeling the lack of support."

"At least he has Declan." Bianca offered Amy a glass of sweet tea.

"Yeah, but as you said, Declan isn't his father."

"I'm sorry I said that because Declan's a great guy." She grinned and cocked her head. "I see how well the two of you are getting along. Is it weird rekindling a love affair with your high school boyfriend?"

"Not as weird as you might think." Amy chuckled. "I suppose I never had one of those 'what was I thinking' moments when it came to him. It was more like, 'Where have you been all this time?'"

"Yeah, well, we didn't all have gorgeous jocks as our high school boyfriends."

Amy frowned. "I know it sounds fun, but in those days he was very committed to the sport. More committed than he was to me. The yearbook photos of our glory days don't tell the whole story. Behind the scenes I was lonely a lot of the time. But that's how it had to be then. He's different now."

"How did the kids take the news about you two?"

Amy had shared the news of David hiding at the park when he'd heard about Rob's girlfriend.

"Well, because they reacted so negatively to Shannon, we...decided to wait."

Actually, she had pretty much decided, without consulting Declan.

"And Declan... He's okay with that, being your kept man? Your dirty little secret?" She tossed her hair as if this was funny, or sexy, or titillating somehow.

A streak of pure hot fury coursed through Amy, and she had to bite her tongue from saying worse. "He's not my— you know what? Declan is a grown-up, and he gets it. His first concern is the kids, too."

"Sorry. Yeah, that wasn't funny or cute." Bianca lowered her head. "Not many guys would be willing to stay in the background. I was just thinking of Mark but we both know he's a hothead."

"He doesn't ever take it out on you or the kids, does he?"

Not that Amy had ever seen any evidence, but those types of matters tended to stay hidden. It would be wrong not to at least ask.

"No. But after the other day, I suggested anger management therapy." She took a big gulp of sweet tea. "And… I think we're going to also do marriage counseling."

The news surprised Amy. "I thought you guys were doing well."

For some time after the divorce, she'd wondered how Bianca and Mark kept their marriage working when they'd been married longer than Amy and Rob had. She'd seen them as the paragon of a healthy sexually dynamic marriage until she'd heard about some of the unhealthy bits not long ago.

Bianca chewed on her lower lip. "Yeah, well, when the only time you have good sex is making up after a bad fight, you need to take a hard look at that."

"Yeah, that…makes sense."

"Look who I'm talking to. I bet you two are going at it like rabbits every chance you get."

"Well, it's…new." A hot flush went through Amy.

"I have to make my marriage work. It's not like I have a hot ex-boyfriend waiting in the wings."

"Declan wasn't waiting for me," Amy protested. "He was dating someone."

"You know what I mean."

"Mom, can we have some ice cream sandwiches, please?" said Matthew, surprising both of them.

Bianca took a quick glance at the digital clock. "I guess it won't spoil your dinner. Sure, but only one."

"Thanks!" Matthew grabbed two from the freezer and ran back up the steps.

"Did you find any good pitching clinics for Matthew?" Amy asked dutifully.

She understood how important it had become to Bianca and pride in her son's talents was healthy. They talked baseball and Little League, avoiding talk of marriages, both failed and still hanging in there, until it was time to head home.

On the way, they picked Naomi up at Mom's. She had with her a little potted fern she'd named "Fern."

"I picked her out at the garden store," Naomi said proudly. "Gramma says Fern can live inside in my bedroom. She doesn't need much sun."

"That's dumb," David said.

It wasn't until that moment that Amy realized he'd barely said a word to her since he got in the car.

"Why?"

Amy didn't have to look in the rearview mirror to see Naomi's lower lip quivering like she was ready to cry. She heard it in her shaky voice.

"David, that's not a nice thing to say to your sister," Amy said as they turned into their development.

"Flowers just die. You have to have a green hand to make them live and you don't have a green hand," David said.

Amy bit back a laugh. "Actually, that's just an expression and I think you know it. Plus, it's green *thumb*, not green hand. It's what we call a metaphor."

"Whatever," David said with attitude, but being a twin who did adore his sister, a moment later he patted her shoulder. "It's a cute plant, though."

"Thanks," Naomi said with a sniffle. "I think so, too."

Obviously, Amy needed to have another talk with her son. Naomi was such a sensitive soul, but particularly tuned in to her brother. His opinion mattered to her. He had to know how invested his sister was in his viewpoint and he'd never been purposely cruel.

Partially, Amy wondered if this new attitude was also part of a rite of passage and David was approaching yet another growth spurt. He did seem too young to have reached that rebellious hormonal state of preteens, which God help her, wasn't that far away. A shudder ran through her.

It's the divorce.

Yes, it probably was the divorce, but Amy also couldn't fall into the trap of blaming that for everything. Nor could David excuse away bad behavior because his parents were divorcing. Speaking of which, where was her "Parenting: Not for Wimps" T-shirt when she needed it?

Once they got home, Naomi quickly gave Fern a drink of water in the kitchen sink, then skipped to find a place for the flowerpot in her bedroom. David hunkered off to his room without another word. Amy started dinner because tonight she'd invited Declan over. She figured neighbors could have dinner together and the more exposure the children had to Declan, the more they'd get used to him being around.

"Dinner will be ready in about an hour," Amy announced from the hallway between their rooms. "I've invited our neighbor, and I expect you to both be on your best behavior."

"Which neighbor?" David, who'd been sitting in his bean-bag chair, sat up straighter.

"Declan, of course. He's coming over after his shift at work."

Naomi clapped. "We never had a neighbor over for *dinner* before!"

"Yes, well, we're in our new house so we're going to start doing that more often."

"Why *him*?" David said.

"Why Declan? Because he mows our lawn—"

"But we never asked him to do that," David interrupted.

"No, but it's nice that he does because it saves me the time. Plus, he came over once and fixed the Wi-Fi, young man!" Amy pointed to David. "Not to mention that he's helped you with baseball."

"He's nice," Naomi said. "I like him."

God bless Naomi, who would probably find something redeemable in Ted Bundy.

"Do *you* like him?" David addressed Amy.

"Me?" Amy touched her chest. "Sure, I do. We already told y'all we were best friends in high school."

"Don't *you* like him, David?" Naomi said, no small amount of surprise in her voice.

"I guess." David shrugged. "He's a good baseball player."

So, "Dec" had now become nothing but a good baseball player. All right, so David *knew*. Well, he knew something, but Amy couldn't be sure what he knew. He *suspected* something going on between her and Declan, and coming off the experience of Shannon and Rob, he didn't like it. That made sense. Amy would continue to keep it friendly and chaste with Declan in front of the kids. But for how long, exactly? Would Declan wait for months, weeks, years? More to the point, would this *ever* be okay with her son? Maybe not. And yet they couldn't hide or be discreet forever.

She thought of how Bianca had referred to Declan as her "dirty little secret" and a slice of fear knifed through her. If any man ever kept *her* a secret, if any man thought of her in the sense she was someone who should remain hidden, she'd be gone. Done. Her parents taught her to first believe in her own self-worth. Her father had modeled that and so had her mother. She couldn't expect Declan to forever be relegated to a little side action every other weekend. He wanted, expected and *deserved* to be a part of her whole life.

All the literature she'd read about single parents dating said a child shouldn't be introduced until the relationship was solid. She was already committed to Declan, sliding into their shared past easily and effortlessly. She loved him, and he loved her back. He defied all the written expectations of dating after divorce. There was no chapter on "proper time-lines to introduce the kids to your first love when he suddenly lives next door."

So, Amy was going to wing it.

She cooked the lasagna noodles and browned the ground beef, adding the store-bought jar of marinara sauce. Amy brought out her colorful bowls and plates, and set the table, trying to give the children the message that Declan was their guest of honor. He would be in their lives, whether they liked it or not, because he was her *person*. They'd get used to the idea. That was final. It was like eating their vegetables and limiting sugar. In this instance, she would play the Mom card.

"I'm going to put a flower at each setting. I'll pick some from outside. Gramma taught me the best ones today." Naomi went skipping outside.

"David, how are you going to help?" Amy asked.

He gazed at her from under hooded lids.

His body language said: *I will help our guest to the door.*

"I'll go help Naomi," he said. "Sometimes she can't reach."

Off went her growing boy, already two inches taller than his twin.

After layering the casserole and sticking it in the oven, Amy texted Declan with a warning:

I think David heard something about us or saw something. He's not feeling too friendly about you today. It's very out of character.

The bubbles of a response forming appeared and then seconds later, Declan's response.

Should we cancel? I can grab something here for dinner and maybe see you later tonight.

She grabbed her phone so fast she left a streak of sauce on it.

No. You're coming to dinner and that's final.

He replied:

Okay, boss.

She smiled and went about the business of shredding cheese and layering the casserole. Meanwhile, Naomi and David finally came in with what amounted to some beautiful weeds they'd pulled from their backyard. No matter. Amy was a big fan of Texas wildflowers even if these fell more on the side of wild than flowers.

"Beautiful," she said.

Naomi carefully washed all the dirt off her purple flowers, dried them, then placed one beside each plate.

David, feeling his duty was done, made himself scarce and probably wouldn't reappear until either Naomi needed him or dinner was served.

While the casserole cooked, Amy went to change into something more dating aspirational. However, she changed twice before deciding on another pair of her plain jeans and a clean T-shirt. This was what she normally wore around the house, and if she dressed casually, David might not deduce this was an undercover date with her new boyfriend. She also went light on the makeup and put her hair up in a casual ponytail. Declan wouldn't care. He'd once told her she looked *better* without makeup. At the time it made her think she probably didn't wear enough makeup or know how to apply it to emphasize her best features. Now, she appreciated it as a comment from a man who'd loved her just the way she was.

She heard Declan's truck pull up next door and a short while later he knocked on their front door.

"I'll get it!" screamed Naomi, running out of her bedroom like her pants were on fire. "It's our guest!"

"Inside voices," Amy said with a smile.

Nice to know someone besides Amy was excited. For her part, Amy stayed back, restraining the excitement coursing through her at seeing Declan. Given, he'd been in their house before and he was not a stranger to them, but this would be the first time he'd spent an extended amount of time in their home. He'd be in a now-familiar setting, one that the kids had only previously enjoyed with Mom and Lou.

Amy straightened silverware neurotically until Naomi appeared in the kitchen, holding Declan's hand, tugging him behind her.

"Mommy, our guest has arrived!" Naomi announced. "And he has something."

Declan flashed the smile that changed his face from wicked to boyish. "Is this all for me?"

"Yes!" Naomi danced around the table until she wound up in front of Amy.

Amy braced her hands on her daughter's little shoulders. "Naomi and David picked the flowers from our backyard."

"We can just add these to the bunch." Declan produced a bouquet of red roses from behind him.

"They can be our centerpiece, Naomi," Amy said. "Aren't they beautiful?"

"I love them," said Naomi. "Gramma says roses are the queen of flowers."

"Here, I'll get a vase." Amy filled it with water and stuck the roses inside.

David finally emerged. "You brought *flowers*?"

Oh, right. Flowers were a statement of sorts, especially

red roses. But David wouldn't necessarily know that. He only knew that Rob brought her red roses for Valentine's Day and her birthday and whenever he felt he was in the doghouse.

"They're so pretty and red," Naomi said.

"You never brought *flowers* before," David said.

"They're roses," Naomi said.

"I know. So what?" David shrugged. "He still never brought them before."

"My mom taught me to bring something when I was invited for dinner," Declan explained.

"It's good manners," Amy said. "And he's never been over for dinner before."

"Can we eat now? I'm starving," said David.

Amy took it as a good sign. He wasn't going to hide in his room or take off on another scare-your-mother-to-death expedition.

"Sure, you two wash your hands and we'll eat."

David followed Naomi as they went to the hall bathroom.

In two seconds, Declan was by her side at the refrigerator, where she was taking out the salad bowl.

"How can I help?" His hand slid over her waist.

"Here, you can take the salad to the table." She handed it to him without meeting his eyes but when he didn't move, she looked up into his deep green gaze. "I'm sorry about this. He's being a pill."

"Don't worry about it. I've got thick skin. If some guy came sniffing around my mother when I was nine years old, I don't think I'd have cared for it, either."

The refrigerator door safety between them, she reached to glide her palm across the rough beard stubble of his jawline. "But you're not 'some guy.'"

"Well, don't forget that to him, I am. He's loyal to his father, which believe me, I can understand. The fact that he's angry with him now doesn't change the fact he loves him. He always will, no matter how much Rob manages to disappoint him. I understand better than most that father-son relationships can be challenging. There's so much expectation on both sides."

"You and your father."

He'd talked about it a little, and she'd sensed the looming tension between them when Mr. Sheridan showed up at the first baseball practice.

"We're going to be okay now."

"Oh, Declan. I'm so happy for you. It gives me hope for us, too, that someday we'll straighten this blended-family thing out. David can love both Rob and me, separately. I want to move on and start my new life."

"Hang on to that hope, Tinks. Hang on tight."

Chapter Twenty-Four

Dinner was a tense affair, with Naomi giving her brother sidelong looks as if she was somehow trying to communicate with him through their magical twin bond. No doubt she wanted to know why her brother was suddenly not fond of Declan when a week ago he'd been, ahem, to borrow a phrase, his biggest cheerleader.

"Can I be excused?" David said.

Amy blinked in surprise. "What about dessert? It's a lemon tart pie."

Yes, she was trying to win her son's approval through his stomach.

Declan had been nothing but friendly through this whole dinner and he deserved to be acknowledged by her son. He deserved to be accepted with open arms. She had resisted many times the urge to hold his hand, just to touch him like a lover would. No. She would bide her time before she could demonstrate any physical affections for him, and even then, her children had never been particularly fond of PDA.

"That's fine," Declan said, nudging Naomi. "I don't think David wants any pie. More for us."

"Yum!" Naomi laughed and held up two fingers. "I'll have two slices."

David didn't laugh but also didn't leave the table. Amy

served her family slices of the pie she'd bought from the bakery in town. Talk revolved around how hot the day had been, always a topic in south Texas, then Naomi's fern named Fern and eventually quite naturally slid into baseball. Because it was summer, after all, and the Astros were playing the San Francisco Giants next week. Declan stated his high hopes even if everyone called him a dreamer for thinking the Stros had a chance against the amazing Giants.

"I like the Giants because their colors are better," Naomi said happily. "Are they the ones with orange and black? Just like Halloween."

Declan clutched his chest. "Don't tell me we've lost another Stros fan to the colors!"

"Naomi, you can't like a team because of its *colors*!" David shook his head, but he did chuckle for the first time. "Besides, the Astros have orange, too."

The conversation devolved from there and before long they were discussing video games and music, the children and Declan poking fun at Amy's love of country music and Chris Stapleton in particular. They felt very much like a regular family. Her children and Declan. He just fit. He would always fit with her, in any situation, so this should not be any different. The tough part would be getting David to understand and accept that his parents were never getting back together. All those years, she'd had an enviable relationship with Rob. She'd loved him, he'd loved her, they worked well together, their children were perfect and their family unit stayed solid for years. But now that she was back with Declan, she couldn't imagine how she'd ever let anyone take his place. No one was quite like him, no one owned her heart and soul the way he always had.

After dinner, Declan stayed to help with the dishes, perfect man that he was. He rinsed the plates and handed them to her because she had a particular way to load the dish-washer and didn't want her first disagreement with Declan to involve terrible dish arrangement.

"How was work?" she said, accepting a glass tumbler from him.

"It's always weird to work the early shift. A different crowd. Tippy and Ted came in and he always likes talking baseball with me."

"Did you stay after to give your pep talk?"

He shrugged. "Debbie wasn't there, and the rest hightailed it out after their shift."

"They don't know what they're missing."

He simply smiled at her, that easy smile that had always felt like a secret tucked between them.

At the evening's conclusion, she chose not to push her luck and simply walked Declan to the front door. A stroll next door with him would invite too many questions from curious little eyes and ears.

"I thought that went well but I apologize if David was a bit grumpy."

"Baby steps."

Smiling so wide her cheeks hurt, Amy slowly shut the door behind him and silently wondered how she could be feeling as giddy as a schoolgirl at her age.

"Do you like him?"

Amy startled. This time the voice was Naomi's. She turned to answer her girl, whose voice wasn't angry or accusatory. She'd simply asked a question, maybe even because she recognized the vibes obviously written all over her mother's face.

Amy took a deep breath. "Yes, honey. I like him very much."

"Oh. Is it kind of like Daddy and Shannon?"

"Um, yes. It's just like that."

"I thought he was our neighbor."

"Well, he *was* just our neighbor. You're right."

"You like him because he's nice, right? And funny sometimes, and he likes you, and helps you and isn't ever mean to you."

And also, he's incredibly hot and delicious and his kisses make my knees dissolve.

But TMI for her daughter, who at least seemed to understand the basics. She wasn't falling for that "if he pulls on your pigtails and is mean to you, he probably likes you" business. Amy would raise her daughter to believe she should be treated like a partner and an equal, the way her parents raised her.

"That's right. He's good to me and I think that's important, don't you?"

Naomi's head bobbed up and down. "I liked a boy at school last year."

"You never told me."

"He's really smart, maybe smarter than me."

"Oh, that's not possible."

Naomi didn't catch the joke. "No, really, he reads a ton of books, like me."

It sounded like a match made in heaven except it had arrived too soon. But one never knew, she supposed. This boy could wind up being Naomi's first love. Good Lord, she didn't want to think about that. Her baby girl was *nine*. Could she please stay nine and sweet forever?

"I don't think David likes Shannon and now he's not going to like Declan." Naomi spoke with wisdom. "But I'm not sure why."

Amy cupped her daughter's sweet face. "He thinks if Shannon and Declan weren't around, things might be different. I think he's mad that we can't all be together like we used to be. You, me, David and Daddy."

"I get sad about that sometimes, too. Is it okay if I'm sad?"

"Yes, baby, it is always okay to feel the way you do. I will never stop you from being sad about this. It's very normal. What do you do when you feel sad?"

She shrugged. "I just think of the good times. But... I like to be happy."

It seemed her daughter might be an emotional savant in addition to intellectually gifted.

"Right. Me, too. I think whenever we can choose to be happy, we should. It's just that sometimes that's hard."

Amy took a deep breath and decided, well, why not tell Naomi the whole truth.

"You probably remember how sad I was after Daddy moved out. Remember when Gramma came over every day for a while because I was sick and had to stay in bed?"

"You were sad." Naomi nodded and lowered her gaze. "I know."

"I was kind of sick with sadness, which happens sometimes. But then one day you came in and handed me a pretty rock you found outside. You asked me if I'd go outside and help you find more." She brushed aside the strands of brown hair at her daughter's temple. "And I couldn't say no to that invitation. So, I got out of bed and pretended to be feeling better. The next day it was a little bit easier pretending, same as the day after that. All of a sudden one day I wasn't pretending. Every day you make me so glad to be here. To be your mother."

"What are y'all talking about?' David entered the room, eyes narrowed.

"We're talking about how sometimes we feel sad, but we try anyway. Kind of like fake it till you make it. Before you know it, fake becomes real. You'll never stop feeling disappointed if you didn't get something you wanted but that doesn't mean you can't find a way to be happy again."

"What about trying to fix something if it's *broken*?' David said.

Leave it to her son to up the stakes.

"Yes, that's important, too. We try to fix things, but then when we can't, that's where the sadness comes."

"All I wanted was for you and Daddy to try to fix it so we can all be together again."

"We did try, honey."

"Maybe not hard enough," David huffed. "Is Declan your *boyfriend* now?"

Boyfriend seemed like a very small word for everything Declan was to her, but she'd have to stay with simple.

"Yes, he is. He's not going to be your father because you already have a great one. But I do want him to be part of my life and yours, too."

"Do you still love Dad?" David's voice was soft and thin. "Because he loves you. He told me so."

It was good to know Rob had discussed this with David, too, and probably right after the meeting with his new girlfriend. This is where words mattered, and she'd choose hers carefully. There were many types of love, and her children didn't have to hear descriptions of each one. They just had to understand that neither she nor Rob was ever going to stop loving *them*. And this required understanding no matter what there would always be a connection between their parents.

"I will always love him in a special way."

David nodded like he understood for the first time. "Okay. I get it."

The employment offer from the school district came through, a far more generous one than Declan expected. Of course, he would not only be working as a teacher but spending a great deal of his time coaching the baseball team. The commitment would mean there was no way he could manage to work part-time at the Salty Dog. Certainly not if he ever wanted to see Amy on a regular basis. Teenaged Declan would have expected her to sit back and wait for him to give her attention when he could, like the overinflated-ego jock he'd been. Now he understood if he had something special and priceless, he better not let it shatter.

On the day he signed and accepted the offer, Declan went into work early so he could speak to Cole Kinsella, who was one of the three owners of the bar. Declan hated to leave them short-staffed the way they'd been just a few weeks ago when a cocktail waitress quit. But with the turnover in the industry, they wouldn't be surprised. At three years, Declan was practically a veteran. The only staff member who outranked him was Debbie.

Declan busied himself with inventory behind the bar until Cole waltzed in, his yellow Lab named Submarine hot on his heels. Though rarely seen in public anymore, Sub had been a fixture around the boardwalk and particularly the Salty Dog since the days when Cole and his friends took over the bar.

Cole waved at Declan on his way to the back office. "Hey, you're here early."

"Yeah, boss, can I talk to you for a minute?"

Cole stopped in his tracks and so did Sub, panting happily in Declan's direction. Whoever said dogs couldn't smile probably hadn't met Sub.

"Sure, come on back."

Declan followed him into the wood-paneled office. He hadn't been back here since he was hired. A surfboard still stood in the corner of the room but now instead of the office of a bachelor, there were touches of family everywhere.

On the bookcase behind him were at least ten framed photos of Valerie, and his and Valerie's son, Wade. On the desk sat a photo of him and Valerie by the beach smiling into the camera.

Sub found his corner on a comfortable dog bed where he had toys. He would also be in on this meeting.

"What's up?"

"I hate to do this to you, but I'm going back to teaching and coaching. I've got an offer at the local high school and it's a good one. I'll be coaching the varsity baseball team there starting in the fall."

Cole leaned back in his chair. "Well, it's about time."

"I'm sorry to leave you short-sta—what?" Declan wasn't sure he'd heard right.

Cole laughed. "Don't get me wrong, I'm going to miss the best bartender I've ever had but hate to see a talent like yours wasted. You should use those coaching skills where they can really make a difference."

"Ah, you heard about my late-night 'inspirational' talks?"

"Are you kidding? Debbie couldn't stop talking about it when you first came on. She said I could learn a thing or two from you." Cole smirked. "As you know, Debbie doesn't hold back."

"No, sir." Declan chuckled.

"She's definitely going to miss you. The rest of us will, too, by the way. I appreciate the notice."

"I would offer to work part-time until you find the right fit, but if I do that, I'll only see Amy at work."

Cole quirked a brow. "You two are in a relationship?"

"It's new," Declan admitted, not sure why he'd even brought up the subject. He and Amy had been nothing but professional at work, often leaving separately and deciding it was nobody else's business. "And very serious."

"Good. I'd expect nothing less from you," Cole said. "My mother was a single mom. If you aren't serious about a single mom, you have no business being with her."

Declan nodded. "This time I won't screw things up."

"This time?"

"Amy and I are high school sweethearts, believe it or not. I know, weird! When does that ever happen?"

"Not so weird." Cole pushed the framed photo of him and Valerie at the beach toward Declan. "That's me and Valerie quite a few years ago."

Declan picked up the frame and examined it closely. They both looked young. The two were fresh-faced, young enough to be teens, with a dreamy gleam in their eyes and a love that seemed palpable enough to seep through time.

"I thought you two have only been married since shortly after she got back from Missouri."

Cole nodded. "We were kids, too, the first time we fell in love. I joined the navy, she went off to college and married someone else. I was engaged to another woman. Fast-forward and after her divorce, she came back to take care of her grandmother. You better believe I wasn't going to ruin my second chance."

"I never knew that. Glad it worked out the second time." He set the frame down. "That's inspirational."

"It's called compromise. You'll find you're much better at this when you're both grown-ups who are able to put someone other than your own wants and needs first."

"That's what I'm hoping. It's complicated, of course, because she has the kids, and they have to come first."

"Well, as my wife will tell you, it's important for a woman to put *herself* first once in a while. Valerie learned that the hard way after we had our son. Suddenly, her life became teaching and all that goes along with being part of the community, me, our baby, her grandmother, the restaurant, our friends. She was about to tear her hair out by the roots, and you know she has a lot of hair." Cole chuckled. "One night she was upset about a conflict, and I point-blank asked her… what do *you* want to do? And she said she just wanted to stay home with me and Wade, so that's what she did. She called up the friend asking her to be part of a fundraiser and used a word she's using more often. *No.* Sorry, but no."

"You know what? That's pretty good advice."

Cole grinned. "Well, don't forget I was a bartender, too."

Chapter Twenty-Five

By the time the weekend rolled around again, and Rob took the kids, Declan was dying for his Amy fix. He'd learned later that after his dinner with the family, Amy had come clean with the children and told them she and Declan were dating. But they'd mutually decided it would be best to take it slow around the kids, limit the PDA and leave the deep affection for after hours, closed doors and weekends. He'd been over a few times to watch TV with them, and the problem with these summer hours was that the kids stayed up late. Amy assured him it would be different come fall when school started up again. Bedtime would be eight then, leaving plenty of time for adult fun.

Eventually, they'd have every weekend together, but it would take a ring for that to materialize. Declan was ready to go ring shopping, but he'd decided not to scare Amy off. She'd just come out of a marriage, and probably didn't want to pole-vault right back into another one. Were it all up to him, they'd elope and get it done in Vegas tomorrow. He didn't need a big wedding, just his life with her and the kids to start immediately.

They were both scheduled to work the entire weekend, which would cut into some of that time, so he was pleasantly surprised when Amy showed up at his door on Friday afternoon. She wore jeans and a cami top with those thin straps, her hair down, her eyes shimmering, lips lush.

"The kids just left."

He hauled her inside, never able to resist her eagerness. They were kissing before the door was closed. He turned and shut it with one hand while busy kissing the breath out of her.

"I missed you so much."

She jumped into his arms, straddling her legs around his waist, climbing him like a tree.

He carried her into the bedroom, where she slowly slid down the length of him. Then she surprised him by pulling off his T-shirt in the middle of ravishing his mouth with her wicked tongue. When her fingers glided up and down his back, he thought he'd lose his mind with lust. Her fingers settled on the waistbands of his jeans and there was no shyness in her now. Her lips were soft and warm. While she was busy undressing him, he unzipped her jeans and tugged them down over her hips. She stepped out of them, pushing them aside with her feet, and he nearly swallowed his tongue when he saw her underwear.

His Amy, his sweet and shy and conservative Amy, wore a plunging black bra and a matching thong that barely covered her. He took a moment to enjoy the view, the milky softness of her curves. Her long and luscious legs.

"Wow."

"I went shopping for fun underwear," she said. "For you, mostly."

"Thank you."

"No, no. Thank *you*." She took his hand and led him to bed. "You're the only one who makes me want to blow my lingerie budget just so I can see your face when you take off my clothes."

"It will always be my pleasure to relieve you of your clothes." He grinned. "Slowly."

And, as it turned out, they were both late for work.

To Amy, the weekend passed in a glorious state of domestic bliss. She and Declan were definitely playing house, and for the sake of ease, they were mostly staying at hers. His toothbrush and shaver had migrated to her bathroom, which hadn't seen evidence of a man in ages. Now all the pain of the past year, all the grief at the loss of a marriage dissolved. She was happier than she could ever recall, the blush of love coloring every minute of her day. Had someone told her in the dregs of her despair after Rob left that she'd be this happy again this soon she wouldn't have believed it. It almost seemed unfair to be this happy because she hadn't done anything to deserve it.

She woke up on Declan's arms late Sunday morning after their late-night shift the night before. He cooked her breakfast, too, and then they wound up sitting next to each other on the couch, each with a laptop. Amy was still studying for her certification test and Declan was researching lesson plans. He was also—he wasn't kidding her—working at a strategy to take their team to the state division. There were phone calls to Mr. Sheridan, who had his own ideas and input. Declan took notes. Amy couldn't help but think all of it was very familiar.

Once, she and Declan sat together side by side on a couch but at that time they were the students. Soon they would both be the teachers. Full circle. She was so proud of Declan for going back to teaching, not allowing that one horrible experience to take away the joy he found in molding young minds. He would make a difference that would be felt for decades to come, she was sure of it.

But when they didn't once go out all weekend, Amy worried. It occurred to her that most girlfriends might want to go out more than she did.

She crossed her leg over his and got his attention. "Am I boring?"

"Boring?" He squinted. Declan wore glasses whenever he used the computer, and they made him adorably geeky in a way he could never achieve otherwise. *"You?"*

"I don't drink, I don't dance and I'm not big on going out to eat." She listed them off one by one. "I thought I'd do more of that when the kids got older but somewhere along the way I became a homebody. Maybe I always was."

"You're not boring, babe. This is what I signed up for. Guess who else is secretly a homebody?"

"That's *right*. Isn't that what you said to me on the first day I moved back in? How you also wanted to get married and have children."

"On the first day we met again, you mean."

"I confess I didn't think you really meant it."

"Now you know better." He squeezed her thigh. "I've always wanted what my parents had. Love and a partnership. I got all the drinking and sowing my oats out of my system in college, anyway."

Later, they ate lunch together, a quick ground beef and vegetable stir-fry that Declan threw together.

"Are these tater tots?" She asked.

"Yeah. Why?"

"Delicious." She wouldn't have thought they belonged in a stir-fry before today.

They washed the dishes together, Declan rinsing, Amy stacking. They already had their routines, and to Amy they were as comforting as melted butter on a cinnamon roll.

Rob texted after lunch, letting her know they were on their

way. Knowing it would be a week or more before they could be like this again, Amy squeezed every last moment of to-getherness. She insisted on sitting side by side on the couch as they watched old reruns of *Friends*. To them, it was feel-good comfort. They'd both pretty much grown up watching it as kids and it was funny to know the actors were now so much older than on the show. In fact, Amy and Declan were now the age of the characters.

"I should get going," Declan said, lifting her hand to brush a kiss across her knuckles. "They'll be back any minute."

"Don't go," Amy said, reaching for his arm as he moved to get up.

He turned. "I thought we—"

"We're not doing anything wrong. You can be over here with me in the middle of the day watching TV or, you know, whatever." She smiled.

"Yeah, well, we spent an entire weekend doing whatever."

"I'm not hiding you. What we have is nothing to be ashamed of."

"I know, sweetheart. Look, I'm a big boy. It's about the kids. We don't have to shove it in their faces that I'm in love with their mother and shagging her every chance I get."

"Not that," she said with an eye roll. "We don't have to make that obvious, but I would think TV-watching together is allowable. Holding hands. Etcetera. And so forth."

"Whatever you say." He tugged her by the waist and pulled her into his arms for a kiss.

The doorbell rang just as they were breaking apart.

"Here we go," Amy said, squaring her shoulders. "United front."

Naomi's smiling upturned face greeted her. "How's Fern? She probably missed me. I'm going to go give her a drink of water."

Naomi rushed inside and down the hallway.

"Hey, Rob." Declan came up from behind Amy and offered his hand. "Declan Sheridan."

"Oh, hey." Rob shook Declan's hand. "Good to meet you. Heard a lot about you. Amy, can I talk to you outside for a minute?"

"Um, sure." She threw a look at Declan, hoping he'd distract the kids.

Rob probably wanted to complain about something or the other if he wanted to talk outside. Maybe he didn't like that he'd found Declan making himself at home, but hey, this was her house now.

"Why don't we throw the ball around outside?" Declan suggested, motioning to their backyard.

"I'll go get my glove." David went toward the bedroom.

Amy followed Rob outside. "What's up?"

Far from tearing into her, Rob dragged a hand through his hair and awkwardly shifted his weight from one foot to the other.

"I'm... Okay, this is hard. Just bear with me. I have something to say."

Amy crossed her arms in an automatically defensive position. "Go ahead, but if this is about Declan—"

"No, it's not. This is about you and me."

"You and *me*?"

"Look. I made a mistake, Amy. I want another chance. Let's get back together, make a home again for the kids."

For a moment, Amy couldn't take in a breath. It was too cruel to suggest this now. They'd *sold* their home, which now belonged to another family.

"We sold our home."

"Then I'll buy us another one, a better one. We can start over, you and me, and the kids. We—"

"What are you *talking* about? We're divorced. What happened to Shannon?"

"It didn't work out, but that's not important. I still love you, Amy, and David said you told him you still love me. This could work. We gave up too quickly. We didn't really try to fix our family, and our kids deserve that. We *owe* them that."

The words were like bullets, each one hitting a major artery. Those were *her* words, said before their divorce, when it seemed Rob had lost his mind. She'd wanted to fight for them, to solve their issues. Rob had not. Except now he did, somehow. Now that she was finding her way to a new life, a new career, with a man she'd fallen in love with all over again, *now* Rob wanted to fix their family.

When she finally spoke, her words were salty. "I wanted to work on our marriage, but you didn't."

"Yes, but—"

"You said, and I quote, 'I don't want to be married anymore. You can't fix that by staying married.' *Your* words."

"I know, my mistake! I own it."

"Honestly, I can't help but think this has something to do with the fact that I'm dating Declan."

Rob shook his head. "It's not that. Even before he showed up, I was already regretting this divorce."

"No, you weren't. You signed up for the dating apps and rented a condo with a swimming pool. You were in your 'bachelor era.'" She made air quotes.

"For about two minutes and then I slowly started to come to my senses."

Those were words she wished he'd said about a year ago but they were too late now. He had to be joking that after putting her through everything she'd give him another chance.

"I don't know what you expect from me now. We're divorced. The kids are just starting to get used to the idea and now you want to come in and upset everything. When *you* wanted the divorce, I didn't make you the bad guy. I didn't tell the kids the real reason we were divorcing is because you didn't want to be married anymore. I hauled out all the platitudes, all the vagueness, followed all the advice when I really wanted to tell them, 'Talk to your father! It's his fault.' No, I didn't do that, and I'd appreciate it if you return the favor now."

"You won't even *consider* it?"

She threw up her hands. "There's nothing to consider!"

"If you won't do it for me, Amy, do it for our kids. They both want us back together. They want things how they used to be. You've always put the kids first, which is what made you a fantastic mother."

Below the belt. Way below.

Rob knew her far too well. He knew how best to exact the maximum amount of damage. He knew how and where to slice, and which veins bled the heaviest. She'd do anything for her children and Rob knew it well.

He studied the ground, regret pinching every feature on his face. "I couldn't have picked a better mother for my children."

"Stop. This isn't fair. I'm not the one who wanted the divorce."

"I know, because you understood better than I did that we belong together."

"Not anymore, we don't!"

"We could change that if you'll give me a chance. I told the kids when we get back together, we'll go on a vacation to Disneyland again."

"You did *what*?"

So, he was going to make her the bad guy! "You told the children?"

"I had to be honest. The first thing I had to do was apologize to them for wrecking their home."

"As usual, you forget to make these things age-appropriate."

"I made the mess, I have to fix it." Rob slowly walked to his car and swung open the driver's side door. "Talk to the kids. And think about it. I'll call you."

Talk to the kids? It was just like Rob to put it in those terms. She was not going to talk to the kids about this. They didn't get to make these decisions, no more than they got to make the one when they divorced. So, yes, Rob had now put her in the position of having to break her children's hearts when she informed them that no, she and Daddy were not getting back together.

Chapter Twenty-Six

Declan had a sense something was off with David, but he couldn't put his finger on what. It could be that he worried his parents were out front arguing, but from here they couldn't hear anything. They threw the ball back and forth, David's strength notably improving. He was also catching the ball so easily that Declan threw him a few curveballs and made him work for it.

"I'm going back to coaching a team after the summer," Declan said by way of conversation.

"Little League?" David threw the ball back to him.

"Our local high school's varsity team."

"That's cool."

"That's where your mom and I first met. Who knows? Maybe I'll be coaching you someday."

"Maybe. If I don't quit baseball."

Declan caught the ball and hesitated before throwing it back. "Why would you quit?"

"I don't know, no reason." He shrugged.

But he looked, for lack of a better word...*guilty*. There was more to this story. Maybe his thoughts were running toward giving up the sport and he regretted all the time and effort Declan had put into helping him.

"If you ever think about quitting, talk to me first."

Naomi joined them outside. "Are y'all going to play catch *all day*?"

"Do you want to try?" Declan offered. "No reason why you can't play, too. I might have an extra glove laying around somewhere."

"I don't want to play ball." Naomi crossed her arms. "I want to hunt for fairies!"

"Fairies?" Declan chuckled.

She reminded him of Amy more each day.

"Either that or I want to solve a mystery," Naomi said. "Like Nancy Drew."

"We don't have a mystery to solve around here, unless it's why weeds grow so easily when flowers you plant need to be watered every day or they die. That's above my pay grade so I'll help you find the fairies." Declan threw one last ball to David. "Is that okay with you?"

"Yeah." David threw his glove down, then he gave Declan what he could only describe as a self-defeated look. "I'm really sorry."

"Sorry for what?" Declan said.

"And if you don't want to help me with baseball anymore, I'm not going to be mad at you."

"We'll play catch again later, okay?"

"Yeah, sure." But David went inside, the sound of the screen door slapping loudly in his wake.

Declan turned to Naomi, hands on his hips. "Where should we start our search?"

"Over here in the bush. I saw some ladybugs and they might know the way." She pointed in the direction.

"Of course. They're also small. Makes sense."

"Yeah. Small bugs probably would know where all the fairyland creatures live." Naomi knelt and dug at the base of a bush. "Yoo-hoo! We're looking for fairies."

"A little softer," Declan said. "I don't think they like it when we're loud. Just whisper."

"Oh. Okay." Naomi slid a finger over her mouth in the "zipping it closed" move.

They didn't find any fairies, but Declan suggested instead they make a little home for them. Naomi gathered pebbles, leaves and sticks and fashioned them into mini furniture for them.

The screen door slapped open and closed again a few minutes later.

"What's going on out here?" He looked up to see Amy, cupping her hands over her forehead, shading her eyes against the sun.

"Lookin' for fairies." Declan stood and brushed the dirt off his knees, thinking how easy boys were compared with girls.

All you needed to do was kick or throw a ball around, but girls were a hell of a lot more creative, it would seem.

She'd obviously had an argument with Rob, going by the worry in her gaze, the tightness around her mouth. Yep. They'd argued.

"Everything okay?"

"We'll talk about it later," she said, further confirming it.

Declan had already accepted that Rob would be a part of his life, too. He came with the territory. He came with Amy.

And Declan could handle him.

Later that night, once the kids were asleep, Declan walked outside with Amy.

The summer night was clear, the stars shining bright above them. He held Amy's hand and sat on one of the steps, pulling her down next to him. His life was coming together in all the important ways and for the first time in so long he felt settled.

"What's up? You've been quiet all night."

"You won't believe this. Rob just sprung this on me to-night."

"Is he giving you a tough time about us?" He threaded his fingers through hers.

Declan would have expected no less. It might be one thing for her ex-husband to move on, but it would be another one watching *her* move on with an ex-boyfriend. Declan had already determined to make friends with Rob, despite what he personally thought of him. For the sake of keeping the peace, he'd keep his less-than-charitable thoughts to himself. He figured they would never be the best of friends, but Declan could get along with almost anyone.

"Believe it or not, tonight he told me that he wants us to get back together. He said he wants another chance."

The shock hit Declan hard, reverberating through him. This is the one thing he hadn't expected. He hadn't planned for this. But damn it all, of course Rob wanted Amy back, because this was *Amy*. Only an idiot wouldn't realize what he'd lost.

"What about Shannon?"

She shook her head. "I don't know. It already didn't work out."

Something unnamed bothered Declan now, niggling at the edges of his mind. And then he found the end of that thought, clear as the evening air. Amy wasn't laughing. She wasn't talking about how ridiculous the idea was now, after they were already divorced, for crying out loud.

Because Declan was speechless, Amy kept talking.

"He said we never tried to fix our marriage, and the thing is, he's right, we never did. We should have, and I wanted to, but he said no. He just walked away, gave up, and now he has the gall to suggest we try again. For the kids, for our family."

"Okay." He let go of her hand, whether out of self-preservation or not, he didn't know, but this wasn't the time to analyze. "Is that what you want to do?"

"No. I love you, Declan." She tugged on his hand, bringing it back to her.

He realized in that moment he had a chance but knowing Amy... His heart told him he was still going to lose this battle.

"I get it. It would be good for the kids if their parents were back together. David would be very happy."

And suddenly the apologetic looks in David's eyes, the way he'd actually told Declan that he was sorry... It all made sense. Poor kid. On one level, he felt remorse for Declan's inevitable loss. David expected what everyone else did.

Amy would choose her children and that meant choosing their father.

"But where does that leave me? I'm going to be miserable without you." Amy moved closer to him on the step.

He had a lot to say about how miserable she would be without him, because he'd done everything to make himself indispensable to her, but she would have to make this decision on her own.

"You're never going to *be* without me." Declan drew her close, framed her beautiful face in his hands. "You'll always have me even if I'm on the sidelines as a friend. I'll always love you. I'm going to be here and I'm not giving up on us. But I know you too well. You want to save your family."

"I do, but that doesn't mean I want to lose you."

"Still, I have to let you try. I wouldn't be much of a friend if I didn't."

"Noo." The sound coming out of her was like that of a

wounded animal. "It's not fair after what he's done. I can try but it will never be the same. That's not a marriage. That's like…my children being held hostage."

"Hey, those are my arguments." The sentiment was exactly right and on point.

He tried to chuckle, but it wasn't coming. Instead, a desperate ache filled his chest. All that sense of being settled, of utter and complete contentment, was slowly leaking out of him.

"I'd do anything for my children, but it just isn't fair to expect me to do this. Not now."

"But if he'd come back sooner, you *would* have tried."

She didn't answer because the answer was of course, yes, she would have tried to save her family. And it made sense to Declan. It was one of the things he loved most about her. She didn't give up on people. Sure, it was coming back to bite him now, but it was one of her best qualities.

"We can't move forward with this hanging over our heads." He let his arms dangle between his legs, a sense of defeat spreading.

"What do you mean by that?"

Still, he'd never been one to give up without a fight. He'd been taught to play fair, however, even if nothing seemed equitable about this. On one side stood Rob with their children, the real weight in all this. On the other side stood Declan, alone.

He got up, sticking his hands in his pockets so he wouldn't be tempted to take her into his arms. So he wouldn't be tempted to remind her who was here first, whom she truly belonged to.

"Take a week and think about this. Decide. And if you choose your family, I'm going to always be here. I'm going to be here when you need me. I'm going to be there in the background, watching and making sure he treats you right. I'm going to be with you no matter what. You won't lose me. But this has to be your decision."

She didn't speak but covered her face. The sobbing started soon after, and he had to force himself not to turn back, take her into his arms and comfort her.

Declan walked across their shared lawn, and it was by far the longest twenty feet he'd ever walked.

Two days later, Amy was still a mess of tangled emotions and thoughts. Declan wanted her to take a week, and she would, but she didn't see how she could wind up having answers in such a short time. She might never know the right thing to do. Already she missed Declan desperately. Someone had cut out her heart and expected her to walk around and live and breathe without the organ so vital to life.

Today Bianca had picked up the children to take them to the boardwalk. When Amy told her friend what Rob now wanted, her first reaction was selfish: "Oh my gawd, it will be just like old times again," followed by, "Oh," when she'd taken a good long look at Amy. Her eyes were pink and puffy, almost like the days just after Rob moved out. She was now unhappy in reverse.

"Sounds like you have a big decision to make," Bianca said, then offered to take the kids for a day.

Mom showed up on Amy's doorstep that same afternoon.

"How are you, sweetie?" She hugged Amy, setting her back to get a good look at her. "Oh dear."

"I don't know what to do." Amy turned and headed back to the couch and her box of tissues.

Her mother followed her to the couch and sat next to her. "Do you want my advice?"

"Yes!" Amy said.

"Rob has asked you to choose between him and Declan. One of them is like choosing your children, and the family you once had. The other one is choosing the man you fell in love with while Rob was busy being an ass. Now I ask you, my darling—why should you choose *either one of them?*"

For two days, she'd thought of nothing but what her heart wanted versus what her logical brain told her was the better choice. She'd never entertained the idea of choosing neither one of them.

"But… I love Declan."

Mom sighed. "I see. And I do understand. It's like the new and shiny brightness of being in love for the first time. But over time, love can wane and ebb and flow. Remember that a marriage, or any long-term relationship, is work. You haven't had to work for Declan yet. But you might have to, someday. It's not all going to be a bed of roses in your second marriage, either."

"It's not the shiny and bright thing. I know we'll have issues. But he's selfless and he's loving and he's perfect… for me."

"And then there's Rob."

"The father of my children." Amy sniffed. "I can't change that, nor would I want to. But… I don't appreciate him putting me in this position. I didn't want the divorce but now it's too late."

"Exactly. If he wanted you back, he should have wooed you, not issued what comes down to the start of hostage negotiations."

"Exactly." Amy reached for another tissue and blew her nose. "But I always said I'd do anything for my children, and am I now supposed to walk away from trying to be with their father? It's what they want. Do I have the right to take it from them? That's selfish, isn't it?"

Mom snorted. "What? You don't think you're allowed to be *selfish*?"

"No, I'm not. Not for many years yet."

"You did such a great job when you and Rob divorced keeping the children out of it. You understand that they can't make these grown-up decisions and it was never up to them. Was it hard for them to have their home split up? Of course, but they are resilient, and good kids. When it comes to our children, mothers will always choose them over ourselves. But you have to ask yourself at some point if that's wise. Let me ask you this—do you think it might be important to them to grow up with a mom whom they know is happy?"

"I would hope so, but they're still young. Right now, they're the center of the universe because they're not emotionally mature enough to understand their parents have needs of their own."

"But someday soon they will be. Do you think they'd rather know that you made a choice that made you happy, and not a long-suffering one that essentially turns you into a martyr?"

Amy perked up because it sounded for the first time that someone had given her the permission to do what she'd wanted to all along.

"Don't think of this decision as choosing between your children and Declan. Why not choose *yourself*?"

Once Amy realized exactly what she'd do, she didn't want to wait the rest of the week. She also didn't want to tell Rob yet. Let him wait and fester and stew. He'd made her agonize those first weeks when she'd begged him to work things out for the sake of their family, and he hadn't listened. Rob chose Rob.

Amy had tried to save her marriage and failed. But, as

one of her mother's favorite quotes went, "Every flower must grow through dirt." And Amy had grown and realized that one day her children would grow up and leave the house. They'd have their own lives and friends and interests, and they were not going to hand her an award for being the world's most selfless parent. They would be grateful for her love and support even though it would probably be many years before they'd verbalize it. And while they were off at college or the Peace Corps or whatever they decided to do, she'd be home with the man she loved.

Yes, in the end, she chose herself because her happiness and joy mattered, too.

She wouldn't always put herself first, but she would now, at the start of her new life.

Amy sat on the top step of Declan's porch, but it was midnight before Declan pulled up and shut off the headlights of his truck. She sat on her hands, trying to tamp down the wave of ecstasy coursing through her. She hadn't seen him in two days, and he looked a little like the sun. Bright. Golden. Her star. Part of her wanted to run toward him, to launch herself into his arms. But she would play this cool and let him know she'd made the decision with the amount of thought he'd wanted from her.

She couldn't look away as he moved toward her slowly, warily.

"I thought we said one week."

"Yes, but I don't need any more time. I'm sure."

He moved toward her almost wearily and in that moment she knew.

He had no idea of how much she loved him or that she would choose him a million times and not just once. She stood and took a step down to meet him before she stopped herself. Perfect. He was two steps below her and this evened out their height so she could look him in the eyes.

"It was an easy decision to make. I chose myself."

He quirked a brow. "Actually, that sounds like a good choice."

"It is. When I choose myself, it makes life far simpler. I love you, Declan Sheridan. And I choose being happy today, and tomorrow and ten years from now when my kids are grown and out of the house."

Finally, he smiled, his relief palpable. "I wanted to tell you to choose yourself first. It's something a friend of mine told me recently. Sometimes you have to say no to everyone else and yes to yourself. Everyone who knows you and loves you realizes you deserve to be happy. You deserve everything."

She pressed her temple to his, raked her fingers through his thick hair and leaned into the strength of him. "I honestly can't believe you thought this could go any other way. It's you. It's always been you."

"I'm not conceited enough to think I deserve you."

"But you do, and I hope you realize choosing myself means I'm choosing us. Because you make me the happiest I've ever been."

"That's all I've ever wanted."

Then she kissed him and sealed the promise of their future.

Epilogue

"Here, David, catch!"

The paper lunch bag went sailing past Naomi and he caught it midair. There were some advantages to having a baseball player in the house.

"Peanut butter and jelly?" David asked, stuffing it in his backpack.

"Of course." Amy turned nervously for one last check in the mirror before all three of them were out the door.

Conservative royal blue dress. Check. Low heels. Check. Hair tamed and pinch of lipstick and blush for color. Check. A month into the school year, they had a nice routine going but this was the first time Amy would be working at Charming Elementary School as a substitute teacher. She'd gotten the call last night and hardly slept.

"Are you seriously going to be a *teacher* today?" Naomi asked in awe.

"Not your teacher, of course. I'm teaching the second graders today. Their teacher is sick with the flu."

"Oh, this is so exciting!" Naomi said with her classic enthusiasm.

"Yeah. I hope none of my friends figure it out," David muttered.

He would get used to it. He couldn't fool Amy. Deep down

he was proud that his mother would now be a teacher even if he'd prefer it be another school. He probably worried he'd be demoted all the popularity points he'd scored by being good friends with *the* Declan Sheridan. The school district practically threw a parade in his honor when he accepted the position as varsity head coach.

In the end, David took the return to their new normal in stride. He confessed to Amy that he'd guilt-tripped Rob into trying to get their family back together. And Rob, being Rob, saw an opportunity to stop doing the hard work in a new relationship with Shannon and wanted to return to the safe cocoon of the old, tired and worn. Thank goodness she'd chosen herself.

The truth was David liked Declan so much he felt guilty about it. Rob finally grew up a little when he told David it was okay to like "mommy's new friend." Of course, mommy's new friend was a whole lot more than a friend and the kids knew it. Rob continued to simplify things when it suited him, and he probably wouldn't believe Amy had moved on until she remarried.

She wasn't in a hurry, except that she wished she and Declan could live together. Every time she got her nerve up to suggest it, Declan changed the subject. She was a little worried but not seriously so. It was difficult to doubt his love for her when he reminded and showed her every day. Usually, he was off to his job as head coach and teacher a lot earlier than they were and it would be nice to see him every morning, but that would come in time.

Amy and her children separated in the hallway and went to their individual classes. She checked in with the principal, a nice man in his fifties who had already promised to hire her full time as soon as a position was open. For now,

Amy filled in as substitute teacher and still worked at the Salty Dog.

"Boys and girls, this is Mrs. Holloway," Mr. Boone announced. "Let's welcome her."

"*Ms.* Holloway," Amy corrected him.

No longer married to Rob Holloway, thank you.

"Hi, Miss Holloway!" the kids said loudly.

They were adorable, the little angels. Except for the one boy who asked if she'd marry him. He seemed a tad precocious. The morning passed quickly, and she took them out to recess, read to them, then helped them through a spelling worksheet.

An announcement came over the PA. "Amy Holloway, please come to the front office."

Amy had no idea what could have gone wrong. Perhaps there was an issue with her certification.

Valerie Kinsella, the third-grade teacher, appeared in the doorway. "I'll handle them until you get back."

"I've no idea what's wrong."

"Probably something with the paperwork, you know how it is." She winked.

Amy did not but chose to trust the process. Ahead of her and just before she reached the office was a bit of a crowd and... Declan in the center of it. Oh, good grief, had he scheduled a visit or something and she'd been unaware? Perhaps a spirit meeting? Did they do those in grade school? But then the crowd separated, and she saw her mother, and Lou, Dan and Lorna Sheridan, Finn and Michelle, and...her children. Both of them, one on either side of Declan.

"What's happening...?" she said.

Then Declan dropped to one knee and there was no more confusion. No doubts. Only the joy of seeing her person, the one she loved the most, giving her another one of her dreams.

"Mommy, I didn't know this was happening today!" Naomi squealed.

Declan chuckled, as did everyone else.

"Amy, would you marry me?" Declan said, producing a little black box.

"Yes!"

She didn't need to see the ring, she didn't need to have a lavish wedding, she didn't need anything but this man and the new family they'd have together.

* * * * *